THE EMPEROR OF THE MOON AND STARS

BOOK 3

IN THE CHRONICLES OF GIL-LAEL

N. R. WILLIAMS

The Emperor of the Moon and Stars

This book is a work of fiction. The names, characters, places, and incidents are products of the writer's imagination or have been used fictitiously and are not to be construed as real. Any resemblance to persons, living or dead, actual events, locale or organizations is entirely coincidental.

ISBN 978-1-7366859-3-8

Dedication:

I dedicate this book to my family and critique partners without whom I'd be less of an author. And, to my readers. May you be inspired to make your dreams a reality. All my love and appreciation.

Author's Note:

In my research, I learned that Gypsies originated in Pakistan and were a migrating peoples ending up in Egypt for a time. When they traveled to Europe, the people there labeled them Gypsy as an insult, combining Pakistan and Egypt in the name. They refer to themselves as Ramoni, and view the term Gypsy as big an insult as the 'N' word is for our black friends. In this book, the Ramoni people are healers and greatly appreciated.

The Asian peoples are a combination of Japanese and Chinese traditions. They carry scimitars instead of swords, because those are cool swords.

My concept is that people from our world traveled to this world through a portal during medieval times. You can read about it in, The Beginning of a Legend, A Chronicles of Gil-Lael Novella.

Table of Contents

Arrival	Chapter 1
Tour	Chapter 2
Coronation	Chapter 3
Decoration Committee	Chapter 4
Trap	Chapter 5
Romani	Chapter 6
Fire	Chapter 7
Hidden Treasure	Chapter 8
Duplicity	Chapter 9
Taxes	Chapter 10
Changes	Chapter 11
Birthday	Chapter 12
Geisha House	Chapter 13
Cave	Chapter 14
Guilt	Chapter 15
Friend-Brother	Chapter 16
Rumblings of War	Chapter 17
Missing	Chapter 18
Found	Chapter 19
War is Imminent	Chapter 20
Assignment	Chapter 21
Troubles, Details and Plans	Chapter 22
Price	Chapter 23
Possibilities	Chapter 24
Unknown Forts	Chapter 25
Divorce	Chapter 26
Fear	Chapter 27
Announcement	Chapter 28
The Cao Zhen	Chapter 30
Traveling	Chapter 31
Strategy	Chapter 32
Kidnap	Chapter 33
Romani Justice	Chapter 34
Dragon	Chapter 35
Emperor of the Moon and Stars	Chapter 36
Epilogue	
Maps	

Arrival

Chapter 1

Wind rippled the square sails as the vessel sliced through the ocean, blowing Jonathon's brown hair into his face and tickling his ears. He brushed it away. Sunlight reflected off the water and sails, causing a dance of shadows along the wooden bow. He squinted at the distant land on the horizon, breathing deep. The smell was of sky and water, and the taste was all salt.

Dolphins played a game of leap and chase, cutting through the water just ahead of the ship titled, Her Royal Majestés Ship, Queen Michelle. No one who gazed at Jonathan would know by his clothes that he was of royal blood. He wore brown trousers and a white cotton shirt. His boots were hidden beneath his pants, and he hadn't attached his gold-hilted sword.

Before him was the blue outline of land rising and falling along with the ship. Shea-Talon. He was to be its king.

A hand settled on Jonathan's shoulder. "We will soon make landfall," Healden said.

Jonathan turned his eyes from the horizon to his father. "Oui." His father's thinning white hair caught the breeze and wrinkles pressed into his flesh around his eyes and mouth.

Healden smiled at him, and Jonathan knew he meant to be encouraging.

"It will be difficult in the beginning, but you will soon come to love the people and the land." Healden tapped his shoulder and removed his hand.

Jonathan turned his eyes back to the horizon and didn't say anything. There would be nothing easy about this transition. He didn't even have a wife to see him through as his twin brother Eamon did.

Hours later, the H. R. M. S. Queen Michelle arrived at the Capital City, Aya. Water lapped at the sides of the ship, making her rock. Having been at sea for the better part of three months, Jonathan barely felt the movement. The heavy salt air was moist on his skin.

Many Shea-Talonian ships were docked at the wharf. Their front was squared off rather than coming to a point as the Gil-Laelian vessels did. The Shea-Talonian ships held three tall masts and their sails were rectangular. They reminded Jonathan of humpback whales coming to the surface with their tails raised.

Land. He turned his eyes toward the dock and adjusted the sleeve of his navy-blue jacket with gold trim. Warehouses made of wood lined the dock. They rested on tall pillars with ladders that lifted to the door several feet above the ground. Their roofs were either tile or sod and had the distinct Asian curve at all four corners that he had seen in his mother's world. He imagined that on a normal day, many carts and wagons would line the dirt road along the wharf, and workers would load or unload goods. But today wasn't a typical day. Today their new king had arrived.

About a thousand Gil-Laelian soldiers lined the dock before the buildings facing them. Some were on horseback. There were also three carriages, two open and one covered. A man and woman stepped out of the covered carriage. Jonathan watched as the man gave the woman his arm, and they stepped onto the boarding platform. The man had gray hair that curled around his ears and over his forehead. He wore a red jacket that came to his waist and black pants that did little to hide his bulging belly. The woman's hair was gray as well and swept up into a French bun. She wore pink and had matching ribbons in her hair. This seemed odd to Jonathan for a woman of her age.

They stepped off the plank onto the bridge and approached Jonathan's parents, High King Healden and Queen Michelle. Jonathan moved to their side as the man and woman bowed and curtsied.

"*Majesté*, what an honor. I am Governor Odo Marlon, and this is my wife, Faye."

"A pleasure, Marlon. May I introduce Queen Michelle and our son, Prince Jonathan." Healden set his arm around Michelle's waist. She was richly attired in shades of lavender silk. Healden wore his navy-blue jacket like Jonathan's.

A large wave struck the ship causing it to rise and fall suddenly. Faye Marlon promptly fell in a pile of skirts and uttered, "oh."

"Are you alright, my love?" Marlon bent and gave her his hand.

Faye stood. "I beg pardon, Majestés."

"I am glad you aren't injured," Healden said.

"Majesté, the people of Shea-Talon have worked hard on a greeting. May I suggest that we head out?" Marlon said.

"Of course, Marlon." Healden gave Jonathan a slight nod, and they followed the governor off the ship.

Each door of the two open carriages was embellished in gold with the symbol of 'The House of Calimar,' three falcons above a tree and stars above that. Jonathan, having a love for horses, was immediately drawn to the Romani Vanner mares. They were tall, white splashed with brown, and had long, flowing manes and tails and featherings of hair on their fetlocks.

He inspected the four hitched to his own carriage, running his hand along a firmly muscled shoulder. “Beautiful,” he whispered to the mare.

A lieutenant in Gil-Lael’s army stepped forward and bowed to Healden, Michelle. and then again to Jonathan. “I am Lieutenant Saville; my men will escort you through the city. There is a grand platform in the center where you might wish to address the Shea-Talonian people.”

“Very good,” Healden said.

Jonathan stepped up into his open-air carriage and selected the seat facing the driver. No one sat facing him. The lush interior featured navy-blue velvet cushions and a Telaneasse carpet across the floor in bold colors depicting a tree and three falcons in flight. He faced the front and took in the Shea-Talonian driver. His straight black hair was pulled back into a long braid. He wore a gold silk jacket with brown pants and a brown triangular hat with gold roping.

The carriage turned along the wharf and headed east. His parents rode in the first carriage, which followed the Gil-Laelian soldiers. The pungent smell of fish was soon replaced by strong incense coming from lanterns that hung from the sides of the building. At the end of several blocks, they came to the main section of the city. The soldiers fanned out to either side and stood before a crowd of people that lined the road. They turned north onto the street made of paving stones. As they traveled, the soldiers marched alongside the carriages while the cavalry rode before and at their rear.

The people of Shea-Talon were dressed in their traditional kimono-style clothing. The men all wore brown with a long coat. The women had on a colorful variety of dresses featuring flowers, butterflies, or birds.

The Shea-Talonians were utterly silent. They each had a long narrow flag in various shades that they waved. Then, as one, they all bowed at the waist, throwing their flags down onto the street, as the carriages passed.

Since the age of nine, Jonathan had been tutored in the customs and language of Shea-Talon. At twenty, he'd studied in the southern country of Telaneasse. The two countries were vastly different. The people of Telaneasse followed the teachings of more than thirty gods. To them, obedience was everything. Those of Shea-Talon valued honor above all. Not just honoring their leaders or family but keeping a set of values that prohibited individual interpretation. The problem with that was that the laws and customs of Gil-Lael didn't always match with the older customs in Shea-Talon. He had a challenge set before him.

The silence of the people was eerie. The only noise was the clip-clop of the horse's hooves or an occasional dog barking. Jonathan had been taught to wave to the people, but no one was looking at him. He turned his eyes this way and that. All along the drive was a sea of bent heads and black hair. The buildings behind the crowd were several stories high, with Asian-style dragons on the flags that billowed out when the breeze hit them. Trees and shrubbery decorated the corners of each building. More lanterns filled with incense hung above the doorways to each structure. The scent made Jonathan's nose itch.

Before they reached the center where he would give a speech, a whistling noise sliced through the calm, delivering an arrow like a flash of lightning. It thudded hard into the door of Jonathan's carriage. More pounded into his seat cushion. One of the horses was hit in the shoulder. Its screams announced the sudden chaos. Some of the soldiers ran into the crowd while others ran toward Jonathan's carriage. The people shrieked. The horses reared and then thundered into a frantic gallop heading toward a group of children. His coachman stood up from the seat and battled the panicked animals. Several soldiers waved the horses away from the people. Jonathan was thrown back against his seat just as another arrow swished past, cutting through his upper right arm.

They rounded a corner. The carriage leaned on two wheels. His parents were traveling at speeds his own carriage couldn't achieve with the injured horse. Jonathan glanced back. Soldiers ran after his carriage. Many of the Shea-Talonian people were falling over each other, and some had been trampled by the Gil-Laelian cavalry. Another sharp turn caused Jonathan to slam into one of the arrows in the seat cushion. It broke off, and slivers found a home in his thigh.

"Damn!" He yanked the wooden piece out and pressed his hand against the wound to slow the bleeding.

They approached a single building on the corner. Jonathan looked up in time to see a shower of arrows rain down upon them. His driver must have seen it too. He swerved to the left. An arrow hit the coachman in the chest, then another. Several bounced off the paving stones making a pinging noise. None landed in Jonathan's compartment. *The attackers meant to capture him. But why then did so many arrows land in his section at first?*

The wounded coachman sat, then fell into the deep foot compartment of his box. He still managed to hold the reins with shaking hands. Jonathan jumped on the rear seat facing him and vaulted over the side, landing in the box. He grabbed the reins just as the Gil-Laelian cavalry reached them. Some of the soldiers turned aside toward the building while others surrounded his coach to protect him.

He glanced at the coachman, who lay unconscious and bleeding. The city disappeared with the next turn that brought them into a field. The road wound in gentle curves that felt like the sea churning from the swift speed he maintained. Flowering orchards filled the air with sweet scents.

Once out of the city, Jonathan took a deep breath and slowed the carriage. Every nerve in his body had tensed, and his heart ached with anxiety. He took a shattered breath and sat on the driver's seat.

He passed a fenced residence and could see the sweeping roofline of the home. A tiled roof with the same Asian arch. So reminiscent of the style he'd seen when his family visited his mother's homeworld and took a trip to Japan and China.

An orchard of cherry trees blossomed beyond the wooden fence and hid the remainder of the house. He turned his gaze away from the trees and looked straight on. Before him loomed a great bluff. As he approached it, the road forked. Jonathan glanced to the side and saw the road twist between forest trees and disappear. Looking back, he saw his parent's carriage heading straight toward the mountain. Jonathan wasn't far behind. The horsemen passed beneath an elaborate arch with a massive Asian dragon leaning over the top. The mountain road turned east sharply and climbed a short distance before turning and climbing the opposite direction. Granite rocks and a thick grove of evergreen trees lined the drive. On the second turn, a brick structure was built into the side of the rock face. It had three tall towers, one on each end and one in the center. A second building that held animals was close by. Several hundred soldiers saluted him.

He pulled the carriage to a stop and beckoned them to assist. They removed the coachman to be given medical care and he had one of the young men join him to take over driving the horses. They resumed.

Jonathan remained in the driver's box. "What is your name?"

"I am Périer, Highness."

Three more turns brought them closer to the top with yet another structure the same as the last.

When they reached the plateau, another Asian dragon leaned over a second arch. They passed through. Jonathan took in a vast flat plain with several buildings, trees, and bushes. Little else registered, though. His leg and arm throbbed, and his head felt as if it would explode from tension. He'd planned on delivering a speech with a promise to improve the lives of his people. Instead, he had been given a bitter dose of the reality of governing a people that viewed him as a usurper.

Tour

Chapter 2

A few hours later, Jonathan watched as his father marched back-and-forth before Governor Marlon's desk and then came to a stop before it.

"Why did you not think to put us in covered carriages?"

Marlon blustered, "Sire–."

"My wife was wounded, and my son was nearly killed." Healden came to a halt and stepped so close to Marlon that the man leaned back on his desk.

"The last up-rising was nearly four years ago, Sire, I didn't think–."

"No. You didn't think. That is clear." Healden resumed his march.

Jonathan leaned against the wall and folded his arms. He was too angry to speak. His arm and leg had been bandaged, but he refused the medicine, needing a clear head.

"May I suggest we sit and go over all the policies and–."

"No!" Healden interrupted Marlon. He stopped pacing to glare at the governor. Then he turned and left the study.

"Later, Marlon," Jonathan said and left the study as well. He found his father in the garden beside the house. An enormous evergreen grew next to where Healden stood. Rather than a full triangular tree, the branches jutted out with the needles rounded in clumps on the ends. He'd never seen such a tree before. Ignoring it, he joined his father.

"I will replace Marlon if you like." Healden ran a hand through his hair.

"He has been here, what? Ten, fifteen years?"

"I believe it to be twelve. He's an imbecile."

"Nevertheless, father, he knows the people. Who our enemies might be."

Healden glanced at him. "True." He moved toward a pond and gazed down at the lilies. "I suspect he will need to stay, at least until you deem his services unnecessary."

"I will watch him and take his advice in measured doses. Perhaps Lieutenant Saville will be a good source of information."

Healden gave Jonathan a half-smile. "When did you become wise, my son?"

"After Sinon Aweirgan nearly killed you, I decided I'd best take my future seriously."

Healden clapped Jonathan on the shoulder. "In a few days, you will be emperor of Shea-Talon."

"Emperor. Seems grandiose."

"Just a different name for king." Healden turned back toward the house. A tall three-story structure.

Jonathan turned beside his father. "Shall we continue our meeting?"

Healden sighed. "*Oui*."

Once within the study, Jonathan sat beside his father at a table. Marlon brought over several maps, rolling one out. He put four heavy-weighted objects at each corner and then sat as well.

"This is the City of Aya. As you can see it is large. The main source of income is here, along the wharf." Marlon pointed his finger at the pier. "There is also a silk manufacturing plant here. And many clothes shops, wine, and liquor merchants, sword-smiths, and other businesses."

Jonathan followed Marlon's finger as he pointed each business out. The silk manufacturing business was at the south end of the city. Aya had to be thirty blocks deep and eighteen blocks wide. Not unlike Terrel, the Capital City of Gil-Lael, vast estates surrounded the town.

"Who lives here?" Jonathan pointed to the estate he had viewed just below the bluff.

"That is Wakisaka, the home of Ose Shigemori. There are rumors regarding him. I wouldn't call him an ally." Marlon frowned.

"What rumors?" Jonathan asked.

"Some say he is the head of Haranobu, but I haven't been able to verify that." Marlon lifted his eyes from the map.

Jonathan had been informed of the Haranobu. It comprised of many Shea-Talonian nobility who wanted to restore the old order and the line of Warwyk. *Puzzling.*

"I thought all of Warwyk's sons died in the war." Jonathan straightened. "How can they hope to restore his line?"

"Through the female line. He had forty-nine daughters. Of those daughters, Warwyk is grandfather to seventy-two men. Most live in the southern part of Shea-Talon and aren't members of any group that might bring harm." Marlon opened a deep drawer in a chest behind his desk. He pulled a fat file out and handed it to Jonathan. Marlon sat once again.

Jonathan opened the file, and began to scan the pages. Finally, after nearly an hour, he looked up at Marlon. "Shigemori isn't listed."

"No, but he is friends with several men who are, and Tamika's mother was Warwyk's daughter."

"Tamika?" He frowned.

"Shigemori's wife."

"But you just said that daughters weren't any concern."

"True, but Tamika is married to an ambitious man. We should watch Shigemori carefully," Marlon said.

After breakfast the following day, Marlon led the tour of the plateau grounds. Queen Michelle joined Healden and Jonathan as they followed the governor. Jonathan had a slight limp from his injury, and his mother's arm was bandaged.

Smooth paving stones lined the path from Marlon's residence and led them northeast to a massive structure made of the same paving stone three-quarters of the way up. A curved roof veranda shaded the porch around the entire building. Wood planks continued to the building's roofline, which was also arched. The planks had been overlaid with gold. The arch beams were red. The flag of Gil-Lael flew at the four points of the roof.

Two evergreen shrubs on either side of the door were cut in the shape of dragons, with their long tongues emerging from open jaws. Spring flowers were in bloom, and the trees were heavy with blossoms. Their sweet scent surrounded them.

Marlon continued his dialogue uninterrupted. "This is the throne room. Shall we?" He stepped up three wide stairs and entered by sliding a plain rice paper door to either side.

Jonathan walked into a massive room close to the size of the building itself. One oversized elaborate chair was placed on a single-tier dais with a red carpet beneath and a red cushion. The chair was carved with a two-headed dragon that extended high over the occupant's head. Rubies were set in the dragon's eyes, while the body was made up of emeralds and gold leafing. The arms and feet of the chair ended in claws.

"Intimidating." Jonathan took a few steps closer.

Rows of colorful cushions lined the side of the room, making a clear path straight to the throne. The only furniture was the throne chair. Not even a single table was present for scribes to take notes.

This awed Jonathan. Soon, he must sit in that chair. *I will have an aching back every night.*

"There's nothing on the walls?" Michelle pointed to the gray stone wall.

Jonathan glanced at the stone interior. No windows, just one way in and one way out. "How do you vent on a hot day?"

"The stone creates a cool environment," Marlon continued. "My predecessor told me that when he arrived here shortly after the war when High King Healden gained the right to rule Shea-Talon, the throne had been ransacked and items stripped from the walls. Only the chair remained, but most of the jewels were missing. I had it refurbished before your arrival, Highness."

"Where have you been taking council?" Jonathan turned away from the throne.

"I have held council in my home."

Jonathan glanced at Marlon and paused. The governor's right eye hand was twitching. *Did he have an illness?* "And these cushions?" Jonathan waved his arms.

"It is the custom in Shea-Talon that those members you appoint to bear witness kneel before you while in attendance."

"What of those who come seeking help?" Healden spoke this time.

"They kneel here, Majesty." Marlon walked to a woven grass rug that faced the throne.

"And the scribes?" Jonathan asked.

"Three men kneel to the left of the throne and write. They bring their own cushions with them." Marlon pointed to the place where those men would be. "Of course, there are guards in attendance as well who stand at the door and line the walls."

"Behind the throne as well?" Michelle asked.

"Just to the side, *Majesté*." Marlon waited while Jonathan walked the room. "Shall we, Highness?"

Stepping outside, Marlon led them past the throne room gardens to the stone path once more. Marlon's residence was directly south of the throne room and had been built in the style of Gil-Lael. A three-story mansion made of brick with a blue-tiled roof. A duplicate building was next door to it.

"And who lives there?" Jonathan pointed to the east-side building.

"Ah…you will live there, Highness. That is until the palace can be refurbished," Marlon said.

"I've sent you a great deal of money over the years, Marlon. What have you done with it?" Healden frowned.

Marlon sputtered and turned red. "I assure you, *Majesté*, it has been well-spent. My predecessor built the home I occupy and its twin. The grounds needed to be repaired and the military guard towers and barracks you saw on the way up the bluff. When I arrived, I continued the restoration of the throne room and upgraded the City of Aya and other cities in the country. I did so, thinking it would go a long way in bringing the Shea-Talonian people onto our side and against the rebels. I also updated the wharf."

"Yet you didn't think to pave the pier road. That would have been my first concern." Jonathan folded his arms.

"It is an ongoing process, Highness. Funds are limited."

"We will need to see the books and accounts of taxes and tariffs," Healden said.

"Of course, *Majesté*." Marlon nodded, folding his right hand over the left to stop it from twitching.

The stone path continued north, zigzagging through themed gardens. Stone gardens with tall boulders and sand raked into waving lines came first, followed by tall grasses. There were ornamental trees, cherry trees, evergreen bushes, and flowering shrubs. They walked past benches, flower beds, and water features.

Jonathan stopped at his mother's side as she gazed down at a pond.

"I've seen these fish before," Michelle said. "In my world when we took the trip to Japan. Do you remember, Jonathan?"

"*Oui*, but I forget what they are called."

Marlon looked from Jonathan to Michelle, frowning. "I didn't know you could travel back-and-forth from this world to yours, *Majesté*."

"The doorway is sealed shut now." Healden stood by Michelle's side, glanced at her, and set his arm around her shoulder.

Jonathan remembered when Uncle Christopher arrived with the news that his grandparents had been killed in a car crash. His parents returned with him for the funeral. They'd given their Colorado residence to Christopher and once back from L'Amérique, his father had the portal between worlds sealed. His mother took out a kerchief and dabbed her eyes.

"The name of the fish." Jonathan tapped his foot.

"*Nishiki-goi*, they aren't for eating." Marlon let go of his left hand. It no longer twitched.

"Of course not," Michelle said.

A small stream ran from the pond over a rocky ledge into another part of the garden. They walked across a decorative bridge and entered yet a different themed park. This one had evergreens cut into the shape of animals. The stream-fed another pond here, which had white water lilies and more fish. Straight on a two-story building could be seen, made of wood with gold overlay that had been hammered for a textural effect. A great carved wooden double door continued the dragon theme. The arched roof was held in place by wooden beams painted red and black, tile made up the roof. Windows decorated with wooden carvings of serpents stood silent watch.

"The palace," Marlon said.

"Impressive." Michelle put her hand on Jonathan's arm. He pulled his eyes away from his new home to look at her smile.

Jonathan turned his gaze back to the palace. He loved Château de Talaith with its white stucco finish and blue roof. There were terraces and porches and balconies and his father's oval office made of glass. Then he realized what was missing. A horse lover, he had to ask. "Where's the stable?"

"There isn't one," Marlon said.

"Where do they keep the beasts?" Jonathan frowned.

"There are two stables by the barracks and guard towers along the route to the top of the plateau."

Jonathan made a slow turn, surveying the many gardens. There was no place within eyesight suitable for building a stable though the land would support growing hay and enclosing several pastures. He'd have to remedy that.

They entered the palace. Carved wooden doors led into all the rooms. However, room after room had been pillaged of contents, and what was left was either broken or burned. Fires had been set, and the walls were darkened with soot. The stairs leading to the second floor were damaged so badly it wasn't safe to climb them.

Stepping around more broken pottery and once beautiful artwork, Jonathan said. "When did this happen?"

"When word arrived after the war with Renwyk, and the people of Shea-Talon learned their king and his sons were dead, they marched on the few guards left, killed them, and plundered the palace. As you can see, nothing remains." Marlon indicated the ruins within with a wave of his arm.

"Where's the kitchen?" Michelle asked.

Jonathan grinned. His mother loved to cook and had introduced several dishes from her world to their chef.

"This way." Marlon led them down a hall to a door opening onto a covered terrace with an open-air courtyard in the center of the building. Unlike the gardens outside, this one was unkempt and overgrown with weeds. When they reached the end, a doorway led them inside the kitchen. As with the palace, it had been emptied of anything useful. The pantry doors were broken and laid askew. The air was heavy with mold. Flour and other food items too old to identify lay scattered and trampled into the tile floor. The only useful thing remaining was the massive fireplace, and even it had missing bricks.

"The repairs will cost a fortune. I can't possibly raise enough in taxes to make this livable soon." Jonathan picked up an old filthy apron before tossing it back down on the floor.

"We need a look at those ledgers, Marlon," Healden said. As always, his expression was unreadable, but Jonathan knew that tone of voice. Things didn't bode well for Marlon.

Coronation

Chapter 3

Tamika Shigemori peered at her reflection in the mirror. She wore a magenta-colored silk dress with lace overlay. Her black hair had been styled in ringlets and was pinned back with two pearl combs. She'd been assured that this fashion was the latest trend in Gil-Lael. Their new emperor had arrived three days ago, and she wanted to be fashionable at his coronation and the evening meal at the palace.

The palace. No one had been to the palace since Warwyk died in the war as Renwyk's ally. The thought made her pause as she remembered the stories her father had told of the days when he had been a young man. And her mother, who had been raised in the palace and knew of its grandeur. Most of Shea-Talon's elite longed for the return of their old ways. But Warwyk's sons had died with him.

After the war and death of their emperor, High King Healden of Gil-Lael claimed the right to the throne of Shea-Talon through the spoils of war. It was one of his sons who would be crowned emperor of Shea-Talon today.

Still, the blood of Warwyk's daughters ran in many families, which made some eager to contend for the imperial crown. Tamika's mother was born of Warwyk's third wife.

The door behind her swung open. Ose entered, dressed in his gray kimono with his scimitar sheathed at his side. Tamika watched his reflection in the mirror. Her husband kept his thoughts close, and she couldn't guess what he was thinking.

"Tamika." Ose stepped close. "Tonight, we witness a new emperor crowned. Let us show him the beauty of our customs."

Tamika turned toward her husband. "This is what they wear in Gil-Lael. I wish to honor our new emperor."

"There is time enough for that. But on this glorious night, I would do honor to our ancestors. Dress as our traditions have taught, for me, my princess."

"As you say, I shall." Ose smiled and kissed her cheek.

After he left, her maid Enya helped her to change into a tight kimono of blue silk embroidered with the cream-colored flowers of the sacred lotus. Lastly, Tamika sat while Enya brushed out the curls from her rich black hair and pulled the strands up, making a high bun in a *shimada* style and added silk ribbons and a silk lotus flower.

When finished, Tamika stared at her reflection. White painted face. Red lips. She appeared as all Shea-Talonian noblewomen did. She slipped her feet into the wooden sandals and took the mincing steps her dress allowed out the door to Ose's side. In silence, he helped her into the carriage, and they drove toward the bluff.

There were still a few families in Shea-Talon who practiced arranged marriages despite new laws abolishing the custom. Tamika's was one of them. She respected Ose but couldn't say exactly how she felt about him otherwise, even after ten years of marriage.

Tamika and her husband waited at the first guard tower as their carriage and persons were searched for weapons. Ose handed over his scimitar.

The coronation of Prince Jonathan took place in the throne room. Only Shea-Talon's elite were invited. The men knelt on the pillows provided while their wives stood at the back in quiet observance.

The gems of the traditional throne sparkled in the candlelight. They waited for Jonathan's arrival. Two additional chairs had been brought in and were positioned to his right. A table waited opposite along with several priests of the Gil-Laelian religion.

The room was crowded with the nobles. Gil-Laelian soldiers stood, at the door, along the wall, and behind the throne.

Tamika had looked forward to hearing Prince Jonathan speak on the day of his arrival. However, the attack had changed that. Years of anger and resentment preceded him. Many had lost hope, and suicide occurred almost daily. Tamika could only hope Jonathan would bring the people together and improve the lives of so many poor and lost souls.

Beside her, the other wives had all dressed in gowns imported from Gil-Lael. Their hair was coifed in a variety of fashionable ways. Tamika was the only one in a kimono. The only one to have her hair done up in the *shimada*. The only one to have a painted face. Her stomach rebelled, and she felt a little sick. If her face hadn't already been painted white, she knew her nerves would have made it so.

Ose had also worn his traditional kimono. Although the other men had dressed as Gil-Laelian men did, in pants and jacket over a shirt. *He will be just as noticeable as I am.*

Trumpets sounded. High King Healden entered along with Queen Michelle. Two guards preceded them and followed. The men all bowed, touching their foreheads to the floor as the royals passed. The women bowed at the waist while still standing toward the back since there wasn't room to kneel. None curtsied, though that was the Gil-Laelian way.

Once Healden and Michelle were seated, the trumpets sounded again. Jonathan entered. Guards escorted him as they had his parents. He wore black pants with a red jacket embellished with golden buttons, tassels at his shoulders, and a gold sash from his right shoulder to his left hip. A sheathed Gil-Laelian straight sword was attached to a golden belt at his side.

At the throne, he sat. Boots peeked out from under his pants.

Now, Tamika had a good look at him. His light brown hair fell to his collar. He had brown eyes and a hawk nose, unlike his father's straight one. He was a handsome man. Tamika hadn't expected that. Shea-Talonian children were taught that the royal house of Gil-Lael were monsters. None of them looked like monsters to her.

As her eyes wandered back-and-forth, taking in Healden, comparing him to Jonathan, she hadn't realized that Jonathan's gaze rested on her. When she did, she dropped her eyes. A tingling sensation spread through her. One she'd never felt before.

Since the war, more than thirty years before, several Gil-Laelian churches had been built in Shea-Talon, but Tamika had never been to one. Now, two of their priests lifted ornate incense burners and began to walk around the throne. A third priest with a tall cone-shaped hat lifted the Shea-Talonian crown, made of gold, embellished with rubies and emeralds in the shape of a dragon, its head center with the tail tucked under its chin and the rest of the body wrapped around in a circle to fit on the head. He advanced toward the throne and placed the crown on Jonathan's head. Next, Jonathan received the dragon ring and the moon scepter. The crown, ring, and scepter were all new. The originals had been lost after the war.

As the priest adorned Jonathan, he spoke in another language Tamika didn't know. *What did it mean?* She supposed the priest was blessing Jonathan.

As the ceremony commenced, Tamika wondered what tradition used to occur. No one still lived who attended Warwyk's coronation.

The two priests with the incense burners returned to the table. The other one stepped in front of the throne.

"May I present, Servant of the Most Excellent God, Judge of the Land and the Seas, Emperor of the People, His Royal Excellency, Jonathan Eoin Healden Calimar I." The priest spoke in Gil-Laelian, turned, and with a wave of his arm, he indicated Jonathan.

Jonathan stood. The two minor priests brought a red cape with an ermine collar and clasped it around his shoulders. Once again, the trumpets blasted. Jonathan stepped from the dais, followed by his parents, and walked out of the throne room.

The nobles stood. One at a time, they walked toward the back, collected their wives, and left. Ose waited. When at last he came, Tamika joined him. Those men who weren't married came last.

Once outside, they walked the path eastward where a large canopy had been erected. There were numerous round tables within the ceremonial tent that formed a u-shape before the long rectangular table at the head. The royal family sat there along with Governor Marlon and his wife. Soldiers stood guard everywhere. Outside the overhang, Tamika glimpsed an orchestra on one side and huge fire pits on the other. The smell of roasted pig sizzled her way.

The Shea-Talonian nobles found their assigned places quietly. Tamika walked just behind her husband as was tradition and found that their table was close to the Emperor. Ose pulled her chair out, and she sat. Then, lifting her gaze, she met the emperor's and quickly lowered her eyes, but not before that strange tingling sensation overtook her again.

Once everyone found their seats, Jonathan stood. Now that he didn't look at her, Tamika studied him.

"My people," Jonathan said. "We have a challenge set before us. The people of Shea-Talon need a new beginning. One that promises peace and prosperity for all. One that will address the wrongs of the past. One that will encourage all the people to prosper." Jonathan had an accent, but his diction was perfect in the language of Shea-Talon.

Ose shifted beside her, and she glanced at him.

Jonathan continued, "You who are the nobility of Shea-Talon are honor-bound to assist me in this endeavor. You shall comprise my High Council, in which you will attend meetings with me twice a week. In this way, I shall hear the voice of my people, for you will bring me their concerns, from minor issues to major ones. I will also open the throne room to all so the common people may come and speak with me on different days twice a week. It is my hope that you will gladly take on this challenge. What say you?"

Tamika had never heard anyone address the concerns of the ordinary people. Their new emperor intended to listen to them. *How would his judgment be? Harsh?* She expected just that, as it had always been.

The tent was quiet. No one spoke. Tamika felt the tension building. Her anxiety kept time with the beating of her heart. *What did Ose think of this?*

Several minutes later, and still, the emperor looked from one face to the other, waiting. Tamika felt shame replace her wonder. *The nobles must support Jonathan. Couldn't they see that?*

She stood. Her heart nearly jumped from her chest.

Lifting her hands to her face and cupping her palms together, she bowed. "Excellency, you have my pledge." She wanted to give him more. She wanted to give him the support of the people, but she could only promise her own. When she lifted her gaze to him, he was smiling at her.

A moment passed, and then, Ose stood beside her. "Mine as well, Excellency."

"I accept your brave and generous offer." Jonathan nodded. "Who will join Lord and Lady Shigemori and pledge their support."

Soon, the entire room stood and gave their pledge.

She sat once more and leaned toward Ose. "He is different, is he not?"

Ose nodded and whispered. “He is. I am not sure how the people will feel about him”

“I think most will like him.”

“But some will not.”

“Why?” Tamika leaned a little closer.

“Don’t forget. He doesn’t have the Bracelet of the Moon and Stars.”

The bracelet of the moon and stars was lost in time, as all the emperor’s treasure had been. The bracelet that the god Ye Tai had brought down from the heavens with him and given to their first emperor, the great Matsui.

Tamika turned aside from Ose. An uneasy feeling made her sick. *Why? What could account for it?* She lifted her eyes again and saw that Queen Michelle stood beside Jonathan with her flute in her hands. Whatever concern had gripped Tamika fell away. The legend of Michelle’s music was known to all. As a child, she’d longed to hear it; now, it seemed she would.

Jonathan spoke again. “May I present Her *Majesté*, Queen Michelle. She has composed a song to honor all of Shea-Talon.” He then smiled at his mother and returned to his seat.

The queen wore a gown of pale blue silk with crystals sewn into the bodice and throughout. Her hair was the color of lemons, fully ripe. She lifted the flute.

The first notes were slow. Then she used short staccato bursts which made Tamika feel as if raindrops were touching her skin. The orchestra joined the queen with the chimes striking as if thunder burst above. This was followed by a violin pulsing and bringing in the melody.

Tamika shut her eyes and gave herself over to pleasure. In her mind, she felt the ocean waves hit the shore, and the wind brought new seasons, the cherry trees in bloom, and the grapevines produced their sweet fruit. Drums changed the song to one where horses galloped over the plains.

The melody lifted, and the queen played alone once more. Tears came to Tamika's eyes as the sensation of healing overcame her. It dissipated the anger she held since her uncle wed her to Ose shortly after her father's death. She'd only been fourteen. Her disappointment led her to be critical of Ose, though she was careful to keep it to herself. The last high note the queen played caressed Tamika's mind. She would do better and be a proper wife.

The Shea-Talonian people didn't clap after a performance; instead, they all stood and bowed. They sat again while servants began to bring in food. Fish, ham, rice, fruit, and the emperor's own wine. Tamika savored the excellent taste and wondered if Jonathan knew he had a vineyard.

Ose became quiet while Tamika enjoyed a conversation with Ohno Arei, an old friend. "I thought we would be in the palace." Ohno ate rice with her chopsticks.

Tamika pulled her eyes away from the royal family, who used utensils to eat. "As did I."

"The music was so unusual. Nothing like what we have."

"I have great peace now." Tamika lifted the tender fish covered in daikon-oroshi sauce to her mouth.

"Oh, as I also did. I thought of my boys, playing with their ball."

Tamika gave Ohno a glance. She hadn't considered that the music would speak differently to others. *What did Ose feel?* She would ask him at another time.

She next tasted the *nasu miso itame*, a fried dish with onion, miso, and sugar. Delicious.

"Why do you not honor the emperor with your dress?" Ohno lifted pickled *hakusai* into her delicate mouth.

"We honor our ancestors," Tamika whispered.

Ohno giggled. "You are silly."

To that, Tamika had no reply.

Dessert arrived. Higashi, a candy shaped into dragons along with *namagashi*. Tamika nibbled at the delicacies.

While they ate, the orchestra continued to play. These men must have traveled with the royal family on the three ships. While their menu had been traditional Shea-Talonian dishes, the music was all Gil-Laelian. Now, she watched as High King Healden led Queen Michelle down to the dance floor. He held her close as they stepped together, turning and moving, forward and backward. The dance didn't resemble anything Tamika had ever seen before. Dances were usually reserved for performers and told a story.

Jonathan stepped down and came to their table. "May I have the pleasure of dancing with your wife, Shigemori?"

Ose frowned. "We do not dance."

"Surely you will make an exception." Jonathan didn't wait but held out his hand to Tamika. Once again, she was thankful for her white-painted face, which hid the hot flush that covered her cheeks. She stood and took Jonathan's hand.

He didn't hurry her, mindful of her tight kimono dress. "Hold my hand like so," he said. "And place your other hand here, on my arm."

She did as he instructed.

"Now, when I step back, you step with me, and when I step forward, you step back."

Tamika studied his movement. At first, her feet were clumsy, and then she found the rhythm. He took such small steps that she didn't stumble. Gazing up at his face, she smiled.

"I want to thank you for having the courage to give your pledge. You led the way while others followed."

"I did nothing more than my duty, Excellency."

"I think you did much more than mere duty. I would like to meet with you and the other women here for a special project. I'll be sending an invite soon."

Surprised, Tamika wondered what Ose would think. "I must ask my husband to grant me permission."

"I will be certain to send him a letter as well."

Jonathan turned her in the dance. He wore a spicy cologne that she had never experienced before. Ose favored a scent that smelled like fresh rain.

When the dance ended, Jonathan led her back to the table. When he relinquished her hand, a sense of emptiness came over her. She pushed the odd sensation down and buried it with thoughts of duty to Ose. As she did this, she noted that Jonathan went from one wife to another and danced with them all. By the time the evening was over, Tamika had experienced numerous jealous moments and chided herself for every one of them.

What special project could the emperor possibly need her assistance with?

The Decoration Committee

Chapter 4

Five days after his coronation, Jonathan stood on board the ship named for his mother, Her Royal Majesty, Queen Michelle. He hugged her. A terrible ache threatened to lock his heart. Most likely, he'd never see her again. Never hear her voice. Never listen to her play the flute. He pulled back and gazed at her beloved countenance.

Michelle lifted both hands and cupped his face. She smiled before biting her lower lip to quell its quiver. "Find someone you can love." She kissed his cheek and stepped back.

Healden hugged him next and patted his back. "I can give no greater advice. A woman to warm your heart and bed." He smiled when he pulled back.

"I will miss you both. Times like these make me wish for the conveniences of your world, mother."

Michelle had slipped through a portal some thirty-two years ago from L'Amérique. They had visited her parents during his childhood in the summer months and at Noel. He knew about airplanes, computers, and cell phones, among many other things.

"As do I," Michelle said.

Once off the ship, Jonathan stood on the dock and watched the sails fill with air and the vessel sailing toward the open waters. His parents waved until the distance obscured them. An hour, maybe longer, Jonathan continued to watch until the boat was swallowed by blue sky and ocean waves.

He joined Lieutenant Saville by the carriage. The dockworkers had all stopped their labor and knelt on the ground with their foreheads touching the earth.

"I will ride." Jonathan glanced at the various horses and men.

"Excellency, it isn't safe."

"Nothing happened on the way here. The people need to see me."

"But–."

"I have spoken." Jonathan took the reins of a fine Norman Cob thoroughbred mare, dark brown with a long mane, from a soldier and mounted.

Saville signaled for the soldier to board the carriage and joined Jonathan. The men formed a guard, and all kicked their beasts into a trot. The townspeople hadn't been notified of High King Healden's departure that day, and so none of them were prepared when the carriages and soldiers passed earlier nor ready to see their new Emperor ride past now. As one, they fell to their knees and bowed.

I must give them more dignity. Jonathan glanced from side to side, but no one looked his way.

Tamika stood before the royal palace along with eleven other wives for their meeting with Emperor Jonathan. A quiet week passed since he was crowned. A week to ponder what he would want all these wives to do for him. Gazing at the palace, she was in awe of its arches, woodwork, and gold overlay. She glanced at the other women as they bent together and whispered. Once again, she alone wore the traditional kimono dress and had her face painted.

Ohno discovered her and joined her side. “Once more, you wear the traditional dress,” Ohno spoke soft, her dark eyes running over Tamika.

“I honor our ancestors.”

“You should think to honor the emperor.”

There was no more time for talk when Governor Marlon opened the massive palace doors and walked outside. “Come in, ladies.” He motioned with his arm.

Tamika entered last, slowed down by her tiny steps. Inside, she found a massive entry under repair. The walls needed painting. The floor was missing tile. A temporary stairway had been built against one wall, and there wasn’t any fine artwork. Emperor Jonathan stood in the center. Beside him, Lady Marlon wore blue from head to toe. Each of the wives approached Jonathan and bowed before turning aside.

When it was Tamika’s time, she bowed and hesitated a moment before opening her purse. Within was an origami crane she had made. “For you, Excellency.” She glanced at the others. None had brought a gift. *Will His Excellency think I’m seeking favor?*

Jonathan smiled, took the crane, and held it up for inspection. “This is lovely. Thank you, Lady Shigemori.” His eyes fell to hers.

Tamika felt a flush warm her. His eyes crinkled slightly at the corners and were filled with humor. She didn’t understand why.

Once she had joined the others and turned back, she found Governor Marlon beside his wife.

“As you can see,” Jonathan motioned with his arm. “The palace needs repair. And I, need assistance.”

Tamika couldn’t help but compare him with Ose. Jonathan spoke in a deep baritone, while Ose’s utterances were a tenor. Jonathan was perhaps seven inches taller. His light brown hair had golden highlights. His skin was fair, while Ose looked like all other Shea-

Talonian men, with black hair and buttery skin. *Why did any of this even matter to her?*

"Lady Marlon will give you a tour. At the end, we will meet again for lunch. At that time, I would like you to present me with your ideas on how to paint and finish the rooms. Until then, good day." Jonathan walked around the group of women and left along with Marlon. The emperor still held her crane. Tamika smiled.

She followed the other women as they walked past one destroyed room after another. Sometimes entering them. She stepped over broken furniture, touching ripped wallpaper, and glancing through broken glass to the outside. The stale odor of dust and mold permeated the entire place. Lady Marlon's voice rose at the end of each sentence as if she uttered exclamation points. After the twentieth time, Tamika wanted to shout at her, but she wouldn't do that. The annoyance had given her a headache, or maybe it was because she'd skipped breakfast, too worried to eat. *And why should she be nervous?* She didn't know, and so she frowned and studied the rooms.

On the upper floor north end, they entered yet another bedroom triple in size with pink and purple wallpaper. Chiffon drapes ripped in many places, hung haphazardly across the ceiling. Tamika knew at once that this had been the concubine's bedchamber. Emperor Warwyk had many wives and concubines of all ages. The youngest being eight. Her own mother had been born of Warwyk's third wife.

Will Jonathan carry on this tradition, or will he follow the traditions of Gil-Lael? One wife and no concubines.

Tamika paused at the huge north end window. Jonathan stood some distance away with several men mapping out a large plot. What would that be?

Ohno joined her. "What are they doing?"

"Building something."

"That is plainly seen. But what?"

Tamika didn't answer. She could only guess.

The tour lasted another hour before they left the palace and walked through the gardens to the same outdoor tent they'd sat under over a week earlier: fewer tables, this time with vases full of peonies. Jonathan sat at the head table with the Marlons on his right.

He stood. "Ladies."

All the women rose from their chairs and bowed.

"Please, that isn't necessary." Jonathan waved his hand, indicating they should all sit. "We will eat, and then I hope to hear your thoughts on improvements to the palace."

Ohno nudged her. "He is so strange, don't you think?"

Tamika glanced at Jonathan and discovered he watched her. She bowed her head and swallowed the fish she was eating. "I think him handsome." *Why did she admit that?*

"Oh yes, he is handsome, but also so different." Ohno giggled. "He likes you."

"He doesn't. I just stand out in the traditional–."

"Dress and ghost make-up with that awful red lipstick. He probably wonders what you look like with it off."

"Perhaps." Tamika lowered her gaze and wished Ohno would stop babbling about every little thing Tamika did. She felt out of place as it was.

She continued to eat while Ohno began to talk with the woman on her other side. By the time Tamika finished the fish and moved onto the fresh berries, her headache disappeared.

Once the tables were cleared, Jonathan stood again. "Ladies. I'm all yours."

Many laughed at such a statement. Fear momentarily spread through Tamika until she saw Jonathan smiling. *What sort of man was he to let women laugh at him?*

Lady Nomiya began. "I think the walls should be painted purple to honor your Excellency."

"Perhaps you would prefer red, Excellency?" another said.

"Or blue."

Several others mentioned types of wallpaper which led to an argument between Nomiya and Suda.

"All know that purple is the royal color."

"No, not in Gil-Lael, it is blue."

A third woman piped in. "Our national color is red. It should be red. The roof is red."

"Ladies, please," Jonathan said. "I do not want just one color."

"Furniture is also important." Ohno stood to speak.

"Furniture comes later," Nomiya pointed out.

"His excellency needs a bedchamber first," someone said.

"No, a kitchen."

"No, he must have a study."

"A courtyard."

"A room for his concubines."

Tamika lowered her head and shut her eyes. The suggestions came in rapid succession, and she feared her headache would soon return. A sudden blast from a horn brought a few shrieks. Chairs made a creaking noise as the women sat once more. Tamika lifted her gaze to find Jonathan standing. He waited. The women quieted. He continued to wait. Then…

"Lady Shigemori."

Tamika felt a sudden rush as if she were alone with the emperor. No one else mattered. She held her breath as he met her gaze. "You alone have said nothing. What do you think?"

Tamika swallowed and lowered her eyes. She stood. *What did she think?*

"Excellency, I think the palace should reflect your interest and goals for Shea-Talon. What is your favorite color? Do you enjoy hunting or perhaps sailing? Do you wish to extend the traditions from your homeland or do you wish to embrace ours? Perhaps a little of both."

As she spoke, Jonathan began to smile.

"Lady Shigemori, I am appointing you to head up the Decoration Committee. Ladies, you will meet twice a week at the palace, present your ideas to Lady Shigemori, and she will make all final decisions." He stepped away from his table and came to her. Lifting her hand, he placed a kiss on the back. "You and I will meet to go over the suggestions you approve at the end of each day."

Tamika swallowed. His touch made her skin tingle. *Why did he kiss the back of her hand? What could it mean? And what would the others think?* "As you wish, Excellency." She bowed and folded her hands together, rubbing the place he had kissed with her thumb.

Ose awaited her when Tamika returned home. She greeted him with the customary bow.

"Come." He turned and led the way into the tearoom.

She knelt on the cushion opposite him. Ose's black hair was pulled back in a knot, with the rest of his hair falling past his collar. Most men in Shea-Talon cut their hair rather than continue the ancient tradition of *chonmage*. Not Ose; he held onto tradition as if it were his life force.

Tamika poured his tea and then her own. He gave a nod, sipped the tea, and set the cup down. "I want to know what happened?"

"Lady Marlon gave us a tour of the palace. After that we had lunch, and then His Excellency wanted us to share ideas on how to decorate."

"That is all?"

"We are to continue to meet on Tuesday and Thursday."

"Why?"

"There is much work to be done, and the emperor requires assistance." Tamika lifted her cup and took a sip.

"Why women?"

"Do you wish to help decorate the palace?"

"No. I don't think of such things." He finished his tea. "Since you will see the emperor twice a week, I want you to observe the changing of the guard. Where do they stand? What do they do? And report it to me."

Tamika frowned. "I will be in the palace. The emperor doesn't live in it. How am I to know where the guards are?" She wanted to ask why he wished to know this, but a wife didn't question her husband, so she remained silent on this matter.

"What do you mean, he doesn't live in the palace?"

"It was vandalized."

"Explain." Ose tapped his cup with a finger. Tamika dutifully filled it with more tea.

"The palace is in shambles. Torn wallpaper, broken windows, and furniture."

Ose's brows pulled together over his angular eyes. "I seem to recall stories about this. Many were angry when Warwyk didn't return. I am curious about our new emperor, though. If you have a chance to be around him, tell me what he does, how he behaves."

Ose stood. Tamika bowed but didn't say anything. *Why does he ask this of me? Could Ose be a member of the Haranobu? Besshou, let it not be so.*

When Ose left, Tamika went to her room and removed her make-up, slipping out of the kimono and into her riding outfit. The trousers and top were like a man's kimono except in color. Today, hers had been pale blue.

Once changed, she left her home, and walked toward the stable, pausing to peer up at the mountain.

The two towers beside the barracks on the way up to the summit were visible. At the top, rising above the trees, were two identical houses, made in the fashion of Gil-Lael with stone and blue-tiled roofs. Tamika noted how the houses were situated, making her think they appeared like eyes staring down at her. The throne room couldn't be seen, nor any other buildings.

She sighed and continued her trek to the barn. Time to visit the Romani and purchase more medicine. She'd been caring for the poor and sick for many years now. *Would the emperor do something for them?*

Trap

Chapter 5

Jonathan dipped the brush in paint and paused as he considered the view. He stood on a platform carved out of the existing rock. From it he could view the sea. Far below the bluff wall, the ocean crashed against the shore. The canvas was nearly complete. In it, clouds swirled above the ever-moving waters, and a pod of whales rose from the depths.

No one stood near. There was no need for guards. The only way up to the top of the bluff had two guard towers along with the barracks and fortifications occupied by hundreds of men. He was incredibly safe and equally lonely.

Footsteps made him turn. A guard escorted Lady Shigemori toward him. She wore a lavender kimono with enormous peonies displayed on the material.

Jonathan set aside the painting materials, took off his smock, and walked to the top of the stairs. Lady Shigemori bowed.

"My Lady, please, come and sit with me." Jonathan went to one of the stone benches carved along the wall. The guard turned and stepped away, giving them privacy.

Tamika climbed the stairs and came close to Jonathan, handing him another origami, this one in the shape of a deer.

"Thank you." Jonathan appreciated these small tokens more than this woman would ever know. She brought a new one every time she came, and he now had close to two dozen. He displayed them on several silver platters in his office.

She sat on the bench near his. "A beautiful painting, Excellency."

"Thank you." Jonathan gazed across at his work. He saw every flaw.

"The kitchen and courtyard are now complete," Tamika said. "The dining room is ready for furniture. But the craftsmen are still completing the woodwork in the entry."

"That is good news. The dining table I ordered from Gil-Lael should be here by week's end."

Tamika lowered her eyes, and Jonathan studied her. The make-up she wore made her face look like a porcelain doll.

"Will Your Excellency be ordering all your furniture from Gil-Lael?" Tamika lifted her eyes. They were round, unlike most of the people who had narrow eyes. Hers were dark brown, almost black. And her nose was a little longer than others he'd seen. He'd noticed this before, of course, but for some reason was struck by it again today.

"I'd like to find a local craftsman."

"There are several who live and work in Aya. Yoshiyori studied in Gil-Lael. You may prefer his work."

"Yoshiyori, you say. You'll have to introduce him to me. Instead of coming here on Tuesday next week, I will pick you up at ten in the morning, and we will visit him."

Tamika glanced away. "Shall I send notice?"

"No, we will surprise him."

She nodded and ran her fingers along the outline of one of the flowers in the dress.

"Why do you dress like that? And paint your face? When I studied the history and traditions of this land, I learned that painting your face was no longer practiced, and few wear the traditional dress unless it's a special occasion. Am I in error on this?"

Tamika lifted her eyes to his once more. "No, what you say is true." She hesitated and then continued. "My husband is somewhat old-fashioned and insists on me dressing in the traditional way when I leave the house."

"Ah…I see."

A long silence followed. Jonathan stood and walked to the stone wall that came to his waist. There he could see the ocean. Birds flew from their nest in the cliff wall and plunged toward the water, snagging small fish and taking them back to their dwellings.

He wanted to keep Tamika close, but the truth was, he barely knew her. She didn't talk about herself or Ose, and he found it difficult to question her without offense. *Shea-Talonians were easily offended. Would Tamika be offended too?*

Jonathan turned to find her studying him. "If there is nothing else, you may leave."

She stood. "Thank you, Excellency."

Back home, Tamika settled on the cushion before their dining table, a raised slab of wood just above the floor. Ose soon joined her, and she poured his tea.

"How was your meeting with the emperor?" Ose lifted his round cup with no handle. Delicate iris flowers were painted on it.

"The kitchens and courtyard of Katatsune Palace are complete, and the dining room is waiting for furniture. I think His Excellency is happy with the progress."

"I find it odd he should worry about the courtyard before the rest of the palace." Ose set his cup down just as Tamika took a sip from hers.

"The doors between the dining room and courtyard will completely open, so guests have a view of the garden. In warm weather, tables are placed in the courtyard, so his excellency can eat there if he likes."

"Ah…I see."

"The walkway from the kitchen to the dining room is along the covered veranda of the porch adjacent to the courtyard as well." Tamika poured more tea for both.

"Does the emperor have a table? And cushions?"

"A table is arriving from Gil-Lael soon. I don't think the emperor will have a low table. Instead, he'll probably have chairs, as is the custom in his homeland." Tamika gazed at their dining room, which was enclosed by moveable paper walls. The only decoration was the tiny vase that held a few flowers on their table.

"What is he like?" Ose set his empty cup down.

"He is an artist. I saw his painting today."

"An artist? An odd pursuit for an emperor. Hunting, fishing, falconry, those are noble endeavors."

Tamika said nothing for a long time. Her mother had taught her that women shouldn't speak unless spoken to. Tamika wasn't quite so dutiful as that, but if she couldn't think of something positive, she kept silent.

"Is he getting all his furniture from Gil-Lael?" The tone Ose used seemed harsh. Surprised, Tamika lifted her eyes.

"He expressed a desire to meet local craftsmen. I am to introduce him to Yoshiyori on Tuesday morning."

"Yoshiyori, you say?" Ose nodded. "He does good work." He pushed back from the table. "Tuesday? What time?"

"He is picking me up at ten in the morning."

"Ten." Ose stood. Without saying more, he turned and left.

On Tuesday morning, the royal coach passed through the entrance of Wakisaka, the Shigemori estate. Jonathan gazed out the window at the impeccable landscaping. Lemon trees lined the drive and would soon bear fruit. A pair of peacocks hurried off the road. When they rounded the corner, the house came into view. The structure was one story, with a porch around the building. It was painted in peach tones with trimmed evergreen bushes and wisteria trees artfully placed.

The Shigemoris were waiting on the porch. When the carriage came to a stop, Jonathan stepped down. Tamika wore a simple rose-colored skirt and cream blouse. No white makeup marred her beauty, and her lips were brushed in soft pink. Her black hair had been done in ringlets. Jonathan was pleased to see her dress in modern clothing with no white paint on her face, but her curls struck him funny. He couldn't help his smile but made sure not to criticize. The last time his sister wore ringlets, she was eight.

They approached, and Ose bowed while Tamika curtsied. Though Jonathan could tell, it still seemed awkward to her.

"Good morning," Jonathan said when they stood before him once more.

"Excellency," Ose said. "I wish to accompany you, that I may be sure of my wife's protection."

"I have brought guards with me."

"I fear the Haranobu. They have spies everywhere and may have set a trap. However, I am skilled with my sword, Excellency, and prepared to offer my life in protection of you both."

Jonathan studied Ose. Marlon suspected him of being one of the leaders of the Haranobu, a group of rebels who wanted to restore the old line as emperor. Since Warwyk had lost all his sons in the war between Renwyk and Healden, Jonathan wasn't sure how the old order could be reestablished unless it was through the female line. He'd seen the list of men who could call Warwyk grandfather. *Should I worry about his granddaughters as well?* A question he'd asked himself repeatedly.

"Another guard is always welcome." Jonathan pondered where to put Ose. If he was a traitor, having him in the royal coach and armed was problematic. But, at the same time, he didn't want to shame Ose, especially in front of his wife.

"One moment." Jonathan turned and walked toward the back. Lieutenant Saville dismounted his horse.

"A word." Jonathan led the way further on from the soldiers who waited. "Shigemori wants to accompany us, to serve as his wife's protector." He spoke in Gil-Laelian.

"Oui," Saville said.

"I hesitate to give him access to the coach. What advice may you offer?"

Saville studied Shigemori for a moment. "Offer to allow him to ride beside me in the lead."

Jonathan frowned. He wondered how Shigemori would view that. He nodded and walked back to where the couple waited.

"My Lord," Jonathan said, reverting to Shea-Talonian speech. "Lieutenant Saville has offered you a place of honor riding beside him."

Ose turned his eyes on the Lieutenant. Jonathan noted a flash of anger that Ose quickly suppressed. Then, without speaking, Ose nodded to his servant. "Saddle my horse." The man bowed and left.

While they waited, Jonathan used the opportunity to talk a little with Ose. "Tell me, My Lord, what do you produce on this estate?"

Ose glanced at the soldiers, preoccupied with some thought, and then answered. "I grow barley and buckwheat."

"There is a market for such grains. Where do you sell it?"

"Both are used in cereal, but I also own an shōchū plant. Have you tried it?"

"I have not." Jonathan watched Ose. The man tapped his foot with impatience. *Why?*

"I shall send you a bottle of my best."

Ose's servant came around with his horse. He mounted, and Jonathan turned to Tamika. "Shall we?" He held out his hand.

She turned her eyes from Ose to Jonathan's and smiled. "Excellency."

Jonathan took her hand, and immediately, he felt a surge of warmth spread through him. *Oh, Great Créateur, she is married.*

Once they were both in the carriage, he tapped the side, and Lieutenant Saville led the way toward the gates of Wakisaka with Ose beside him. Tamika opened her small purse and removed a dragon origami from within, handing it to Jonathan. He smiled and held it up to examine the delicate folding of the paper.

"You'll have to teach me how to do this sometime."

"My pleasure," she said.

"The color you selected in your skirt suits you."

Tamika looked down at the fabric and ran her fingers over it. "It is pretty and the fashion so different from ours. I won't miss the tight kimono."

"Tell me what you know of this man, Yoshiyori."

"I only know that he is skilled in furniture making. I have no need of furniture, so I haven't been to his shop, but my friend, Ohno, has. They are building a Gil-Laelian structure on their property and will be furnishing it in the style of your homeland. What I saw of Yoshiyori's work there is beautiful."

"Indeed. And…Ohno is married to?"

"Bito Arei."

"Oh yes." Jonathan visualized the man. The Shea-Talonian people were short in general, but Bito Arei only came to his chest.

Tamika gazed out the window. Now that he had a good look at her without make-up, he realized that her features weren't as pronounced as most.

"How did you come to marry Ose?"

Tamika turned her dark eyes on him. "My uncle arranged it."

"Your uncle?"

"Yes, after my parents died, I went to live with my uncle. Before the end of summer, he had arranged my marriage to Ose. I knew Ose before that. He was my brother's friend."

"Was?"

"Yes, my brother died in a hunting accident the year before the fire. My parents and sister perished in the fire. I wasn't home when it happened."

"I am sorry for your loss."

"It has been eleven years. I miss them, but at least I have our home here. There are many happy memories."

"Your parents owned Wakisaka?"

"Yes." Her fingers folded together, and she looked up at him while keeping her head lowered. "I don't want you to hate me."

"Why would I hate you?"

"Because of my mother."

"I can't imagine anything that would make me hate you." Jonathan immediately thought she would tell him some horrific tale.

"My grandmother was Warwyk's third wife."

"I see. Then your mother was his daughter. She had property as well."

"More than property. My mother was a favorite. Warwyk gave her land, money, and jewels."

"Do you wear any of them?" Jonathan felt a sense of relief that she admitted her bloodline. If there was danger from the Shigemoris, it didn't come from Tamika. She was too honest.

"Ose locked everything away when we married. They are all his now, including our home here."

Jonathan frowned and peered out the window. They drove along the main street, passing one shop after another. He remembered the law that transferred married women's possessions to their husbands, but he didn't have to like it. It seemed wrong.

"How old were you?" He looked at her again.

"I don't understand?"

"How old were you when you married Ose."

"Fourteen."

They pulled up to a shop with a large window that gave a view of the interior. The footman opened the door and bowed. Jonathan stepped out and then turned, offering his hand to Tamika and helped her down.

A small table and chair had been placed outside the shop. More furniture could be seen through the window. The footman was now at the shop's door and stood with it open. Ose and Lieutenant Saville joined him.

"Shall we?" Jonathan went into the shop.

Several workers labored at the back and stopped immediately when Jonathan walked through the door. They all fell to their knees and touched their foreheads to the floor. One stood back up and came forward.

"Excellency, what an honor. How may I help you?" The man had gray hair that he kept in a long braid down his back.

"Yoshiyori I presume."

"Yes, yes."

"You have been recommended to me. Please, show me around."

Yoshiyori immediately led the way showing off his work. The furniture was made of many types of wood, including cherry, mahogany, oak, walnut, and pine. There were rich brocade fabrics on the sofas and chairs. And a choice of claw feet on the tables or more simple designs.

They spent more than an hour listening to Yoshiyori and examining the quality of his work.

"Impressive." Jonathan stood in the middle of the shop. The workers had resumed their labor, and the sound of hammers and sanding could be heard. The entire place smelled of freshly cut wood and furniture polish. "I would like to retain your services, Yoshiyori. I have an entire palace to furnish."

Yoshiyori squared his shoulders and stood a little taller. His smile softened the lines of age that graced his face. "Thank you, thank you, Excellency."

"This is Madam Shigemori. I have requested her help in refurbishing the palace. You will work with her, and she will select all the furniture I will need."

"Yoshiyori." Tamika bowed to the older gentleman. Then, everyone started bowing all around, and Jonathan gazed at Saville, who appeared a little amused by the spectacle.

Once a meeting with Yoshiyori was arranged at the palace, Jonathan turned to leave. As they walked toward the shop door, Ose came near.

"Thank you, Excellency, for giving so much honor to my wife."

"My pleasure." Jonathan stepped through the open door, his footman to the side. Ose and Tamika followed close behind. Saville had already left and waited by the coach.

As soon as Jonathan cleared the overhang, he heard the whizzing of arrows. Three slammed into the coach. Another grazed his cheek. The horses reared and took off, galloping through the street. Across the way, a dozen men or more held up their scimitars and shouted, "*Shi Xun*!"

Jonathan turned and shoved Tamika toward the shop door. "Go back inside." He pulled his sword and saw Ose do the same. He turned back toward the rebels, slicing his blade across one man's sword arm. Ose fought on one side of Jonathan and Saville not far from him. The Gil-Laelian soldiers moved to block more men from reaching Jonathan, but they were outnumbered.

He killed a man and then another. More came. The Shea-Talonian rebels pressed him back toward the shop. Ose engaged a man trying to cut through two others to reach Jonathan from the side. Jonathan noticed a man slip past, a knife in hand. He turned. Tamika hadn't gone back inside the shop. *Damn. I must stop this man.*

The enemy stood between Jonathan and the lady. A thrust with his knife, and Jonathan felt the blade cut his arm. Another jab and he managed to press the man backward.

"Go inside," he yelled at Tamika, but she seemed paralyzed.

Another man came at him from the opposite side. "*Créateur*!" Jonathan cried. A quick stab with his sword put one man down. He turned just as the one with the knife hopped backward to avoid Jonathan's killing blade. The glass of the door to the shop shattered, and the man fell against Jonathan's sword, trying to deflect the lethal shards.

Tamika turned. Blood squirted from her wrist, where a piece of glass was embedded.

"I have your back," Saville called.

Jonathan dropped his sword, jumped over the dead man, and caught her. She clutched his arm with her good hand, her eyes filled with tears. "Jona…" she whispered as she fell. He went down with her, gently putting her on the ground. He ripped material from Tamika's petticoat, pulled the glass out and wrapped her wrist tight, and then held it up so gravity would help slow the bleeding. His fingers coated in her blood; he felt as if his own life were being spent as her face took on a gray hue. He put his hand on Tamika's forehead. She was cold and clammy but not dead.

Ose joined him. "Tamika." He reached for her.

"Here." Jonathan handed Tamika's arm to Ose. "She cut her wrist in the glass. You must hold it up and keep the bandage tight, or she will die."

Ose took her arm.

He turned back and found the fighting had ceased, and the dead or injured Shea-Talonian rebels far outnumbered his men. Saville stepped over one of them to come to his side.

"You're injured, Sire."

"A minor cut nothing more, but Lady Shigemori is severely injured." A lump caught in his throat. He had been foolish to come when Yoshiyori could have been brought to him.

"What are your orders?" Saville asked.

"Do we have a suitable place to hold the injured rebels?"

"*Oui*."

"Then, arrest them and interrogate them. We must learn who their leader is."

Romani

Chapter 6

Twilight changed the hue of the sky, from pale blue to deep purple. As Jonathan gazed out over the ocean, a breeze touched his hair with invisible fingers. The scent of peonies floated his way, and he shut his eyes. He'd been raised in a land where nearly everyone loved his father. Only twice in recent years had the throne been threatened. The war with Renwyk before he was born and then by Sinon Aweirgan. Now, he received reports of skirmishes almost daily, and he'd been in two. Shea-Talon wasn't an easy country to rule.

Today, he made a colossal blunder. He regretted his stupidity. He'd wanted to leave the palace grounds and have an adventure. But in so doing, he'd put his own life and that of Lady Shigemori at risk, and now she was injured and may die.

Tamika. The thought of her made his heartache. He was cursed. Always attracted to married women, but Tamika was in a league all her own. Her husband, Ose, had proven himself a loyal subject today. That was good. Someone he could depend on. But, on the other hand, if Ose was a traitor, he could have him executed and, in time, marry Tamika. He wanted her. More than any woman before. But he couldn't just do away with her husband. That would be an obscenity.

Jonathan turned to the sound of footsteps. A guard approached with a noticeably short man in tow.

"Excellency, this is Master Mossé," the guard said.

Master Mossé bowed. He was dressed in brown pants with a matching jacket and a burgundy cape tied around his neck. He removed a wide-brimmed hat to reveal long curly hair. "His Majesté, High King Healden the 1st, has sent me to you, Excellency, to examine your books." He climbed the three porch steps and pulled a letter from an inner pocket.

Jonathan took the letter and turned it over to see the emblem of the House of Calimar pressed into the wax seal. He opened the letter and read his father's message introducing Mossé.

"I see." He studied the man as he looked up at him. A pug nose rested between two brown eyes. "Leave us," Jonathan directed the guard. "Come, sit and tell me how my father managed to send you so quickly?"

Jonathan took one of the stone benches and watched Mossé waddle to the one next to his. He lifted himself up, rolled to the side, and sat, his legs dangling off the edge.

"His Majesté called on me when his vessel arrived in the port city of Clérisseau and hired me. I left the next day, two months ago now."

The City of Clérisseau had sprung up about twenty years earlier as trade between other nations increased. Jonathan had departed for Telaneasse from there when he left to study art.

"How long have you applied yourself to the study of numbers?"

"I took a shine to it early in my schooling and have worked with several esteemed members of the Numeral Society."

"How much did my father tell you?"

"Only that you needed a professional bookman."

Jonathan gazed at Marlon's house a short distance away and wondered where to put this man. If Marlon was stealing, this little man might be in danger rooming at the mayor's house.

"Do you have a first name, Mossé?"

"Grégory, Sire."

Jonathan turned back to him. "Grégory, the palace is being renovated. I live in one of those houses." He pointed. "I hope you will agree to take one of my rooms there."

Grégory opened his mouth and then shut it. Then after a moment, he said, "I'd be honored."

"I'm about to tell you something which you cannot repeat. Are you capable of keeping secrets?"

"*Oui*, of course."

"Good. I am concerned that Governor Marlon has been stealing money from the treasury. I will need an accurate count of the monies and a search of the books to see if you can find any falsehood. Are you able to do that?"

"*Oui*."

"You must not eat with or discuss anything with Marlon. I don't trust him. Eat only in my house. He lives in the other one. I will also require regular meetings with you to learn what you have discovered."

The look on Grégory's face bordered on comedy and tragedy. His brows were thick and pulled so close together that they formed a single line over his eyes while at the same time his mouth was curled down at the ends. Jonathan smiled, hoping to reassure the fellow.

"Don't fear, I will appoint you a personal guard." Jonathan stood, and Grégory followed. He came to Jonathan's waist.

"I will have someone give you a tour. But for now, I'm hungry. Are you?"

"Oh, *oui*, I am."

Jonathan ate breakfast at his manor house the following morning and watched Grégory shovel eggs into his mouth.

"Do you know much in the way of taxation, Grégory?"

The man put up a finger to indicate a moment, swallowed his eggs, and washed them down with a gulp of tea. "No, Sire. I've never worked with the taxing of goods or people."

"Then you will need to learn, but first things first. I will assign you a scribe, and you will both go to the treasury and count the gold and silver coins there. I need to know how much I have. There are also land titles and fishing vessels as well as an army and navy. I need to know the exact numbers and uses of each. Once you've done that, I'll have you look at the accounting books and review the tax system."

"Very good, Sire."

"Do you know the language?

"I fear not."

"Then, you must learn. I'll appoint a tutor. What about a wife or children? Did you leave them behind in Gil-Lael?

"No, I'm not married."

Jonathan nodded and resumed his meal. After attending business, he mounted a horse, collected a contingent of soldiers to guard him, and rode out. The ride to the Shigemoris was short. He knocked on their door and waited. Soon a servant opened the door, fell to his knees, and pressed his forehead to the floor, speaking without rising. "Excellency."

"You may stand." He waited a moment. "I wish to see Lady Shigemori."

The man nodded and showed Jonathan in. The windows in this room were open, allowing natural light to spread onto numerous large plants in pots. There was no furniture, just cushions on the floor. And nothing on the walls either. He remained standing.

Somewhere outside, a drum began to beat a series of taps. Odd.

Time stretched thin. Jonathan didn't understand what was taking so long. Then at last, the door slid open, and Tamika entered. She was wearing riding pants and a casual cotton top. Her hair had been pulled back in a ponytail, and her wrist was still bandaged.

"Excellency." She curtsied. "My apologies, I was halfway through the forest when I heard the drumbeat letting me know I was needed."

"Where were you going?"

"I visit the Romani on Wednesday to collect herbal remedies for the sick."

"Romani, you say. I didn't know there were any in Shea-Talon."

"Oh yes, we have quite a few."

"I'd like to meet them. Shall we?"

Tamika's eyes widened. "You wish to go with me?"

"Yes."

A moment later, they were both outside. Jonathan told the soldiers where they were going, and soon Tamika led the way with twenty soldiers following. Around the house, they headed north, passing a pond garden and then a vegetable garden with the stables on the other side. The forest spread just past the property. No fence blocked the way.

Jonathan trotted beside Tamika as they passed under white alder growing beside aspens. Occasionally a deer would raise its head while eating to peer at them and then flee into the brush.

"I must admit, I'm surprised to see you up and about after yesterday's accident. How's your wrist?" Jonathan glanced her way.

"It aches a little." Tamika held up her hand.

"You might have died."

"But I didn't."

The sunlight splashed through the trees and created shadows that collapsed across her face as they rode. Jonathan glanced up at the leaves. "Tell me a story."

She looked at him. "What kind of story?"

"Something that happened when you were a child."

Her brows pulled together, and she gazed straight ahead for a moment. Then smiled and turned his way.

"When I was little, my parents had a pond with the N*ishiki-goi* fish. I used to love to sit and watch them. My older brother loved sneaking up on me and more than once caused me to swim with the Nishiki-goi. Then, one day I heard him coming, and I moved quickly to the side. He took a tumble and swam with the Nishiki-goi that day." She lowered her gaze.

Jonathan chuckled. "I can picture it. I, too, have siblings, and we were always causing mischief for each other."

"It is your turn to tell a story."

"Hmmm…I once captured a skunk without getting sprayed and put it in my older brother's room. But of course, those beasts smell so strong that there was stink on my clothes, and I was caught. Liam couldn't sleep in his room for weeks."

"I have never heard of a skunk."

"A creature from my mother's homeworld. The portal near the *château* leaked, and the skunks passed through. Father had every one of them hunted down and killed."

"A portal into the queen's world? Did you ever go there?"

"Indeed. We spent many summers there with my grandparents and *Noel* too."

"What is Noel?"

Jonathan smiled. "A holiday to celebrate the birth of our Savior."

"It is part of your religion?"

"Yes. You also have such holidays, don't you?"

"Oh yes, my favorite is the Dance of Dragons to celebrate the arrival of *Ye Tai."*

"He is your number one god, is he not?" Jonathan watched her smile.

She lowered her eyes. "Yes, the highest god."

"Ah, I believe I read the story."

Jonathan turned his gaze into the forest. The Shea-Talonians had many gods, and each had its own strange story of power.

The trail turned around a rock and wound downward. Soon, they came to a clearing where numerous painted wagons made a circle. A central fire had been recently put out. Smoke slithered in the breeze and disappeared. Jonathan held up a hand to halt the soldiers behind him.

Tamika urged her mare forward a little. "His Excellency, Emperor Jonathan, to meet you."

A moment later, several men emerged from the forest. Bows were made ready, but the arrows weren't notched. Jonathan watched them. Their dark hair curled, and nearly all wore it long. Their shirts were multi-colored with belled sleeves over brown pants. The women followed with brightly colored skirts and linen tops that tied at the collar. Coins were strung in their hair, and heavy make-up was applied to their faces. They looked nothing like the Shea-Talonians, and Jonathan surmised they came from a similar place as his ancestors.

The group of more than a hundred people was joined by an older woman who used a walking stick. She hobbled, bent slightly forward with long gray hair.

"Excellency, a true honor. What brings you to our camp?" the woman said.

If Jonathan was honest, he'd reply, curiosity. However, a leader must be…*tactful.* "I understand your people provide healing herbs. I'd like to know more." He dismounted, and so did all his guard. Tamika glanced at him and then dismounted as well.

"What are your names?"

"I am Mariyam." She moved her staff, and the others began to rattle off their names. "Loris. Kourken. Stephen." And more, followed by the women and then the children. "Anoush. Isabella." So, on. Jonathan nodded and knew he'd never remember each one. Isabella was beautiful. She stood next to Kourken.

"Feast," Mariyam said. "Come." She nodded toward Tamika, and Jonathan followed.

The wagon she took them to was painted with bright colors in swirling designs and had two lanterns dangling from the top rear. Three steps brought them to the door. Jonathan had to duck to enter.

The scent of incense lingered. Bookshelves lined with many bottles stood to either side of a table and chairs in the center, and a red tablecloth with gold leaf overlay decorated the table. Mariyam asked, "the usual?"

"Yes," Tamika said.

The woman set her staff aside while filling small cloth bags with ingredients and tying them shut. When she had almost a dozen pouches, she came to the table and set them down. Tamika slipped her several coins before depositing the bags in an oversized purse.

"What will you do with those?" Jonathan asked.

"I take them to the poor who are ill."

"Tamika has a good heart," Mariyam said.

Jonathan smiled. "That she does."

Tamika flushed and looked down.

Once outside again, the smell from the fire pit made his stomach grumble. Children played with sticks and balls, giggling and chasing each other. Men were setting up tables while some women stood over the fire, cooking. Laughter was exchanged along with a hug or pinch on the arm. The soldiers walked along the perimeter, checking the wagons or talking with the Romani. Jonathan heard several of them speaking Gil-Laelian, which surprised him.

Tamika came to him. "Excellency, I must return home, or Ose will be worried."

"I will send men along to guard you."

"It isn't necessary. I come here alone often."

"It would make me feel better." Jonathan signaled the captain over.

"Excellency." The man bowed.

"Select a few men to escort Lady Shigemori home. It isn't far. I'm sure they'll have time to return and join the feast."

"As you wish." He turned to Tamika and motioned with his arm. She glanced at Jonathan before leaving.

He watched as Captain Périer helped her on a horse, and they all rode from camp. His thoughts once more turned dark. How could he deal with Ose to free Tamika? Disgusted by the images that his mind conjured, he kicked a stray ball and walked toward his men.

More than an hour later, the food was ready. Mariyam showed Jonathan a place of honor and sat beside him. The meal's main course was roasted pig along with a variety of vegetables and flatbread.

Mariyam leaned a little closer. "You like her."

Jonathan had been listening to a young Romani woman speak with another. "What? Who?" He looked at the older woman.

"Tamika. You favor her. What will you do? She is married."

"This isn't any concern of yours."

Mariyam smiled. "I may be old, Excellency, but I'm not blind."

Kourken stepped out strumming a guitar, followed by Isabella with a tambourine. She began to dance, lifting the tambourine overhead and shaking it violently, and then twisted this way and that until she knelt on the ground.

"She tells a story with her dance," Mariyam said. "She is showing how the earth shook many years ago. People fell to the ground with the movement of the earth."

Isabella rose lifting the tambourine once more. She rushed forward and bowed low, bringing her instrument forward and holding it with both hands while shaking it. Then she backed up and repeated.

"After the earth sent us to our knees, a great wave rose from the ocean and flowed in. Many were swept away to be swallowed by serpents in the seas."

Now, Isabella ran around Kourken and moved the tambourine from side to side, bending and rising.

"We awoke to find ourselves on a floating island." Mariyam leaned close to Jonathan.

And then, Isabella rushed forward, stopped abruptly, and fell to the ground once more. Kourken finished the song.

"We arrived here, and our island sank. And then many more islands arrived with Tamika's people. And, thus began our lives in this new place."

"Interesting," Jonathan said. "We have a similar tale. The elves brought us here."

"I had not heard that before," Mariyam said.

Jonathan cleared his throat and stood. "I must bid you farewell. Thank you for your hospitality."

Jonathan joined Captain Périer. "They say we should go north through the forest and will shortly come to the road," Périer said.

"Let it be so." Jonathan mounted his horse, and soon they were gone. As they passed beneath the alder trees, his mind returned to Tamika. He was pleased to learn that she helped those who were sick.

Fire

Chapter 7

The manor house where Jonathan lived had three stories with multiple bedrooms. He had a bath attached. Each room was furnished in the style of Gil-Lael. He could guess that Lady Marlon decorated the house since the color scheme was all in pastels. This was not his permanent home, so he wouldn't change it.

Five days had passed since he met the Romani. His routine had settled into a predictable schedule. So far, no urgent request had arrived during his meetings with the nobility, and not one peasant had come to beseech him on their behalf. The week's highlight was Tamika's arrival, but since he couldn't pursue her, that had become painful on multiple levels.

When he'd been fifteen, Lady Delaunay had requested a portrait from him. She took him to an upper floor of her husband's estate. While he prepared his canvas, she went into another room to change and emerged naked. At the time, he'd never seen a naked woman before. She smiled when she appeared, but now, thinking back, he could barely remember what she looked like, only her breasts. She approached and took his hand, putting it on one plump bosom. He could still feel the hardness of her nipple.

He never painted her portrait; instead, she introduced him to pleasure. He continued his affair with her the entire summer. When his father found out, Delaunay was removed from society and sent to live with nuns on an island far from Gil-Lael. After that, Jonathan couldn't help noticing how married women had a certain confidence about them, a particular way of moving and smiling that unmarried women lacked.

Tamika didn't move or behave in any of those ways. He suspected it was due to the honor-bound culture in Shea-Talon. He found Tamika intelligent and compassionate. Qualities he admired. He didn't believe that Ose gave her a second thought despite his demonstrations when they were attacked. He'd invited them multiple times to dinner and, on those occasions, had watched Ose. Not once did he include her in their conversation. If Jonathan addressed her, she gave short, polite answers and kept her head bowed. Ose would steal the discussion and turn it into something he enjoyed. While Tamika displayed honor, Ose had none.

Jonathan left his bedroom. He hadn't hired a personal servant yet and didn't miss having one.

At the end of the hall on the third level was a spiral staircase that led to the flat roof. He climbed it to the landing and opened the door. From here, he could see everywhere.

Smoke, thick and full of leaping flames, was visible. He grabbed the telescope he'd had placed on the roof and peered through it. There, past the city, it appeared as if a home was on fire. Not just any home, but one belonging to…*who*? Jonathan racked his brain.

A few days ago, he'd appointed a man to be his advisor by the name of Umezawa. He was a Shea-Talonian scholar and had brought a map. They both studied this map from the roof, and Umezawa had pointed out various buildings as well as estates belonging to the nobility.

So, who did this estate belong to? Oh yes, Nakagawa Kaku. He could picture him, but more importantly, Kaku was Warwyk's grandson.

Jonathan turned and ran to the stairs. Using the rails, he jumped several steps at a time. He continued to run to the end of the hall and descended the stairway there. Once on the main level, he burst through the front door to find Captain Périer and half a dozen soldiers. They replaced those men who stood guard outside his residence earlier.

"Captain," Jonathan bent for a moment, catching his breath. "There's a fire just past the city. The house belongs to a nobleman. Sound the alarm."

Périer signaled the trumpeter, who lifted his instrument and blew a series of blasts to indicate an urgent need.

Jonathan took one of the horses from a soldier and, together with Périer and the remainder of his men, galloped down the road to the first set of barracks. There, several hundred men rushed to mount their steeds. Lieutenant Saville joined his men, and once more, they headed out.

By the time they reached Kaku's estate, it was a smoldering ruin. More than thirty men and women had soot smeared on their clothes and faces. One approached and bowed as Jonathan dismounted his horse. He released the people from their prostrate obedience.

"Excellency."

"Who are you?"

"I am Satomi. We are servants." He indicated the others with a wave of his hand. We tried to save our master, but the flames were so hot our small effort came to nothing.

"Kaku?"

"Yes, he and his family were sleeping in the house. They are dead."

Jonathan stepped back and turned. The air was thick with smoke making each breath labored. Sheep and cattle grazed some distance away. All the bushes and trees close to the house were nothing but piles of ash. To die in such a manner was too horrible for words.

"How did it start?" Jonathan's emotions coiled within his gut.

"I awoke to the flames in the early hours before the sun. By the time we reached the house, the fire had spread to the entire building. We passed water in buckets and tried to save it, but no luck."

"Saville." Jonathan turned toward the man. "Do an investigation." He spoke Gil-Laelian.

He turned back toward the servants and addressed them in Shea-Talonian. "What will you do?"

Satomi glanced at the others and then bowed again to Jonathan. "We will need to find employment."

Jonathan gazed at the men and women. Enough of the palace was finished that he could use a few servants, but thirty? Could he really use them all?

"Come tomorrow," he said. "All of you. I will interview you and see if there is a place at the palace for you."

As one, the servants dropped to their knees and pressed their noses to the ground. "Long live His Excellency," they said.

Jonathan shook his head, uncomfortable.

Back at his manor house, Jonathan called a meeting with both Grégory and Marlon. When they were ushered into his office, Jonathan stood before a window gazing out at a garden filled with lush red and white flowers.

He turned. "Do we have servant quarters, Marlon?" It seemed a stupid thing he needed to ask but, he couldn't remember seeing anything that resembled such a place.

"Only those few rooms in the manor houses that are small. Before the palace was ransacked, there had been serving quarters separate from Katatsune at the rear. They were burned to the ground. "

"I see. What of the stables? Are they close to being completed?"

"No, I think that will take a year or better."

"Grégory, have you gotten an estimate of our income and supplies?"

"*Oui*, Excellency." He opened a folder and pulled a file out. Jonathan took it from him and opened it. In Grégory's precise handwriting, he read the sum of twenty-seven million Royal Tlokel, a gold coin, each valued at one thousand. In addition, there were thirty-one thousand Honor Som, a silver coin valued at five hundred, and then there was minor currency too.

Jonathan sat and turned the page where he read the expenses of keeping the army and navy, the tally of food storage and cost per month, then the number of horses and other animals and their cost. Page after page had meticulous counts of income and expense. The last page showed the taxes.

He stood abruptly. "Fifty-two percent! Do we need to tax the people fifty-two percent?"

Marlon looked at his feet and fingered his hat.

Grégory glanced at him before looking at Jonathan. "I have not yet determined where this money is going or how it is divided."

"Marlon, get out of my sight."

"As you wish." He bowed and left.

"Come and sit with me, Grégory." Jonathan returned to the desk chair, and Grégory climbed into the one before it.

"This morning, the estate house of Lord Nakagawa Kaku burned, killing both Nakagawa and his family. I found thirty of his servants covered in soot, having tried to save the family. I intend to hire them all. I need your help interviewing them with me and placing them in appropriate positions. We will need housing."

Grégory lifted pudgy fingers and began to twirl the end of his new mustache. A source of great amusement to Jonathan. Except for today, nothing was funny today.

"Tell me true, do we have the money, and do we need to tax my people fifty-two percent?"

"You have the money. As far as the tax, I think it is too high as well. King Healden invested in various sources of income, and by doing so, he was able to keep the tax at a minimum. From what I can surmise of your businesses, chief among them, the winery and fishing vessels are all reserved for personal gain."

"Can these sources be used to earn a profit?"

"Your excellency will have to do an accounting of their actual revenue. For example, how many fish are caught, how much wine is produced, and at what expense."

"Very well. We will visit the winery, you and I. Also, we must visit the fishing vessels, do a count, speak with their captains, etcetera." Jonathan stood once more, unable to sit still for long.

"What of housing?" Grégory asked.

"It will have to be built. But, for now, temporary housing will have to do. Tents." As he peered out the window, his mind returned to Kaku. *Was he murdered? Why?*

Hidden Treasure

Chapter 8

Tamika knelt before the dining table. “Good evening, my Husband.”

Ose grunted something. Steam curled from the teapot. Tamika reached for the vessel, prepared to pour Ose’s tea.

“How was your visit with the emperor today?” Ose lifted the teacup she set down before him. Their dinner was *domburi* with steamed fish. His questions had begun to disturb her. She watched Ose use the chopsticks to eat and wondered how much she should say.

“Did you know that Nakagawa Kaku’s house burned down? He died with his family.” She watched Ose hold the chopsticks midway to his mouth.

“I heard about it.” He put the food in his mouth and showed no reaction.

“Does this not trouble you?”

“I fail to see why I should be concerned. Someone was careless with the stove.”

Summer had given way to autumn, and the nights were cool. A breeze came through the open window and sent goosebumps on Tamika's arm. She shivered. "You knew him. Do you not feel compassion?"

"Nakagawa Kaku had no honor. He ignored the concerns of everyone. I will not miss him and his elevated opinion of himself."

Tamika had her chopsticks poised above the bowl. Rarely had she seen Ose angry? He held his emotions close. But he was angry now.

"What did he say to you?" Tamika couldn't help but wonder about Nakagawa and anything that transpired between the man and Ose.

"That is none of your concern. I am master. Now tell me what the emperor said to you today." Ose reached for the shōchū and poured his glass. He didn't offer any to Tamika.

"The emperor has called off the repairs to his palace. I am to oversee the building and furnishings of new servant quarters."

"What? Why?"

"Jonathan hired all of Nakagawa Kaku's servants. But the old servant quarters were destroyed, so new ones are being built. In the meantime, they are living in tents on top of the plateau."

Ose was staring at her. "Is he insane?"

"He is a kind and generous man."

"He is a fool!" Ose stood. "And he degrades you by tasking you over a project for his servants."

Tamika knew she shouldn't respond…but. "He trusts me."

"You are but a foolish child. Always willing to overlook the faults in others. Jonathan is a foreigner who believes he is entitled to our respect and loyalty. Well, I shall…" Ose stopped. His face had turned red. Without another word, he turned and left. The paper door vibrated when he slammed it, and Tamika felt the muscles in her stomach tighten.

She finished eating in silence, wondering about the events of the day and Ose's attitude. He hadn't changed much since their childhood when he was her brother's friend. She had caught him staring at her while she played, and often he seemed preoccupied with some thought he didn't express. She'd never liked him when she was a child. When her uncle informed her, she was to marry Ose. She cried for a week. All in all, her life wasn't a great burden, and she wasn't unhappy, but she also didn't see much of Ose.

Tamika soon finished and retired to bed. Tomorrow, she would meet with the architect. Jonathan had been clear about the needs he felt were essential in the buildings, and she looked forward to helping him. She loved being helpful. As her reward, he promised to build a hospital and hire more doctors for the people.

Ose laughed. He leaned back and took the cup of shōchū from his favorite geisha. She behaved in the proper way, lowering her eyes, speaking softly, and dressed in black with white face makeup. Her hair was adorned with a soundless cascade of tiny bells.

Ishikawa Natsu, Ose's best friend, joined him in chuckling. A moment later, Ose stopped laughing and leaned closer to Natsu. "Did you hear what he did?" Ose never mentioned Jonathan by name at the geisha house.

"Besides leave for the north country?"

Ose sat up. His frown shadowed his eyes. "What?"

"My wife saw them leave with wagons that carried his belongings. She said he left to visit his vineyard."

"When did this happen?"

"Two days ago. After Kaku's death."

Ose backhanded the geisha, who cried out as she tumbled. He stood. "I must leave."

Natsu grinned, swallowed more shōchū, and joined Ose.

Once outside, Ose marched toward the stable to retrieve his horse. The two men paid the horseman and mounted. Night shadows obscured the road. Both traveled to the geisha house so often they were unconcerned by the quiet. The smell of pines erased the memory of cherry blossoms filling the room where they had been. They trotted far enough away from the property to assure ears wouldn't hear when Ose pulled his beast to a halt. "She didn't tell me."

"Who?"

"Tamika. She didn't tell me he was leaving. We missed our opportunity."

"What will you do?"

"It is time to teach her respect." Ose kicked his stallion, leaving Natsu behind.

Tamika tried to stand, only to fall on her sleeping mat again. Ose had awakened her. Ripped her nightclothes off, beat her, and raped her. The taste of blood from her cut lip filled her mouth. Her body hurt, especially where he punched her or grabbed her.

She managed to sit and then stand. She grabbed the silk robe from her closet, put it on, and shoved her feet into the bamboo sandals. The robe felt as if it caught her emotions and kept them close to her heart. Long ago, she'd learned to hide her passions from Ose. A kind of numbing settled over her.

Outside, the night air was cool on her skin. Only a few flowers remained this October night. She walked carefully along the garden path, her leg muscles complaining of pain. Rounding a tall evergreen, the bathhouse came into view. She held the rails tight as she climbed the stairs. She needed to erase Ose from her body. Cleanse her soul. If only she could leave him. But if she did, she'd lose everything: all property, all monies, all jewels, and clothing, and even her title. Marriage had transferred her riches to Ose. She had nothing.

Hot springs fed the pool in the bathhouse. Tamika slid the door open and stepped inside. A single candle burned on a small table near the door. She used it to light a few more candles in the room, but not all.

The minerals in the steam filled her mouth, removing the copper taste of blood. Jasmine nestled in many jars and mingled with the strong scent of sulfur.

At the edge of the pool, she kicked off her sandals and let the robe fall before stepping down into the hot water. The shock caused her muscles to tighten before they relaxed. But the rip in her vagina from Ose's brutality burned. Tamika eased along the edge, letting the burning sensation fill her mind until, at last, it stopped.

When Jonathan sees the bruises…no, he was gone. He would never see them. She had kept the emperor's journey quiet, and now she'd paid the price.

She'd long suspected Ose's involvement in the Haranobu. When he traveled into town with them and fought the rebels alongside Jonathan, she decided she was wrong. Then the glass broke. But it wasn't Ose who came to her aid. It was Jonathan. Ose saw the accident first. He saw the shard of glass protruding from her wrist. And she saw him smile.

Tamika slipped down to sit on a rock ledge in the pool and let her head fall against the side. She had never known love. Certainly, Ose never loved her, and she didn't love him. Their wedding night had been a nightmare, and she had cried. After several weeks, she finally got used to Ose, but she never enjoyed his body as he did hers. They rarely slept together these days. *Will he visit me more often?* She shuddered.

Recently she had begun to imagine what it would be like to have Jonathan pressing himself inside her. Touching her in all the tender places. "Jonathan." She whispered his name and shut her eyes. "Jonathan, will you save me?"

But Tamika was practical. *I am a married woman whose husband doesn't love her. Whose husband is the head of the Haranobu.*

Her admission that Ose was the leader of the rebels finally allowed her to release the pent-up emotions that raged within. She cried.

The sunrise greeted Jonathan with a sense of urgency. Three days had passed since they left Katatsune Palace. Now, thoughts of Tamika came to him along with deep concern. *Was she alright? Had something happened?* Whatever the difficulty, it must wait until his return.

His troupe set out directly after breakfast, riding at a leisurely pace. At noon, they stopped for lunch. The surrounding countryside held leagues of rolling hills. Yet, as he peered in every direction, he didn't see a single structure. For a country that dated back for more than a thousand years, this seemed odd.

"Who owns this land?" He turned his attention to Umezawa.

"You, Excellency. This is all part of your vineyard."

"My vineyard? I see no grapes or buildings. Only ground full of weeds, bushes, and a few trees."

"The vineyard itself is much further on. This land has never been properly tilled."

"No, it has not. You." Jonathan pointed to a soldier. "Bring a shovel and dig into the dirt. I wish to see the soil." He followed the man and watched. The earth held so many weeds it took several attempts to bring up dirt without thousands of tiny roots. Jonathan knelt and grabbed a handful of brown soil mixed with clay. After a few minutes, he stood, brushing the excess from his hands.

"Grégory." The small man approached. "I will need your advice on how best to use this land. I do not wish to be an emperor of waste as was my predecessors."

"It will cost a considerable amount, Excellency."

"And to leave it as is?"

"Will be a greater cost to the country."

"*Oui.*"

All during lunch, Jonathan mentally debated the excesses of Warwyk. While he reigned, the people of Shea-Talon suffered. They were no more than chattel to the man's appetite. According to all he read, Warwyk lived in obscene luxury, had hundreds of women, countless lands, most of which lay idle, and made war as the mood took him. All the while, the poor of Shea-Talon starved and died while struggling to get by living in the gutter.

Governor Marlon hadn't done enough to address the problems of Shea-Talon leftover from Warwyk's rein. Jonathan must find a way to alleviate the suffering. How he wished he had a telephone as they did in L'Amérique. He'd call his father and discuss the problems with him. But alas, the modern world of his mother's homeland was but a dream in this one. He must send letters and then wait months for a reply. The Peregrine falcons were another choice. Flying a hundred leagues in an hour, their speed was unmatched by pigeons. But one sentence or two in the note he could compile would hardly be enough to address his many concerns.

Their journey continued until sunset when they made camp.

Three days later, Jonathan looked up at the arch over the entrance and recognized the symbol for Emperor, but the other was lost on him. Despite his years with a tutor, he found the written words of this land a true challenge.

As they rode up the hill, they passed fields of grapes. This time of year, they'd all been harvested. After some time, small rock huts came into view with a larger barn-like structure further back. Ruts lay deep in the dirt road, and Jonathan was careful to guide his stallion away from the edges. The smell of dirt and rotting leaves filled the air.

At the top of the hill, the ground evened out, and they rode onto paving stones. Numerous men and a few women lined the road wearing gray kimonos with no difference between the men and women. He called a halt and dismounted. The people dropped to their knees, touching their foreheads to the ground. All said at once, "Excellency."

"You may stand."

They did.

He approached, and when an older man saw him coming, he bowed again and the others followed. They continued several times.

"Please."

They still bowed.

"Enough."

Bowed again.

Jonathan looked toward Umezawa. He nodded and clapped his hands three times. The bowing stopped. But then all of them fell to their knees and put their noses in the dirt.

Jonathan sighed. "I command you to all stand. I would speak to the man in charge."

Their faces lifted, they gazed at him with various expressions of concern. Finally, it was a young woman who stood first and helped an older man rise.

The older man approached. "I am Oto. How may I be of service?" Oto came to Jonathan's shoulder, a little heavy with a round face. His gray hair was pulled into a long braid down his back.

"What do you do, Oto?"

"I am the Wine Master. This is Goto. He is the Vineyard Foreman and my daughter Egawa." Goto stepped forward, a broad-shouldered man with black hair and exceptionally angular eyes. Egawa smiled, and when she did, Jonathan saw tiny dimples in her cheeks. Then, for a moment, her eyes met his before they dropped.

"I am happy to meet you all. This is my Advisor Umezawa, Master of Books, Grégory Mossé and Lieutenant Saville. Please, show us around and explain how things are done here."

Now that Jonathan stood on the flat hilltop, he saw that the stone houses were arranged in a circle. Off to his left were several one barn-like stone structures. Oto led the way with his daughter and Goto close by.

Before the buildings were five large round wine presses and, to the side, numerous tables with benches, large barrels were stacked outside the buildings between huge arched doorways.

"This is where we press the grapes." Oto looked his way and motioned toward the round presses. Jonathan knew this already but kept quiet. He didn't want to discourage Oto from telling him everything.

Grégory waddled near him, taking notes as he went. Another man held the ink bottle for Mossé to dip his quill into.

They entered the first stone building and followed two men who held torches and went before them, lighting wall sconces. The scent of grapes lingered. Oto led the way toward the stairs. Soon, they were all following him down into the cellar.

In the belly of the building, down multiple rows of storage cases, were more oak barrels. "This is where the wine is aged." Oto pointed as he spoke. "The date is burned onto the lid of each barrel."

"What kind of wine is this?" Jonathan peered at the symbols, and once again, the meaning was lost on him.

"We only make Tsutsui wine, Excellency. A white wine with a fragrant bouquet. This was the wine that the Great Matsui, our first emperor, brought with him across the great ocean. Our grapes date back to his time. We do add different fruits when we press the grapes for different flavors. This has peach added. Others have apple or pear."

As Jonathan took this information in, he realized there were hundreds of barrels in just this one room.

"These are this year's production," Oto said.

"How long is it aged before you distribute the wine?"

Oto stopped and gazed at him. "The wine is aged for three years, but only you may drink of it and offer it to your guests. We have no distribution."

"Only the emperor? How many barrels for just this year?"

Oto gazed at his daughter. She nodded before speaking. "It was a good year, Excellency. We have two hundred barrels of each variety for this year."

"How many bottles does each barrel fill?"

"Each will fill seven hundred bottles."

"Seven hundred? And you have two hundred barrels of each type, and there are three types, bringing the total number of bottles for this year alone to…" he hesitated. "420,000 bottles. And only the emperor may drink it?"

"Yes, Excellency. Does this not please you?"

"We have double that number of just white wine,"Otto said.

"Double!" Jonathan turned to Grégory, who was smiling. "Yes, of course, I am pleased. Just surprised, that is all."

"Come, there is more." Oto stumbled, and his daughter was quick to catch him before he fell. The older man appeared sickly. His hands trembled while his daughter led him to a nearby chair.

"Please forgive, Excellency." Egawa looked up at him from her position leaning over her father.

"Are you ill, Oto?" Jonathan stepped a little closer.

"He is old," Egawa said. "It is hard sometimes. But he is still capable."

"I see." He glanced at Umezawa.

The Shea-Talonian scholar approached. "When workers can no longer do their job, they are put out along with their families," he said in Gil-Laelian.

Jonathan frowned. Another barbarism left over from Warwyk. "Egawa, how long has your father worked here?"

"He was born here and has labored since a boy of nine. He followed both his father and grandfather in the business."

"And now he doesn't have a son but a daughter, is that it?"

Egawa lowered her eyes and looked away.

Jonathan took two steps and set his hand on Oto's shoulder. "I will not put you out. Do you wish to continue living here or is there somewhere else you want to live?"

The older man raised his eyes, and Jonathan read wonderment there. "Excellency, my prayers have been answered."

"Have you trained someone to replace you?"

"Women are not capable." This was the first time Goto had spoken.

Jonathan turned toward him. "I disagree. Women are sometimes more capable than men. My mother went to university and saved many during the war. She continues to compose music, and her healing gift is known to all. My mother, a mere woman." He turned back to the older man. "Is there someone who can replace you, Oto?"

"My daughter knows all."

"Then, your daughter may replace you if she wishes. Please, continue the tour. Goto, will you see Oto to his home that he might rest?"

Goto came forward and bowed. "As you wish, Excellency."

Egawa smiled. "This way."

She led them forward, preceded only by the men who lit the sconces. Each building stored reserves of wine, thousands of barrels, all connected by tunnels. When they reached the middle, they came to the room where the wine was transferred to bottles, and in the last basement, the bottles were stored. Millions of bottles. All labeled with the year and which emperor ruled.

Jonathan stood in the center and made a slow turn. "May I guess that the emperor was never able to drink it all himself?"

"That is true. Some emperors consumed more or held more dinner parties in which they shared. But as the vineyard grew, more and more bottles were left untouched, and so we have added a lower level for storage." Egawa stepped between rows. "Come."

He followed along with the others. They descended another set of stairs and followed Egawa to the farthest end. There, she removed a dusty bottle from the shelf. She used a nearby cloth to wipe off the dirt and handed it to Jonathan. Once again, he studied the symbol. This one looked a little more familiar.

Umezawa approached. Jonathan handed it to him. His mouth opened, he looked up at Egawa and then back down. "This is impossible."

"What?" Jonathan asked.

"That is the first bottle we ever made for Emperor Matsui when he entertained the god, Ye Tai."

"Is it still good?" Jonathan took the bottle back. Thousand-year-old wine.

"I fear it is not good to drink after two years."

Jonathan looked toward Grégory, who wrote on his pad, and then gave it to him. It read: There are billions here.

"Most is no longer good for consumption," Jonathan spoke Gil-Laelian.

"That which is too old to drink will still be good for collectors, and with 420,000 bottles each year, there is plenty that you can sell."

Jonathan nodded. "Shall we eat, Egawa? I would like to share the two-year-old vintage with all."

Duplicity

Chapter 9

Katatsune loomed out of the darkness. No lantern swung from its overhang, and there weren't any in the gardens surrounding it. But the manor house Jonathan called home was well lit. He dismounted his stallion.

Home! He hadn't thought of the plateau as home until this moment. He stretched, saddle sore and exhausted from his trip.

"Allow us to go in and make sure all is well before you enter, Excellency," Saville said.

"You think I'm not safe on top of this fortress?"

Jonathan gazed at Saville. He looked as exhausted as Jonathan felt. "Go ahead."

Saville took four men with him, entering the manor house with drawn sword. Jonathan waited with the six men Saville left behind, along with Grégory and Umezawa.

They'd been gone nearly a month. Six hours ago, he'd given the order to continue and not make camp. At this moment, all he wanted to do was go to bed. He would wait to hold council meetings until he was sure of what he wanted to do.

They had remained an additional three days at the winery. He walked the property with Goto and listened to his explanation on how the process went to harvest. He learned the winery employed hundreds of temporary workers and bought bottles and corks from a factory in the south of Shea-Talon. The barrels were used over and over, and no new barrels were purchased in quite some time. He ate with these people in their communal kitchen/dining room located in the center of the huts, and he'd played the violin for them. That last, he did more for himself. His mind was so jumbled with facts and possibilities, he found it difficult to sleep. The music helped clear his mind and eased the tension he felt.

Saville and his men came out of the house. "All is well."

"Take your men and go to your quarters. I appreciate your service." Jonathan walked toward the manor house. Grégory and Umezawa followed. Both stayed in their own quarters in the manor house. There were guards in the place as well. Jonathan climbed the stairs and saw two Gil-Laelian soldiers outside his bedroom door.

Once inside his room, he pulled off his boots and shed his clothes, lying down without washing.

Sunlight streamed through the bedroom window. Jonathan lifted his head. He was sprawled naked on the bed. Sitting, he pulled on a robe and rang the bell for his manservant, Miyake. One of those who had come to him after Kaku's death. He waited at his southern-facing window overlooking the bluff to the road and Wakisaka estate. Tamika. *How was she? He must see her soon.*

As in Gil-Lael, Shea-Talon's important houses had running water, hot and cold, along with porcelain tubs, sinks, and toilets. With the need to house both Grégory and Umezawa, Jonathan had moved to the third floor. His bath was down the hall. Shedding the robe, he stepped into the steaming water and sat.

"What time is it?"

Miyake knelt beside the tub, soap, and washcloth in hand. "Well past noon, Excellency."

As if on cue, Jonathan's stomach rumbled. "Give me the soap and go to the kitchen and bring back a roast beef sandwich. No, make that two sandwiches along with whatever fruit they have and ale."

Miyake nodded and left. In no time, Jonathan was clean and dry. He let out the water and returned to his bedchamber, nodding at his guard. Once there, he selected brown pants and a white shirt, padding around the room barefoot. Miyake returned with his lunch.

When he first arrived, he had to teach his Shea-Talonian chef how to make sandwiches and pizza. Now he ate a sandwich nearly every day for lunch and pizza once a week for dinner. Grégory appreciated these meals, but not Umezawa, who ate fish several times a week. Jonathan sat at the small round table in his bedchamber and devoured his lunch.

Now that he was fully awake, fed, and dressed, he went to his study and called for Grégory to join him. He began to trust Grégory with more than just bookkeeping and found the little man wise. However, while Umezawa knew the local traditions and customs well, he wasn't Gil-Laelian, and Jonathan never fully trusted him, especially when making important decisions.

The fire in the hearth sent out sparks, and the scent of applewood filled the room. Grégory arrived, pushing a cart laden with his books. Jonathan sat back in his seat and watched as Grégory put the cart next to his chair and climbed on it.

"I want to discuss your calculations in regard to developing more land for wineries." He watched as the little man moved the stack of ledgers around until he found two of them.

Opening one ledger, Grégory set it on Jonathan's desk along with the second. "This one is a calculation of how much you could potentially sell your wine for. A total can be calculated once you set a price and how many bottles. The other one is a summation of all the land as yet not developed."

Jonathan pulled the first book toward him and read, turning several pages. "I think we should offer the wine to existing local vendors rather than opening new stores. That would save considerable time, and since they already have customers, they would know best how much to order."

"I agree." Grégory nodded. "The last page listed under each year will give you the total number of bottles and the flavor. How many bottles do you want to sell and what year?"

"Hmmm…" He pondered the number. "I must hold a meeting with the vendors. Grégory, prepare to write an invitation."

Grégory left his seat to go to the small desk Jonathan installed for his use. While the little man did this, Jonathan stood and went to the window looking out over a garden. The flowers were dead now, and the trees had turned brown. A drizzle began to fall, hitting the window in soft pelts.

"How long do you think it will take the vendors in the south to arrive?" Jonathan asked.

"It's going to get cold. Does it snow here?"

Jonathan turned to peer at Grégory, whose back was toward him. He walked around the small desk and pulled up a chair. "It doesn't snow except in the mountains. Rain will be the worst."

"And the roads?"

"The main road, Tadanao, runs north and south the length of Shea-Talon and is made of bricks."

"Still, it is quite a journey," Grégory said.

"*Oui*, a thousand leagues or more. My guess is some will need more than a month's notice to pack and travel."

"And we will need time to send the invitations."

"The falcons can make the journey in a day."

Grégory tapped his fingers together and stared at the ceiling. A smile twitched around Jonathan's lips as he watched his friend.

"Then six weeks is my guess, and the note must be small to fit the bird's capsules."

"That is fine. Each station along the way has a royal scribe."

In the end, they decided on the first week in December, and Grégory prepared twelve small notes, which instructed the scribes to send out invitations to all the liquor vendors in their area. Next, he created actual invitations for the local vendors, and Jonathan signed and sealed each.

"Now, we will discuss the development of new wineries."

Jonathan returned to his desk, and Grégory moved from his small table and climbed into the chair before Jonathan's much larger desktop.

"I have thought about this for some time." Grégory tapped his fingers together again. "We can invite wineries from foreign countries to develop their wines here. By doing so, we avoid the cost, the country benefits since all other wines have traditionally been banned from selling here, and you can charge a percentage on the sale of each bottle. If you lease the land to the foreign wineries, rather than selling it, you have yet another source of income that didn't exist before."

"Grégory, I will write my father and thank him for sending you. You're a brilliant man with numbers."

They continued their discussion for a little longer before eating dinner together in the dining hall with Umezawa.

"I will get you a list of wineries and what wines they make within a few days, Excellency." Grégory cut into his roast chicken.

"Excellency," Umezawa paused with chopsticks hovering close to his mouth. "No one else may sell wine in Shea-Talon. No one else may taste the emperor's wine without his say. It is our tradition."

"Tradition." Jonathan used his fork to scoop up a little rice. "Old traditions must make way for new ones. I am Emperor, and what I say about this tradition will change its face and allow for many positive things to follow."

"As you wish." Umezawa drank a little of the wine they'd brought back with them.

"Grégory, we meet again tomorrow to discuss taxes." Jonathan wiped the remnants of his meal from his mouth, stood, and left.

In the morning, Jonathan once again watched as Grégory looked through the stack of books he'd brought. He wanted to know precisely what Marlon had been up to.

Grégory passed him a large ledger. "You will note on the next three pages that Governor Gauthier decreased taxes over time from 32 percent to 20 percent."

Gauthier was the first man his father had appointed after the war.

Grégory continued. "When Marlon arrived, he increased taxes every year until we now have 52 percent."

"What is the basis for the tax?" Jonathan flipped the page. "Everything?" He looked up at the little man.

"Oui, the people, pay taxes on their income as well as on everything they buy. It is all 52 percent."

"And what did Marlon spend the money on?"

Grégory riffled through more books until he had three of them out. "This one lists the amount of tribute sent to High King Healden. This one lists the amount used to improve several things from the harbor to roads. Finally, this one lists Marlon's expenses as governor."

Jonathan pulled paper from his desk and opened an ink bottle before sharpening his quill. "Five percent is sent to my father and another 5 percent for repairs. Twenty percent is for Marlon's expenses. Did you know my father pays Marlon a salary?"

"No, I didn't." Grégory frowned and leaned forward. "How much?"

"He sends ten gold hilts a year, which equals double that amount when exchanged in the Shea-Talonian royal tlokel."

"That is a fortune."

"Where does the remainder of the tax funds go? 22 percent?"

"I have searched through every book, but I can't find it."

Jonathan stood abruptly, pushing his chair back. He began to pace. "We have 22 percent times 12 months unaccounted for. How long has this been going on?"

"As far as I can tell, there has always been a slight discrepancy from day one of Marlon's governorship. It has grown from 1 percent in his first couple of years to 22 percent in the last seven."

Jonathan went back to the window. Anger made his nerves tense. "Ten gold hilts is far more than the tribute Marlon sent home. He keeps his wage from my father and steals from the people of Shea-Talon. Send for Saville."

Taxes

Chapter 10

"Bring the Master of Ships to me immediately!" Jonathan stood, setting his fist on the desk, and leaned forward. Captain Périer bowed and left.

"Lieutenant Saville." Jonathan sat once more and pulled out his quill, took a knife, and sharpened the point. "Must I teach your men who is emperor and who is not? Why didn't anyone think to send a falcon with this news, or at the very least inform me on our return?"

"Marlon gave an order to not disturb you, and they obeyed."

Jonathan dipped the quill in ink and began to write. When he finished, he sprinkled sand on the page to dry the ink and then dusted the sand back into its box. Then, standing, he handed the page to Saville. "Share this with your men. No one gives any standing orders but me."

"As you wish, Excellency." Saville bowed and left.

Jonathan stood and went to the window. "How long have you known?" He turned halfway to peer at Grégory.

"Not long. I suspected something like this. When you gave me the order to bring the information on taxes yesterday, I spent a long night searching the books to see if I could find the missing money."

Jonathan turned back to gaze out the window. Marlon had taken the first opportunity to flee Shea-Talon. *Where had he gone? Probably not Gil-Lael.*

Tamika Stepped down from the coach and paused while the carriage moved further on where it would wait for her. Jonathan's manor house had a lot of soldiers coming and going. She noticed Captain Périer mount his horse and gallop away with three other men. Several others arrived, dismounted their horses, and tied them to posts.

He must be back. A jealous pain settled in her heart. *Jonathan didn't summon her. He no longer cared about her.* She shook her head and forced reason into the emotional cloud in her mind. *Stop yourself. He has just returned, and something has happened, that is all.*

She turned and walked toward the rear of Katatsune, where the servant quarters were being built. There were five buildings in all. The first three were nearly complete, another had the outer shell done, and the fifth only a foundation. She'd imagined this would take more time, but Jonathan hired hundreds of builders to speed things along.

Tamika entered the tent where the architect Akira worked and bowed. He did the same.

"You may enter the first two buildings now and tour the interior," Akira said once he stood upright.

"Will you come with me, Master Akira, and explain your vision for the accommodations?"

"I will."

They left together. The layout of the buildings was shaped like an 'X.' The first of the two-story buildings was about a league away from the palace. Situated behind them and centered was a one-story building that would serve as a kitchen and dining room for the servants. Behind this would be two buildings in the same style as the first pair.

Akira opened the door of one of the completed buildings for Tamika, and she entered a large room on the main floor. Windows gave a view of the gardens that surrounded the palace.

Akira began the tour. "His excellency requested that each building would have a common room where the servants would be able to enjoy each other's company. And wants all of it furnished in the manner of Gil-Lael. This doesn't make sense to me."

"Yes, those are my instructions. I'm guessing he wants to change our style of living." Tamika made a slow turn-taking in the pale green walls and hardwood floors.

"Why?"

"Why not?" Tamika turned her attention to Akira. "I would love to have a feather bed and a chair to sit on at the table."

Akira stared at her for a moment before continuing. "His excellency also mentioned a ping pong table be brought along with other games. I made room for this but do not understand the need."

Tamika smiled. "He wants people to be happy. He is a kind man."

Akira grunted. He moved toward one end. "There is a flight of stairs leading up on either side." He climbed without waiting for her, and she had to hurry.

The remainder of the tour was the same. Room by room with Akira complaining about Jonathan's kind treatment of servants. He left her pondering what she should do first. *Should she meet with Jonathan?* Her body felt the usual surge of warmth with the thought. She walked along the path, between the buildings, past the tent where Akira bent over his table and drawings. When she stood facing the manor house, she noted that no one was rushing around any longer. She approached the guards at the door and bowed.

"May I speak to his excellency."

The man looked down at her while remaining stiff. "Your name?"

"Tamika Shigemori."

He clicked his heels and gave a stiff bow before disappearing into the manor house. Tamika turned and gazed at the landscape. She read that the leaves turn bright colors with the frost before winter in Gil-Lael. Here, in Shea-Talon, leaves simply turned brown and sagged on the branches until spring arrived in February. She'd love to see autumn in Gil-Lael.

The soldier returned. "His excellency begs your forgiveness and asks that you return tomorrow at noon and have lunch with him."

Tamika felt as if Ose had just punched her. "I will return, thank you." She bowed once more and struggled to walk away in a calm, unhurried manner.

The entire ride home, she debated what she had done to displease Jonathan. She second-guessed every decision she'd made with the palace and now with the servant quarters. *Or maybe it was because she was married to Ose. Had Jonathan thought Ose was the head of the Haranobu? She couldn't blame Jonathan if he put her away and never spoke to her again. But...he had invited her to lunch. Would he do that if he never wanted to see her again?*

Tamika felt a headache press between her eyes. She must control herself. Tonight, she would have to tell Ose, Jonathan was back.

In the last three hours since he sent Captain Périer to bring the Master of Ships to him, Jonathan had time to collect his thoughts. He dismissed Grégory and felt conflicted at having to send Tamika away. He wanted to see her. To soak up her ever-calm demeanor, yet he couldn't afford any distraction, and she was that.

When the door opened, he turned. Périer entered along with an elderly man who was hunched and walked with a cane. Jonathan could tell by his hobble, the older man suffered from gout, his feet so swollen, the flesh spilled over the edges of his slippers.

Périer bowed. “Excellency, may I present the Master of Ships, Yonezu.”

The older man bowed, holding his cane so tight his knuckles turned white. “Excellency.”

“Yonezu, please take a seat.” He motioned to the chair before his desk and walked around to sit opposite. Périer brought over an enormous book and set it down on the desk. Jonathan gazed at the engraved symbols on the cover and recognized the one for ‘ships.’ He pushed the book back toward Yonezu.

“When did Governor Marlon leave?”

Yonezu reached for the book and lifted it. His hands shook so violently Jonathan thought he might drop it. He placed it on his lap, pulled out a pair of reading glasses, but had difficulty putting them on. Then, turning pages, he started from the back. As with everything, Yonezu’s trembling fingers made it troublesome for him to search through the book.

“Here it is. The governor left on October 3.”

“Did anyone go with him?”

“His wife and three servants.”

“Were the servants from Shea-Talon?”

“No, they were from Gil-Lael.” Yonezu pulled his reading glasses off and took a kerchief to wipe his eyes. The book slipped off his lap and fell to the floor, making a thudding sound. “Forgive my clumsiness.”

Jonathan lifted his hand and signaled Périer to retrieve the book. He did so, handing it back to Yonezu.

“Where did he go?”

“He told me he intended to return home, but the ship’s captain filed papers to head to Telaneasse.”

Telaneasse. Jonathan studied in Telaneasse. He knew the king well. He would send a falcon and request Marlon’s return.

"And the name of the ship and her captain?"

"Captain Ishihara of the ship Wakamatsu."

Jonathan wrote both names down. "Thank you, Yonezu. Before you go, may I ask about your health?"

The Shea-Talonian people were adept at keeping a tranquil expression. Jonathan learned to study their mannerisms and looking for the smallest of signs.

"I am well enough."

"Who is your employer?"

Yonezu lifted his eyes to Jonathan and looked down. "You are, Excellency."

"I am?"

"The Master of Ships is a government job, Excellency," Captain Périer said.

"Ah. Yonezu, you have served well, but it is time for a younger man to replace you. Therefore, I would like you to recommend someone for the job."

Yonezu gave a mournful cry. "Please, Excellency, I have a wife." Périer shifted his weight. Jonathan glanced at him and them back at the older man. "

"In Gil-Lael, older people receive a pension so they can retire and not lose their home. I will enact the same law here. You will have money for all your needs, Yonezu, do not fear."

"Forgive, Excellency, I don't understand. How might I receive money without working?"

"You have done your duty and worked all these years faithfully. As a reward, you will receive money so you may retire and spend the rest of your days in the comfort of your home."

"But how will I buy food?"

"With the money you receive."

The frown on Yonezu's face told Jonathan that the man still didn't understand. "You must trust me. Now, will you provide me the names of those you believe could do your job and be loyal to the crown?"

Yonezu nodded.

"I look forward to receiving them." Then, Jonathan dismissed Yonezu and gave instructions for him to meet with Grégory and provide him with the information.

Now he was alone, Jonathan sat to write King Tripada Pathak of Telaneasse and ask that Marlon and his wife be returned as prisoners.

Changes

Chapter 11

The following morning, Tamika set out through the woods toward the Romani camp. The damp, cold morning smelled of wood and wilted leaves. Moisture clung to her skin and clothing. Her horse nickered. His breath left a film that slowly disintegrated into the moist air. No one rode beside her.

Winter settled its shroud down in the Capital of Shea-Talon. Every day it rained and hung heavy in the saturated air. Only once in her life had she seen snow. The memory of the trip her family took to the mountains when she was a child traveled through her mind but was soon replaced with growing anxiety. Ose had become more and more abusive. She believed it was because Jonathan favored her and ignored her husband. Her encounters with Ose were tinged with brooding silence or ripe with shouting and blame. His accusations of adultery were unfounded. He was absent from her bed, though that wasn't new. He favored the *Geisha* house. She knew what he didn't tell her. That this house was the *onsen geisha*, prostitutes.

Tamika had suffered two miscarriages and given birth to a stillborn child early in her marriage. The more she knew Ose, the less she wanted his child. To ensure the possibility never occurred, she traveled to the Romani camp once a month. Perhaps she could forgo this errand, but though Ose's visits were rare, they still happened, and she would take no chances.

The heavy smell of campfire began to cling to the soggy air. She turned toward the valley where the traveling people lived. They were watchful. Soon several men emerged from the fog armed with drawn swords. As soon as they saw her, they put their weapons away.

Both men gave a nod rather than a bow. "Lady Tamika," one said.

She didn't care he hadn't addressed her by her married name. "Kourken."

He helped her from the saddle. "You come early today."

"Yes, I have an appointment with the emperor at noon."

As they walked toward Mariyam's wagon, other camp members greeted Tamika, offering encouragement or small treats. She knew each one of them well, having come here for years.

Mariyam emerged from her wagon. "My child, it is good to see you. Come inside." The older woman beckoned.

Tamika climbed the steps and entered. Candles illumined the inside. Mariyam's bed curtains were drawn, and the sheets pulled down. The scent of many herbs lingered in the air. A small iron pot in the center of the wagon burned wood and made the compartment warm.

Mariyam locked her door. "You may disrobe now."

Tamika did so and laid down on the bed for her examination. Mariyam brought over a small table and placed a bowl and pair of large tongs on top. Next, she opened a jar and pulled out a peach pit.

"Do you have any discomfort?" Mariyam pushed Tamika's legs apart.

"Sometimes, but not often."

"You must tell me if it hurts you. Then, we will do something different."

Tamika clutched the sheets tight between her fingers as Mariyam inserted the cold tongs and pulled out the used peach pit, placing it in the bowl. As she worked, a tear slid down Tamika's cheek. She examined the constellations painted with fluorescent color on the ceiling. If anyone ever found out about her birth prevention, she would be criticized and shunned.

Mariyam lifted the new pit and rubbed a gel over it before inserting it inside. Tamika shut her eyes. The fresh peach pit always hurt on the way in despite the gel covering the outside. After Mariyam removed the tongs, she pressed on Tamika's belly and lower parts.

"Does it hurt?"

"No." Tamika sat up.

The older woman lifted the small table and put it back in a corner. As she did so, Tamika dressed in her riding clothes.

"Come." Mariyam went to the small round table where she had tea waiting. She poured two cups.

The Romanis didn't kneel on pillows before a small table but sat on chairs or, if outside, logs around the campfire.

"I have been studying your star chart, child."

Tamika gazed into the older woman's wrinkled eyes as she sat.

"Trouble and change surround you. Also, much danger. You must be careful."

Tamika sipped her tea.

"You don't appear surprised."

"No, I help the emperor, and Ose is jealous."

"He is more than jealous, I think. You had me do Ose's chart if you remember. Death surrounds him."

Tamika lowered her gaze. *Death.* "His death?" She lifted her eyes again.

The older woman shut her eyes and sat back. "It isn't clear, but death nonetheless." She stood and retrieved a small envelope bringing it back to the table. "Are you faithful to drink the powder after relations?"

"Yes, always."

"Is this enough?"

"Ose doesn't come to me often, so yes, it is enough."

Mariyam nodded and shut her eyes once more. When she opened them again, she leaned forward with great intensity. "Learn of the emperor's birthday, time, and place. Bring it to me soon."

Unease caused Tamika to set her cup down. She glanced at the envelope with the herbs inside, picked it up, and looked at the older Romani again.

"I don't know if I can find that out."

"You must."

Jonathan gazed out the window in the small dinette waiting for Tamika to arrive. He wore a new navy-blue jacket made of silk and quilted with tiny pinheads throughout. The coat came down below his hips. He was thankful for the extended cover since his anticipation of receiving Tamika caused some discomfort in his lower extremities.

Tomorrow he would hold the first High Council meeting with Shea-Talon's nobles since returning home from his trip. He planned to introduce two new policies. If he shared this with Tamika, would she tell Ose?He wanted her input, but the thought of Ose learning ahead of time made him cautious.

Moisture dripped from the drooping leaves of the hydrangea plant outside the window. As with everything in his gardens, the arrangement of trees, shrubs, and plants obscured his view of the drive. He wouldn't know when Tamika's carriage arrived until she was announced. He checked the mantel clock over the fireplace. Nearly noon. They would have chicken soup, cheese, and sliced ham along with rolls to make their own sandwiches. He looked forward to seeing her reaction since this wouldn't be a typical lunch for her.

The door opened, and his newly acquired butler, Okabe, entered. Jonathan dressed his servants in red jackets with black pants since those colors represented Shea-Talon.

"Lady Shigemori, Emperor." Okabe bowed.

Tamika entered wearing a gray wool dress. She curtsied. "Emperor."

"Good to see you." Jonathan stepped to her side as Okabe left.

Tamika rose and lowered her eyes at once. "I trust you had a good trip."

"It was productive. Come and sit." He pulled a chair out for her and then walked to the other side of the round table to sit across from her.

Okabe, along with several other servants, entered with their lunch. He uncorked white wine and poured it for both Jonathan and Tamika while the others set down bowls, plates with the cheese, meat, and a basket with rolls along with a choice of condiments. They all bowed once more before leaving them alone.

"They do not bow in the same manner." Tamika's brow creased.

"Dropping to your knees and touching the floor with your forehead is demeaning and unnecessary. I have requested my servants not to do so."

A smile toyed with her lips. Lowering her gaze, he watched as she noticed their food. She lifted her eyes to his once more.

He grinned. "I love soup in winter, don't you?" He waited, but she kept her hands in her lap. "To make a sandwich, first you choose one or more condiments, slice open the bread and use your knife to spread the condiment on the bread. I prefer the mayonnaise, but there is also mustard or butter. I recommend that you taste a little of each before you pick." As he talked, he made his sandwich, adding lettuce and tomatoes from his greenhouse garden, plus pickles. "I also like ham and cheese." He made a second sandwich before looking at Tamika again.

She examined her spoon, turning it before dipping it into the mustard and afterward the mayonnaise, tasting each. Then, finally, she made a sandwich with the mustard. Jonathan began to alternate between a bite of his sandwich and a sip of his soup.

"I have never eaten a sandwich before." Tamika smiled after her first bite.

"I'm glad you like it. We rarely ate sandwiches in Gil-Lael. I was introduced to them while visiting my grandparents in L'Amérique."

"You have been to the other world?"

Her tone of wonderment caused Jonathan to look up at her expression. Wide eyes and her mouth formed an 'O'. He smiled. "*Oui*...yes."

Tamika set her sandwich down and scooted a little closer to the table while leaning forward. "What was it like?"

Jonathan smiled, his soup spoon halfway to his mouth. "Loud and overcrowded but fascinating too. We went every summer and for Noel."

"Noel?"

"A Christian holiday in December." He finished the bowl of soup. "I would take you but, after my grandparents died, father closed the portal. Things started leaking through."

"Things?"

"Yes, animals from my mother's homeworld. Father worried that an unwelcome person would find their way in."

Tamika sat back. Her soup was gone, but the sandwich was only halfway finished.

"Please if you're hungry, finish." Jonathan knew custom dictated no one eat unless the ruling monarch was eating.

"No, I am full. It was delightful."

He lifted the wine and poured more for each of them, ringing the bell. The servants entered and took their dishes away before putting down small plates and a bowl of strawberries.

"Strawberries in winter." Tamika plucked one from the bowl. Jonathan watched as her smile spread and her posture eased.

"My greenhouse." Jonathan ate several strawberries while

watching her. Tamika took a bite from the berry and then glanced around the room before returning her gaze to his and quickly lowering her eyes.

"When I was born, it was in our winter house in the south." She lifted her eyes again.

"You were born in winter? I too. In November."

"I in February. Is it the custom in Gil-Lael to have home births?"

"Yes, my brothers and I were born in Château de Talaith. But my mother had complications with my sister, and she was born in L'Amérique. They are far more advanced than we are in the medical sciences."

"What is science?"

"Science is another name for the study of plants and animals, the stars along with many other things."

"I see." Tamika bit into another strawberry. "If your Birthday is coming up soon, will you declare a national holiday on that day?"

"Hmm…" He gazed off to the right for a moment. "I hadn't thought of that. There are so many other pressing things to do."

"I think you should at least invite a few friends."

He chuckled. "That would be you."

"Oh no, there are many who love you already."

"Like whom?"

Tamika wiped her hands on her napkin and used it to touch the sides of her lips. "The Romani, and many, many more."

"I'll think about it." He stood and came around the table, offering his hand to her. She took it and stood as well. "Let us go into my office."

The Manor House wasn't as large as the palace. His office was across the hall. Entering, he sat behind his desk while she sat before it.

"I have met with Akira. He seems over pleased with his architectural designs. What do you think?" Jonathan watched her face. She frowned, looked off to the left, and then back to him.

"He is a master."

"True."

"He had many rooms that were larger than most have for their serving staff."

"Yes, as I requested."

"Game rooms. Bathrooms."

"And what do you really think?"

She paused, looking up at him. "What do you mean?"

"You're holding something back." She shook her head and peered down at the table while setting her hands in her lap where Jonathan couldn't see them.

"Tamika," he said. She didn't lift her gaze. "Tamika," he said again. Then, after a moment, she raised her eyes. "I want you to tell me your honest opinion. I need you to. I don't have many I can trust to do so, and I depend on you."

A tinge of pink ran up her neck to suffuse her face. "Master Akira is a fine architect. There is nothing wrong with his skill, but…"

A long pause. "But?" Jonathan encouraged.

"It is his attitude. He thinks you are spoiling the servants with so many bathrooms, game rooms, and large bedrooms. He doesn't like the married servants, believing mere servants should never marry. I fear most will agree with him."

Jonathan tapped the desktop with his fingers. "Do you know the secret to winning hearts?"

"No, Excellency."

"I think you do. I've watched you with others. You praised Yoshiyori for his furniture, and you dealt with the Romanis gaining their friendship. The medicine you obtain, you take to the needy. I've sent out scouts and have learned a few things about the nobility here in Aya. Most of the people had little to say about anyone and sometimes refused to talk if asked about a particular member of society, but when asked about you, they beamed and spoke words of praise."

Tamika smiled and lowered her eyes.

"The way to win the hearts of men and women is to respect and treat them as if their lives matter as much as a beloved member of your family."

"Not all will love you even so." She lifted her gaze.

"No, not all. Particularly those who wish to take my place."

The next morning, Jonathan adjusted his burgundy jacket. A gold sash ran from shoulder to opposite hip. He wore a sword with a gold hilt, and his polished black boots came to his knees over black pants. The nobles awaited him, sitting on chairs at tables. His scribes had ink and paper waiting, and the entire room was filled by Gil-Laelian guards.

He entered the throne room surrounded by his personal guard as well. The hostel atmosphere hit him hard. Most of these men hated him so much it was palpable and made his skin crawl. But which of them were members of the Haranobu, he didn't know. Perhaps all of them.

He turned at the throne and sat. The dragons just over his head peered at the crowd. They numbered nearly one hundred of Shea-Talons nobles. All who lived in the Capitol of Aya.

"Thank you for coming," Jonathan said.

They stood and bowed. "Excellency."

Jonathan waved them back, watching as the men took their seats. Ose Shigemori sat three rows down just left of the aisle. His face was masked in rage. Of course, the last was speculation on Jonathan's part.

"I have learned of the outrageous tax Governor Marlon placed on you. From this day forward, all persons will be taxed twenty-two percent of your income to be paid quarterly."

Most of the men stood and bowed, saying, "Thank you, thank you." But Jonathan noticed Shigemori still sitting, though he didn't look as angry. Jonathan held up his hand, and the men once more sat.

"Those who make fewer monies will be taxed less, and the poor will pay nothing in taxes that they may have hope of climbing out of their poverty. The tax rate will be supplied to you.

He continued, listing various taxes.

“Are there questions or concerns in this matter?” Jonathan finished.

“Yes.” Shigemori stood. “You have decreased our personal tax by 30 percent, and yet you announce the goods we produce will be taxed. I fail to see, what if any, savings we will receive.”

“My Lord, I understand your concern. However, the taxes on your goods will be but a few Dragon Korunas, and those monies, as I said, will be spent on improvements that will directly benefit you.

“I understand you produce the grains to make Shōchū. You also have distilleries to produce the Shōchū. You will be taxed on both the grains and the Shōchū, but those taxes will build a better distribution network as well as allow more liquor and wine stores to open. Anyone who wishes to open a store may apply for a license and receive a one-time advance of money to get started. This will increase the number of vendors you can sell to and thereby increase your wealth. You may find yourself doing business with a former servant who owns a store.”

Jonathan watched as Ose’s face went from understanding to delight and, lastly, anger. He knew Ose wouldn’t consider doing business with a commoner an advantage. Most of the other men were nodding or looking confused.

“Are there any more concerns you wish to discuss?”

The men glanced at each other and then back to Jonathan. He waited for only a moment.

“There is another matter I wish to address. He leaned forward a little. “I have reviewed the treatment of servants and have come to realize these men and women are let go when they can no longer perform their duties without compensation for their lifelong service. If they have a family to care for them, they stay with their family, if not, they sleep on the streets and starve.”

Some of the men nodded, but no one spoke to confirm or deny this was true.

"No man who works hard all his life should die on the streets. Therefore, all retiring servants will be compensated and given monthly severance pay by you, from this day forward. In addition, you must find all servants you have released from duty and who are unable to work, and you must provide for them."

Most of the nobles jumped to their feet and began yelling. Ose remained seated, his head slightly bent, sneering at Jonathan.

Umezawa stepped forward from the back of the room in a long gray robe with a lacquered red staff. Jonathan had made him, Keeper of the Peace. He carried himself with pride and stood before Jonathan, slamming his staff down three times on the floor. "Quiet!" He bellowed. "Sit down before his Excellency." He then returned to the back of the room while the nobles sat noisily.

"Let me be clear. You will be fined heavily if you do not do this. But if you do, then you may take the expense off your quarterly taxes and receive a portion of those monies back."

Bito Arei stood from his position four rows back and bowed. "Forgive Excellency, may I speak?" He lifted his head and met Jonathan's gaze.

"Yes." Jonathan waved his hand.

"Our wealth has been strained by the taxes you have mentioned. If we must care for old servants, there will be only a few Dragon Korunas left in our vaults."

Many in the room nodded, and some said "true."

Jonathan looked toward Grégory, who occupied the table along with the scribes. Mossé cleared his throat before answering. "Dragon Korunas is the same value as Gil-Lael's Copper Talons."

Jonathan turned back. "For any of you who find yourselves short of funds, you may apply for a small loan which I will provide. You will be required to prove that you need the monies. See Master Mossé, and he will assist you."

Bito Arei sat.

"That is all for now. We meet again on Thursday." He stood and left, walking quickly to his manor house before the nobles left the throne room. Only time would tell him the result of this day's business. Or if such a move would work towards lessening the power of the Haranobu because the people would want to keep him and the changes he was making.

Birthday

Chapter 12

Grégory stood before the cheval mirror in his bedchamber. He smoothed down the black wool of his tailored jacket and admired the way the burgundy collar of his silk shirt peeked through. He'd purchased the suit before leaving Gil-Lael and hadn't had an occasion to wear it yet. Tonight was a grand dinner in honor of the emperor's birthday.

His heart pounded with excitement. The Romani would be there. He'd heard many tales about the Romani and their women, mainly from Claude. Claude Coulomb, a Longbowman stationed here along with many other soldiers of Gil-Lael. He was a bit crass, which was fine with Grégory since he made him laugh. After standing guard for six hours outside the manner house, Claude was ready for a drink, and Grégory happily obliged him. They often took to a room in the basement of the manor house along with several other members of the military and drank themselves into a stupor. He learned about the onsen geisha houses from Claude and that they were willing to take any man regardless of station or the country they hailed from, as long as they had the money to pay.

Born a little man, Grégory had long ago given up on marriage. Most women walked by him while looking the other way. Even though he was little, he was still a man, and his needs were no less than any other man. More than once, he wondered about Jonathan and what he did to relieve his sexual needs. The laws in Gil-Lael demanded the heir to the throne wed by age twenty-nine. Jonathan was older. At least Grégory thought he was. But then, this wasn't Gil-Lael, and Jonathan was emperor. He could do whatever he wanted.

He left his room and held tight to the banister as he hobbled down the stairs. Stairs that were made for normal-sized people. He didn't wear a cloak or coat as he waddled along the paved walkway to the palace. Waddling was his fate. Part of the disease that he inherited as a little man. One that would cripple him when he was old. Two soldiers stood at the palace doors.

"You invited a dwarf?" one of the soldiers asked the other.

He grimaced, glaring at the man. He hated the word dwarf. "I am invited."

Both men spoke Gil-Laelian, and so he answered them in the same. He hadn't seen either of these men before. Several hundred new soldiers arrived, replacing those who had spent the last five years here. Others chose to remain.

Another guard stepped outside when he saw the exchange. "This is Grégory Mossé, the emperor's bookman. A favorite. I'd make a note of that if I were you."

Grégory nodded to the guard while the other two looked at each, both a little alarmed if he read their drawn eyebrows correctly. They stepped aside.

The massive entrance was already crowded. No one was sitting just yet and a line formed to meet Jonathan. Grégory didn't join the queue but waited.

The Romani were easy to spot. In appearance, their skin color was olive. The males wore their hair long past their shoulders, and more than one had a single gold hoop earring in one ear. The women wore colorful scarves to hold their hair away from their faces. Their clothes were often patterned with stripes or flowers. After meeting the emperor, the Romani gathered at the far end, away from the few Shea-Talonian nobles who were there. Grégory recognized the Areis and the Shigemoris. As he watched, Jonathan raised Tamika's hand and put a kiss on the back. He didn't do the same with Lady Arei, and based on Ose's reaction, it didn't go unnoticed. Ose's brows furrowed against his forehead, and the anger Grégory read there matched the occasion when he'd witnessed a dual between two nobles in Gil-Lael. Their hatred for each other had led them to break the law. He was sure, that if Ose had a weapon, Jonathan would feel the blade.

This wasn't the first time Grégory had seen this reaction from Ose. *Did Jonathan realize his attention to Tamika upset her husband?* Watching all three of them now, he decided Jonathan hadn't a clue. *What would this lead to?*

For the next half hour, more Shea-Talonian nobles arrived, and then they headed down the side hallway to the dining room. The entire wall panel opened so you could look out at the garden enclosed within the palace when you sat. Not that there was much to look at in the winter months. The trees had lost their leaves though moss still clung to the side. A few small bushes were still green in contrast to Gil-Lael, where snow would now cover the ground. Shea-Talon was just wet.

A cool breeze entered the overheated room from the garden. It touched Grégory's cheek, and he lifted his hand to brush it away.

The opposite wall held a mural from ceiling to floor depicting the Shea-Talonian god Ye Tai, arriving on a dragon. Grégory thought about all the different gods in Shea-Talon. Instead of one God who created everything, there was the god of war, Shi Xun, one for the harvest, Katou, and even a god of compassion and mercy, Besshou. The rest he hadn't learned the names for.

When High King Healden appointed him Jonathan's bookman,

Grégory bought every written account he could find on Shea-Talon. While traveling to the country, he read them all. He knew about Ye Tai and the Bracelet of the Moon and Stars. An enchanted bracelet. Though the account didn't describe what enchantment the bracelet held. He knew about all the past emperors. The last three before Jonathan were terrible men. At least, in his opinion. They had hundreds of concubine women as well as multiple wives. If they fancied someone's wife, they took her too. *Was this what Ose feared?*

Grégory found himself seated in the middle of a massive walnut table facing the garden. Dragons were carved at the four corners of the table as well as on the legs beneath. Someone had taken the trouble of putting pillows on his chair. He climbed the small step stool and sat like an average man and not so low, his chin touched the edge.

A hand settled on Grégory's back. "It's good to see you, my friend."

He needed no introduction to that voice. Twisting, he looked at Jonathan and attempted to rise.

"No, no." Jonathan smiled. "No need."

"I am well, Excellency. Thank you for the cushions."

"Of course. Enjoy the evening." With that, Jonathan walked toward the far end of the table, where he seated himself in the grand chair with a dragon's head carved at the top.

Dinner consisted of three types of fish and bird, all cooked differently, rice, vegetables, and fruit. Of course, the emperor's own wine flowed from the servants' carafe as they made their rounds. When it came time for dessert, Grégory didn't know if he could take another bite. Still, the luscious cake looked so good, he had to at least try it. Delicious. The sweet, velvety taste melted on his tongue, and he swallowed.

He listened, with little interest to the Shea-Talonian nobles around him. He understood them well enough since he'd been taking lessons. He simply had no interest in the qualities of sword and horse. Little men had trouble riding a horse.

The Shigemoris sat on Jonathan's right while two of the Romanis, an older woman and young man, were on his left. Once again, Grégory was struck by Ose's obvious displeasure. Chopsticks were in use around the table other than utensils, and Grégory thought that good, or Ose would grab a butter knife and try to inflict a mortal wound to Jonathan. Instead, the man's lips were in a pout and his frown looked to be permanent.

Jonathan appeared not to notice. He must ask Jonathan about it. Perhaps he could somehow befriend Ose, learn first-hand what he thought.

On the opposite side of the dining room was a ballroom where they all went after their meal. A three-tier dais was at one end. Alternate the platform was a stage, and around the dance floor were small round tables. Unlike the dining room, this room didn't open to the enclosed garden, but there were doors leading outside. Grégory supposed there would be gardens and pathways beyond in the warmer months.

The Shea-Talonians stood aimless, looking around as if lost. Jonathan took to the stage and waited for everyone to turn toward him.

"Lords, ladies, friends. This is my new ballroom. I will host parties here, one in the spring and fall, where young people can come and dance and meet each other in the hope of finding their future mates. This will be a new tradition in Shea-Talon. One which I hope you will embrace. In Gil-Lael, the summer months are filled with parties, *pique-nique*, and outings where young people are properly chaperoned and able to meet future wives and husbands. Everyone looks forward to the new season, as it is known."

Grégory wasn't sure how he ended up standing directly behind Ose. The man growled under his breath. "He thinks he can force us to become Gil-Laelians."

Recognizing this as his opportunity, Grégory said. "He is naive, my Lord."

Ose turned. A frown gathered his brows together while his eyes stared at Grégory. There was no humor there, no welcoming expression, just stern judgment. Grégory knew all would be lost if Ose turned back without speaking.

"What do you want, Dwarf?" The venom in his words nearly burned Grégory.

"Nothing. I understand your frustration with the emperor. The entire royal family of Gil-Lael is just like him."

"You're one of them. You are his friend."

"I am his bookman, not his friend."

The man standing next to Ose turned, and Grégory recognized him as Ishikawa Natsu.

"I doubt if you understand us, bookman." Natsu folded his arms.

"I was born in Gil-Lael and had to crawl my way into a position of status. Now I am here enjoying many of your rich traditions. Frustration at one's circumstance is a feeling I know too well."

"And what would you do, Dwarf, if your traditions were stripped from you and you were forced to adopt new ones." Ose held himself a little taller making Grégory feel like an ant.

"I would celebrate my traditions in private and honor the new ones in public."

"We have many questions about the emperor." Natsu adjusted his jacket.

"I would be happy to answer your questions." Grégory watched Ose and Natsu look at each other. They gave the slightest nod before turning back to him.

"Perhaps you would enjoy coming to the geisha house with us tomorrow evening?" Ose asked.

"I would be delighted."

Jonathan peered out from the stage. Tamika stood to his left with several of her friends while Ose and Natsu had turned their backs to him a short distance away.

"I am pleased to inform you, the Romani have agreed to perform for us tonight." He motioned with his arms, and several men with guitars joined him on the stage. A servant brought him his violin. "I will accompany them."

He took his violin and partially turned toward the Romani guitarist. A nod from Jonathan and the guitarist began to play. The melody was slow with an extended note, and then Jonathan added a series of plucks from his instrument before drawing the bow over the strings in a long cord that warbled at the end. With that, he played quickly. The melody was haunting, rising and falling. The guitar accompaniment struck a blended chord to Jonathan's emotional tune. Then, Isabella hit a tambourine, jigging to cause the cymbals to chime. She twirled onto the floor before the stage. Bending forward and then backward. Twirling as she danced, all the while beating her instrument with each step.

Jonathan watched her. She was a great beauty, with thick curly hair, lips ready to smile. She sizzled on the edge of excitement, ready to laugh or cry depending on the circumstance. And… she wasn't married.

He lifted his eyes to Tamika. He thought he saw affection there. His fingers held down different strings to receive the desired effect. Jonathan wondered what he could do to win these people over. So far, nothing had worked.

Of course, he knew the Shea-Talonian nobles thought themselves superior to the Romani, so perhaps bringing the two together had been a mistake.

He played two more tunes and then, the music at an end, moved to the small dais in the room. This throne was a duplicate of the one he sat in for dinner. Neither were as elaborate as the one in the throne room, but both still had a carved dragon above his head.

When he first sent out the invitations, he'd intended to instruct the people gifts weren't necessary, but Umezawa advised not to. Apparently, gifts were a tradition that must be followed. Umezawa didn't like the idea of the Romani attending either.

Umezawa stood off to the side with his laminated staff. He hit the floor with it three times. "Come forward with your offerings for His Excellency."

One by one, the lords of Shea-Talon stepped forward. Jonathan thanked each of them, and one of his guards took the gift to a nearby table. For nearly an hour, the men would extol the beauty of their gifts. So far, there were more than twenty porcelain bowls and vases, all painted with intricate detail. Silver trays and pitchers. Landscape paintings. Rugs, bows with a quiver of arrows. Finally, only one lord remained along with the Romani.

Ose had been missing most of the presentation. He appeared now with a highly polished saddle. Carved into the leather was a dragon resting beneath the tree of Gil-Lael with three falcons in flight above the tree. The symbol of the House of Calimar. Jonathan's family combined with the symbol of Shea-Talon.

Jonathan stood, stepped down the dais, and took the saddle from Ose, who bowed. Jonathan ran his hand over the carvings and smiled. He looked up and found Tamika. She had joined her husband, and was smiling. *If only. If only Ose would vanish. He'd sweep her up in his arms and kiss her here and now.*

At that moment, the Romani guitarist, Kourken, walked into the room with a splendid Romani Vanner stallion. All black, the beast had been brushed until its coat shone in the candlelight. Its tail touched the floor, and its head dipped as if to bow. Jonathan gave the saddle to his guard and walked to take the reins of the horse.

"Magnificent." He ran his hands along the animal's muscles and walked slowly around him. The saddle and horse were perfect.

"Have you named him, Kourken?"

"No, you may have that pleasure."

Jonathan smiled and turned back to the horse. "Excellent," he said.

Geisha House

Chapter 13

Several days after the emperor's birthday celebration, Grégory stepped down from the coach he shared with Ose and Natsu. Tall pines surrounded the circular drive. The geisha house stood prominently at the center with a wooden bridge over a wide pond leading up to the door. Grégory expected nothing less than a beautiful garden, even in winter, and he wasn't disappointed.

Ose and Natsu walked side-by-side, over the bridge to the front porch where a middle-aged woman waited. Grégory followed.

"Madam Shiho, may I present the emperor's bookman, Grégory Mossé." Ose turned to the side and waved with his arm toward Grégory.

If Shiho was surprised by Grégory's stature, she didn't indicate it. She bowed to him, and he returned the gesture. "We are honored," she said. "Come." Turning, she led the way inside.

They each knelt on cushions before a tiny table. Shiho vanished, and soon, three geisha emerged, bringing trays with cups and liquor and one with an instrument in appearance similar to a lute. Grégory recognized it as a biwa. The style was a short-necked fretted lute. This one had a flower pattern inserted into the front panel of the wood.

"Shōchū?" Ose met his gaze.

"Yes, please." Grégory watched as the geisha bent to fill his glass. All three women wore the traditional kimono in bright colors, adorned with flowers and a wide band. Their hair was coiffed into a bun with jewels or a fan. Their faces were painted white to enhance their beauty, their eyes outlined in black, and their lips were red.

"To the emperor." Ose lifted his glass, Grégory followed.

The woman with the biwa rested on a cushion a little way off and began to play. Grégory found the music pleasing to the ear.

"Tell us, Grégory, what is the emperor's favorite food?"

He turned his gaze from the geisha to Ose. "The emperor has an eclectic taste, and he favors many different types of food. For lunch, he often enjoys a simple sandwich. For–."

"Sandwich? What is a sandwich?" Natsu lifted his second glass of shōchū.

"Jonathan adopted the sandwich on one of his visits to L'Amérique. It is two pieces of bread spread with a sauce and layered with meat, cheese, and lettuce. Sometimes he has a–."

"Disgusting." Natsu put his glass down. "What man would eat such a thing?"

"Oh, many. I have had them. They are quite good."

"Interesting," Ose said. "I have never heard of a sandwich." He turned toward one of the geisha. "Make our sandwiches." The woman slid past the screen door.

"What else?" Ose's gaze narrowed.

"Well…he favors beef over chicken." He frowned, trying to think of exciting things about Jonathan that wouldn't do him any harm. "He likes brandy. Of course, wine, as you may have surmised."

"And fish?" Natsu questioned, downing yet, more shōchū.

The Shea-Talonians preferred fish to all other meats.

"Yes, of course. Especially shellfish."

"If I were to have the emperor to dinner, what shellfish should I serve?" Ose held his shōchū glass but didn't take a sip.

"I believe lobster and shrimp are his favorites."

"I have heard of lobster." Ose set his glass down. "But I have never tasted it since we don't have those in our fishing waters. But shrimp, we have in abundance."

"The emperor isn't fussy. He will sample something he has never had before."

The sandwiches arrived. Natsu leaned forward and sniffed. Ose tried to pick up the bread, only to have it slip between his fingers and leave raw fish and cheese.

"What sort of sauce did you use?" Grégory looked at the geisha who had brought in the sandwiches.

"Chef used *tare* sauce."

"No, no. That's no good. Something thicker. In the Emperor's house, we use *anavar* or *tinullee*. And the meat should be cooked. Beef or chicken is preferable."

The young woman took their plates and left.

Ose grunted and wiped his hands on a cloth. "My wife has said the emperor loves horses."

"Indeed, he does." Grégory took a sip from his shōchū. "Now that his stable is complete, he is sending out inquiries to horse breeders throughout the kingdom."

"Would he consider nobles who breed their animals too?"

"Why yes, I do believe he would."

The chef entered and bowed to the three men. "I am ashamed. Please forgive. I have no sauce as you asked for."

"Bring me, Madam Shiho." Ose sat back against his legs.

All three of the geisha rushed out the door while the chef remained with a bowed head. Time slowed. Ose tapped a finger on the table. Natsu poured more shōchū into his glass. Grégory felt odd about sitting with these two nobles and discussing Jonathan. When Shiho entered, Ose stood.

"What is your excuse? This man can't serve the required meal. Does he have the right credentials? Does he make excuses for inadequate cuisine? How do you explain yourself?" Then, he backhanded the chef across the face.

The man fell to his knees. "Please, please." He bowed several times.

Grégory stood. "I'm afraid this is my fault. The sauce I mentioned is Gil-Laelian. I will bring the recipe the next time I come."

Ose glared at him, and Grégory half expected to obtain the same punishment as the chef received.

"In the meantime." He put his small hand on the chef's shoulder and met his gaze. "If you have butter, you can spread a thin layer over the bread and place cooked meat and cheese in between. Add lettuce and tomato if you have it. Sandwiches vary to the taste of the one eating it."

The man bowed three times before standing and repeatedly bowing as he backed out of the room.

"My deep sorrow, my Lords. It will not happen again." Madam Shiho bowed as well.

After she left, Ose knelt back down. "You must not be kind to servants."

Grégory settled himself next to Ose. It wouldn't serve his purpose to argue over the treatment of servants. "I'll keep that in mind."

"What else can you tell us about the emperor?"

"In Gil-Lael, the royal family is loved. The king has enacted many policies to benefit the poor. I suspect Jonathan will do the same."

"What kind of policies?"

"There is a program to feed the poor. All nobles must contribute and businesses too. The king has built a hospital and hired many doctors. All are welcome to use the services. Old gowns are given to poor girls, so they can attend the festival dances in spring and fall."

"What is a festival dance?" Natsu downed more shōchū.

"I do believe the emperor brought up this matter in one of his council meetings. Am I wrong?"

Neither Ose nor Natsu answered him.

They were interrupted again by the arrival of more sandwiches. This time the chef brought them and waited, half bent for some measure of approval. Grégory thought he did an good job but didn't want to say so if Ose took issue with him again over his kindness.

Natsu belched, spit his bite of food onto the plate, and then threw it across the room where it tore the paper-thin wall and landed with a crash on the floor in the adjoining room.

"Interesting." Ose set his sandwich on the plate. "Go on."

"High King Healden loves to hunt, but there are some animals he has issued a 'no hunt order' for."

"Why?" Ose ate more of his sandwich and finally drank some of his liquor.

"There are some animals that are scarce in Gil-Lael though plentiful elsewhere. And other animals that are new to the region. The king wants to encourage their numbers, and so no one can hunt them, like the elk."

"What is an elk?" Natsu swayed slightly on his cushion.

"The best way to describe them is to compare them to deer. They are larger, and their antlers push backward instead of to the side." Grégory moved his arms in a demonstration. The chef had left, and only the geisha girls remained with them. "Their call is a bugle noise, like a horn. I haven't actually seen one in person, but I did see a drawing."

"It would seem our emperor is near perfect and has no faults." Sarcasm laced Ose's words, and his gaze made Grégory pause.

He began to realize he had only praised Jonathan and all the Calimar's. It was hard to do anything else since he admired them. But if he was to be successful at this game, he must win Ose's trust.

"Some might say he is weak," Grégory said while observing Ose carefully, but he couldn't tell what the man was thinking.

"Weak?"

Oh, Great Créateur, forgive me. "He prefers married women."

This brought a reaction from Ose. He made a fist and rested it on the table before leaning forward. "Tamika?" His voice was lower, not quite a whisper.

Grégory paused. As far as he knew, Jonathan never slept with Tamika. *If he said otherwise, Ose would be angry. He might trust him, but what of Tamika? What would Ose do to her?* "No, Jonathan has never slept with Tamika. He admires her sense of…design. But there have been others."

"Who?" Ose's voice had become a whisper.

Grégory searched his memories of the women he had met. "Ohno Arei for one and that Romani woman, Isabella."

"Ohno Arei? Arei! And the slut of a Romani, Isabella?" Ose's face became slightly red. "But not Tamika. What is wrong with him? Tamika is far superior to both of those women."

"No doubt, and he does favor her, as I'm sure you are aware. But should he be implicated as her lover, he fears the people will rise up and rebel."

"Yet, for Ohno, they will not?"

Grégory was unprepared for how quickly Ose reacted. He leaned forward and thrust all the contents off the table to the floor with his arm. Then he stood, and marched to the far side of the room, took a potted plant, and threw it across the room. Natsu laughed. The geisha jumped and huddled together.

Straightening his shoulders, Ose turned and calmly walked back to the table. Before he knelt, he clapped, and the geisha left. A short time later, they returned with mats they rolled out. Natsu snorted, stood, and swayed toward one of the women.

"These women are more than geisha." Ose smiled.

Grégory frowned, watching Natsu start to undress. "What do you mean?"

"They are onsen geisha."

"What is the difference?" Grégory knew what onsen meant because of Claude, but he was trying to delay, and he didn't want Ose to guess how much he knew.

"Geisha are entertainers, plying songs and dance for our pleasure. Onsen are geisha who take a more personal interest in men. By telling our wives we are visiting the geisha house, they think we come for polite conversation and entertainment. If they learn we see the onsen, then they will know we are spreading our seed beyond their wombs." He grinned then and stood. "Come, I'm sure you will enjoy the onsen."

Grégory did stand, a little stiff from kneeling. Natsu had already stripped naked and was laughing like a drunken idiot. Ose began to remove his clothes. The women were already naked. The one that had played the biwa came toward Grégory and took his hand. He stared at her tiny breasts, the nipples hard from the chill air in the room. He wasn't keen on being intimate in such a public way. To expose his deformed frame to these two nobles would be a mistake.

"Private." He managed while gazing with effort up at her lovely face.

The woman nodded, took his hand, and led him out the door.

Cave

Chapter 14

Time slipped between the cracks and layers of Jonathan's patience. On the one hand, his calm resolve to see things through reigned. On the other, he wanted to charge Ose Shigemori with some horrible crime so he could have him executed and then marry Tamika.

He took his morning walk along the garden paths of Katatsune Palace. The renovations were ongoing, and he hadn't stepped foot inside since his birthday party. When he reached the far side of the palace, he stopped to study his finished stables. They bore the same style as Katatsune. Curved roofs dominated the buildings, and both were painted red with black tops.

He continued to walk down a slight incline to the stable door. Adjacent land had been fenced to provide his horses with exercise as well as pasture to graze on.

Recent reports indicated the Haranobu had increased in numbers. Jonathan couldn't understand it. *Hadn't he decreased taxes?*

Hadn't he given the elderly a pension? Hadn't he set up programs to feed and house the poor? So why were the people turning against him? Perhaps Tamika could shed light on it all.

The double doors of the stable were open. The scent of hay and horse predominated. There were more than thirty stalls and, in the back, living quarters for the trainers, stable boys, groomsmen, and horse handlers. The coachmen lived in a separate building.

Jonathan had three Romani vanner horses to date, but his favorite was the one he'd received for his birthday almost three weeks ago. An all-black stallion he named Quickflame.

His horse handler, Imari, stood within Quickflame's stall. "Emperor." He bowed.

"Imari, I wish to go riding."

The man nodded and lifted the bridle, pulling it over Quickflame's muzzle. A short time later, the stallion was brought out of the stables, ready for Jonathan.

"Thank you, Imari, you're a good man." He took the reins and turned his horse, heading out the gate.

The bluff on which the palace, throne room, and Jonathan's living quarters were situated was immense. For the most part, all the buildings took up the southern end. West, past the stable grounds, were fields of hay, and further on toward the northwestern edge was a large forest of pine and oak. Jonathan had ridden in that direction to the edge more than once. Today he headed along the western side. An old path with ruts and stone was partially overgrown with knotweed. From his vantage, Jonathan could see past the boulders out to the ocean. He slowed to a trot and patted Quickflame's shoulder.

A breeze lifted off the bluff and touched Jonathan as he passed. When the path became too dangerous to navigate, he pulled the horse to the side, dismounted, took the reins, and walked up a steep incline. A single oak spread its roots over rocks and furrowed deep into the land. New leaves were budding on the ancient limbs. The wind deformed the trunk, so it bent sideways before leaning toward the ocean. Jonathan reached the summit and mounted Quickflame, riding under the massive tree.

He turned his stallion to face the ocean and brought him to a standstill. Past the boulders dominating the edge, he could see waves forming. He dismounted, took the reins in hand once again, and walked to the flat outcropping of stones. There, he was able to peer down to the shore.

Dozens of birds sang and flew out from their nests in the rocky face of the crag. Jonathan stepped closer to the edge. The flat sand was marred by an outcropping of tall pillars breaking past the sand into the sea on his left. To the right, the waves buffeted further in, disappearing before they reached landfall. *Was there a cave?*

If there was a cave, was there a way down? Could you explore it?

He stepped back and rejoined the knotweed opposite the path. Quickflame nickered and nuzzled his arm so that he stroked the horse with his free hand. An outcropping of bushes formed a regular line straight ahead. Once there, he looped the reins around a branch and proceeded to walk the length of the bushes away from the edge. They formed a semi-circle leading him to a man-made opening. The rocks were stacked in such a way that a building of sorts presented itself. Jonathan ducked and entered. The interior was dark. He felt a decline in the floor and stopped. As his eyes adjusted to the shadows, he discerned a table along with a few chairs. Sitting atop the table were several old lanterns. He picked one up and took it outside. Inspecting the lantern, he found an excellent candle within. He pulled a small tinderbox from the saddlebag and, kneeling on the ground, lit the candle.

Returning to the rocky building, he lifted the lantern to look around. The room was small with only the table and chairs. On the floor were dozens of small stones with markings. Nearby a wooden board had rotted, but he could still see painted symbols. He picked it up to examine before setting the panel on the table. This was a game he had seen a few soldiers play called *Sasaki*.

Off to one side, a door led to a stairwell around a deep hole in the rock. Using his lantern, Jonathan peered over the space but couldn't discern the bottom. No railing stood between the wall and opening to steady his hand. His nerves tensed from the danger.

He kept near the wall and began to descend, careful not to slip. On the third turn around, slits in the rock face allowed him to glimpse the ocean. The floor was more expansive here but still uneven and sloped. The little light from the windows and his lantern made the interior gray. Another opening hewn from the rock led into a room, but there wasn't anything there. He returned to the stairs.

His footfalls echoed. By the time he passed the third set of small windows, he could hear the ocean. Another room was located to one side. He ignored it this time. Peering over the circular edge, he still couldn't see anything. His shadow stretched over the wall and walkway from the lantern's light as he continued his journey. Still, the slick floor and lack of a rail made him overly cautious. *What had this place been used for?* He couldn't imagine.

Two more rounds and he saw a flickering gray light when he looked down the hole. He strained to listen. The sound of the ocean reached him, and the air began to taste of salt. He continued. The light changed from gray to yellow. A scraping noise followed by grunts warned he must proceed with care. *Would he find sea lions below?*

Finally, he viewed a rock-hewn arch over a wide entry. The light was brighter now. He rounded the stair and stepped off into another room of sorts. Jonathan expected a pool beyond the opening and a sandy beach beyond that. He almost walked through the door but, at the last minute, paused. Noises came to him. Unexplained and unexpected when there should only be the ocean waves crashing through the cave opening and the bark of animals. His heartbeat increased. His stomach muscles grew tight.

The crack of a whip and cry of a man was followed by, "Work, or I will inform Natsu of your laziness."

Jonathan pressed his body against the wall and inched toward the opening.

The man yelled again, “Back to work!”

Jonathan crept forward. When he peered around the door, he saw a dozen workers dressed in gray kimonos, lifting boulders to clear yet another opening in the cave. Two, no three men stood by in black, each holding a whip. He glimpsed past the second opening, where he made out water pushing against the sides of the cave.

“Use your shovels,” another man said.

Jonathan focused on the men working. From the way the rocks and gravel were positioned, he realized the opening the men were enlarging had been closed, either from a rockslide or intentionally by someone blowing it up. At this point, only one man at a time could squeeze through.

What is the purpose of these men? Of Natsu? Was it Lord Natsu, Ose's friend? Or another?

A worker spotted him and stared. Jonathan pulled back.

The same man who shouted before yelled, “Enemy!” His voice echoing.

A commotion. No time. Feet and voices advanced on him. Jonathan pulled his sword and stepped into the door. Two of the guardsmen abandoned their whips and drew swords. The third stared without moving. The workers gathered together in a huddle.

Blade upon blade. Jonathan used his superior height to drive down their weapons. His straight sword an advantage over the scimitars.He swiped wide through the belly of one of his attackers. That left only the one whose skill of sword was expert. They danced around each other. Thrusting, swiping, metal on metal. Then, Jonathan saw the third man advance, out of his peripheral vision, twirling his whip overhead. He lunged away from the blow, and the whip cracked against a rock. This left him open. The blade of the swordsman pierced his left side. He sucked in air. Pain soared through his nerves. He lifted his blade and came down hard, slicing through his attacker’s skull. His eyes widened, his sword fell, and he crumbled to the floor.

Holding his side, Jonathan turned toward the man with the whip. He lay dead. A worker stood over the body with a bloody shovel. Jonathan raised his eyes to the man.

"Excellency!" He knelt and bowed his head along with all his companions.

Jonathan's sword dropped from his numb fingers. The room spiraled. The lights dimmed and went black as he fell to the floor.

Grégory didn't like running, and he hated riding a horse. He had run from the manor house to the stables watching Lieutenant Saville outdistance him with his men, including his friend, Claude Coulomb.

At the stables, Grégory was helped into a saddle of a white mare. This horse loathed him. She backed against her stall to dislodge him. Now she was galloping to catch up to the soldiers. With every hoofbeat, he was cast into the air only to plunge back into the saddle. His bottom hurt, and he feared he would soon be thrown to the ground.

None of it could be helped, though. When word came, Jonathan was injured, Saville began to bark orders. Captain Périer was sent to the Romani along with several men to fetch a healer.

Grégory passed a soldier whose horse tripped in a hole. The animal stood with its hoof off the ground while the man bent, checking its injury. The party of men and horses was just up ahead.

His horse came to an abrupt stop, and Grégory was thrown from the saddle, landing hard. He screamed, "Oh!"

Claude ran to him. "Are you injured?"

Grégory sat up, checked his person, and gave Claude a frown. "No."

To this, the man started to laugh. Grégory glared at him but accepted his hand and soon stood. "Where is Jonathan?"

Claude pointed to a rock formation surrounded by bushes.

Brushing off his derriere, Grégory walked to the building, passing a dozen Shea-Talonian men. Inside, lanterns were hung on the wall all around a small room. Jonathan lay unconscious on a table. His face was gray, and his shirt was soaked in blood. A crude bandage had been put over the wound.

"You two," Saville said. "Lift him up over a saddle so we can take him back." Two men reached for Jonathan.

"Wait." Grégory stepped in front of the men. "We shouldn't move him until the healer has a chance to examine him."

"When the sun goes down, this place will be freezing." Saville's mouth ended in a purse.

"The emperor has lost a lot of blood. If we move him, he may die from blood loss."

"Or freeze to death in here."

"We could move him carefully…very carefully outside. Bring blankets to keep him warm and light a fire."

Saville looked at Jonathan, then back to Grégory. "Let it be done. You," he said to a soldier. "Pull your blanket and find a good place to lay it on the ground." Saville left.

Grégory turned to Jonathan and put his hand on the emperor's forehead. Hot. Soon several men returned and lifted Jonathan to take him outside. He was lowered onto a blanket near a fire.

Saville was standing before the Shea-Talonians. Grégory joined him. One of the workers was talking.

"We were hired to clear the cave entrance. None of us knew the reason."

"Who hired you?" Saville asked.

"Natsu."

"Lord Natsu? Or another?"

Grégory looked from Saville to the Shea-Talonian.

"We were only told, Natsu."

"And the purpose of clearing the rocks?"

"To open the cave."

"But it's not just a cave, is it?" Saville pulled his sword. "Treason is punishable by death."

All the men fell to their knees and began rocking back and forth.

Grégory set his hand on Saville's arm to stop him. "Did you know the cave gave entrance to an old structure that led to the plateau above?"

The same man as before sat against his legs and looked at Grégory. "No, we knew none of that."

Grégory sensed someone and glanced back to see Claude. He returned his gaze to the man. "Tell us what happened."

The man began to explain in detail what he'd seen. "When I saw the emperor come out from behind the wall, I knew it was more than a cave. The overlords attacked him. I took the shovel and hit one of them over the head."

"You killed that one." Saville didn't ask a question.

"Yes."

Saville put his sword away.

Grégory cleared his throat. "Natsu is a member of the Haranobu. Who is their leader?"

"The Haranobu? They are dangerous, my Lord. We do not converse with them."

"And yet, you cleared away a hidden entry to an old forgotten building for them." Grégory nodded. The pieces were coming together. He turned and walked away. Jonathan would decide what to do with these men when he regained consciousness.

Guilt

Chapter 15

Grégory sat back and rubbed his eyes. He'd pored over every decree Jonathan implemented since he became emperor, and there was nothing that dealt with the current situation. Standing, he blew out two of the candles on his desk and lifted the third. Outside his office, he climbed the stairs and approached Jonathan's bedchamber.

The Shea-Talonian workmen had not been allowed to leave. The council meetings had been canceled. And word had been sent out to the people that Jonathan was ill. *All his doing. He befriended Ose.*

He knocked before entering. Jonathan lay in bed, his skin pale. Isabella sat next to the bed. Her grandmother slept in another room, and her brother Kourken did the same.

She rose. "Monsieur."

Isabella was a beautiful woman. "How is he?" Grégory asked.

"He hasn't improved. The fever is bad."

Grégory went to the bed and reached across, taking Jonathan's arm.

"Don't be discouraged. Grandmama says he is doing well for all the blood he lost. I clean the wound every two hours."

Grégory lifted tired eyes to hers.

"You must rest as well, Monsieur."

She walked across the room. "Here, lay on the lounge. I'm sure the emperor won't mind."

The thought of climbing down the stairs to the second floor and his room felt overwhelming at that moment, so he walked to the lounge and climbed into it. Isabella brought a pillow and blanket.

Laying down, he shut his eyes.

"Sweet dreams." She kissed his cheek.

That made him open his eyes.

"Shh…rest," she whispered.

Grégory stood on a mound with forest on either side of the Plains of Gil-Lael. A lone horseman turned his stallion to face him a short way off. The man had armor on and a helmet in the style of Shea-Talon. Around his upper arm, there was a spiral bracelet with a dragon head. He lowered his sword and charged.

Grégory couldn't move. The horseman drew closer. The sword was positioned to impale him.

He caught his breath and sat up. For a moment, he felt disorientated. *Where am I?* He took in the room, his eyes landing on the prone figure in the bed. Jonathan. The older Romani woman wrung out a cloth in the bowl of water on the nightstand and set it on Jonathan's forehead.

Taking a breath, he slowed his heartbeat. "How is he?" Grégory slid off the lounge and approached. *He needed to shave and put on fresh clothes. Maybe a bath.*

"He is better, Little Man." The woman's accent was thick but not unpleasant.

He neared the bed. “His fever?”

“Not as high, and the wound is healing.”

“Is there anything I can do?”

The older woman’s wrinkled face smoothed in a smile. “Not unless you believe in God, and then you can pray.”

Grégory nodded. “I do believe and will continue to pray. Summon me if there is a change.” He left for his room.

Hours later, Grégory sat back in his office chair and peered up at Lieutenant Saville.

“We waste time,” Saville said. “The Haranobu grow strong. We must question the prisoners and learn who their leader is.”

“You mean you want to torture them.”

“They haven’t answered our questions.”

“High King Healden has banned torture, saying, a man will confess anything and often not the truth.”

“This isn’t Gil-Lael. Governor Marlon allowed it, saying we would never learn anything from these people.” Saville clasped the handle of his sheathed sword so tight that his knuckles turned white.

Grégory looked up at him. “These men killed one of their superiors to save Jonathan. They carried him up those stone steps and laid him on the table. One ran to inform us of what happened. If they were part of the Haranobu, don’t you think they would have killed Jonathan and left him at the bottom in that cave building? Don’t you think they would have gotten in their boats and returned to tell their leader? We wouldn’t have found Jonathan for days, months maybe.”

Saville stepped closer and leaned on Grégory’s small desk. “They know more than they say.”

“Perhaps. For now, it is enough that we have detained them. When Jonathan awakes, you may take it up with him.”

Saville stood straight. "Who are you to give orders?" He turned, marched to the door, and slammed it on the way out.

Grégory had the sickening feeling that Saville would do whatever he wanted.

"Monsieur, Monsieur."

Grégory gasped and sat up in bed, feeling as if he had left his heart behind.

Isabella shook him again. "Come, come, there has been a change."

He slipped from the bed, put on his robe and slippers before hurrying after her. She ran, and he was forced to do the same.

Kourken waited at the stairs. Two powerful arms lifted him up and climbed the stairs two at a time before setting him down in the hall.

Grégory adjusted his robe. "Well, that wasn't dignified."

Kourken laughed. Isabella looked between them. "Come!"

He found Jonathan staring at the ceiling. The sweat on his brow told Grégory the fever was back. Kourken picked him up again. "Stop that." The man put him on Jonathan's bed.

After clearing his throat and eyeing Kourken with his most stern expression, he turned to Jonathan. "Emperor, it is good to see you awake."

Jonathan turned his head toward Grégory. The far-off gaze that met his made him shudder.

"Tamika?" Jonathan searched his face.

"She isn't here."

"Tamika." Jonathan turned his eyes away once more. His breathing labored, he shut his eyes and whispered. "Tamika."

At a little after ten in the morning, Grégory stood and came around from his desk. “Thank you for coming.”

Tamika bowed in the manner of her people. “When I learned of his excellency’s illness, I was greatly concerned. I have sent prayers and hope he is better.”

He cleared his throat. “Please take a seat. Wine?” He poured them both a goblet of the peach wine before she said anything and handed it to her. Then he sat across from her. “I have a confession.”

Tamika’s calm demeanor gave him no clue as to what she was thinking.

“I must have your assurance that you will not utter a word of what I’m about to tell you. Not to your husband, nor servants, not even to friends.”

“In my life, I have kept many secrets.”

“Even from Ose?”

“Especially from Ose.”

Grégory downed the wine and set the goblet aside. “The emperor isn’t sick.”

Her brows drew together. “Not sick.”

“No, it is far more serious. Jonathan has been injured. Pierced through with a sword.”

“What! How? Will he live?” Tears glistened in her eyes.

Grégory looked away for a moment. *Did Tamika have feelings for Jonathan?* This was bad, unbelievably bad. Her husband was an important noble. One he befriended, looking to learn what he could of the Haranobu. But, so far, Ose hadn’t indicated he knew anything about them, and the lies Grégory told to stay in his good graces had started to weigh on his conscience.

“Yes, I think he will make a full recovery, but at present, he still has a high fever. He calls for you.”

“For me?”

“Yes. Are you willing to see him?”

“Yes.”

Grégory stood. “Then follow me.”

She set the wine down untouched.

For whatever reason, climbing the stairs with Tamika following brought him humiliation. The way he had to balance with his hands and even sometimes sit and roll up the step. At last, before Jonathan’s door, he knocked. Kourken answered. The older woman and Isabella were both in the room. It was stifling hot.

“We will leave,” Mariyam announced. She patted Tamika’s hand on the way out.

Jonathan turned his head. His hair was damp and matted to his forehead. He’d thrown off the covers and lay in his long pants. His chest was bare except for the bandage that wrapped around his lower stomach.

“Tamika.” He lifted a trembling hand.

Tamika approached. “Excellency.”

“Please,” Jonathan said and patted the mattress.

“You may leave.” He didn’t look at Grégory.

He nodded and left. At the door, he paused. *Propriety said the two should not be alone, but how did one advise an emperor on such a matter?*

Friend-Brother

Chapter 16

Grégory pushed back from the small table inside the geisha house in time to miss the hot tea Ose swept from the surface with his arm.

"Why didn't you tell me, Little Man?"

"Tell you?"

Ose grabbed Grégory's collar and lifted him. "That the usurper was pierced with a sword. Instead, you had us believe he was sick."

Grégory's mind raced. It had been three days since Tamika came to see Jonathan and four days since he kept the appointment to meet with Ose at the geisha house. *Who told Ose? Tamika?*

"I was sworn to secrecy."

"I have befriended you. Allowed you to accompany us here. Let you tour my factory. And in return, I expect you to inform me of every move that…that…that the emperor makes." Ose shoved him backward, and Grégory slid on his bottom against the paper-thin wall.

Catching himself, he adjusted his shirt and stood. Ose was short compared to Jonathan but still towered over Grégory. He looked up, noticing Ose's red face. "I am under certain restraints, as I'm sure you can appreciate."

He stepped away from the wall and glanced around the room. The three women stood off to the side. Natsu held the hilt of his sword still sheathed. Grégory had a small knife, no match for the two Shea-Talonian nobles.

"In any event, Jonathan has recovered and is holding his next council soon. You can ask him about his injury yourself."

Ose tilted his head back and let out a roar. Then, he settled his eyes once more on Grégory. "Leave before I kill you and never return."

Grégory's nerves were raw. "As you wish." He bowed, turned, and left. As he walked along the corridor to the entrance, he heard Ose bellow.

"We had our opportunity."

Natsu answered. "He is not gone yet, be careful what you say."

Grégory paused. *Did he dare? No one was in the hall with him. There were more rooms. But wouldn't his carriage still waiting for him tip-off Ose?*

He left the building, crossed the bridge, and waited below the driver's box for the man to notice him.

"Yes?" He peered down at Grégory.

"Drive a little way off and turn into the woods to hide. I will return on foot to this place."

The man nodded, and the footman helped him into the carriage. Not long after, he felt the wheels roll over uneven ground.

"Wait for me here." Grégory directed after climbing down the steps. He ran between bushes and trees back to the geisha house. Ose's carriage stood off to the side away from the front entrance. The driver was bundled inside his coat with his head bent. It wouldn't take much to awaken him. He was about to run across the drive when Ose and

Natsu appeared at the door to the house along with Madam Shiho. The two walked toward the coach.

Grégory moved between bushes to the carriage and remained hidden.

"What now?" Natsu asked, standing outside the coach.

"The next time I see that disgusting dwarf, I'll kill him." Ose climbed into the carriage.

"He's a favorite of the emperor."

"Yes, I was stupid to believe he would be useful. His information contradicts the soldier."

Soldier...who could this be? Grégory waited until the vehicle turned on to the road and vanished, then he returned to his own carriage.

Grégory woke to banging on his door. He sat. Sunlight peeked through the slits in his curtains. Leaving the bed, he grabbed his robe and answered the door.

Captain Périer stood before him. "His excellency has called a council meeting."

"What time is it?"

"Late."

Grégory nodded and shut the door to dress. His fatigue caused him to oversleep. He needed a bath, but it must wait. Selecting dark brown pants and jacket, he opened the door once more. His gout was acting up, and his shoes were too tight. Périer still stood there.

"Captain," he said.

"His excellency has requested you bring a ledger and twelve *honor som coins* and *two royal tlokel coins*. Along with twelve pouches."

A fortune in silver and gold. What did Jonathan intend to do with it?

Grégory walked beside the captain, down the stairs and to his office, across from Jonathan's. He opened the safe for the money and his drawer for the ledger and inkwell, along with several quill pens and sharpener. Once out the door, more soldiers joined them and kept pace with his hobbling walk.

He found the Shea-Talonian nobility already seated and Jonathan on his throne chair when he entered.

"Thank you for coming, Monsieur. Please sit." Jonathan pointed to a table off to the side and in front of the seated nobles.

Grégory put the things he brought on the table, arranged them neatly, and noted the Shea-Talonian workers who rescued Jonathan when he was injured. Two of them had bloody clothes over their right wrist where their hands used to be. Opposite these men and standing with many soldiers were Saville. Grégory had related to Jonathan what happened while he was unconscious a few days ago.

He sat and opened the ledger.

"Welcome, men of Shea-Talon." Jonathan straightened his back. He wore a red jacket and black pants over polished boots. His sword rested across his knees.

"This is the first council meeting since my illness. Or so you were led to believe. I wasn't ill. Someone paid these men you see standing against that wall to dig an opening to a cave. A cave that had carved stairs leading to the top of the plateau. A rock house that until now I didn't know about. One can only speculate who knew about this cave along with the house and why they wanted it cleared. Rest assured; it will be heavily guarded from here on."

As Jonathan spoke, two men at another table wrote in books before them. Grégory wondered what Ose's face looked like, but he didn't turn around to see for himself. Natsu was there as well. Seated next to Ose.

"These men," Jonathan pointed to the workers, "saved my life." He turned to look at them. "I will forever be grateful." The men bowed several times as all the people of Shea-Talon did.

"While I was recovering, Lieutenant Saville took it upon himself to torture some of you, believing you knew who the leader of the Haranobu was. Two of you have lost a hand because of this. I didn't order this torture." He once again looked at the men. Grégory looked as well.

Jonathan turned his gaze back to the nobles, and Grégory could almost feel the tension rise in the room.

"Torture is outlawed in Gil-Lael. The reason for this is because a man tortured will confess to anything, even an untruth. Especially an untruth. Lieutenant Saville."

Saville stepped before the throne. "Excellency."

"I understand Governor Marlon tortured men and women whenever he felt threatened."

"Yes, Excellency."

"Yet. Monsieur Mossé reminded you that it was outlawed."

"Yes, Excellency."

"I am greatly disappointed in you, Saville. I'm afraid that I cannot simply let this pass. This man," and Jonathan pointed to one of the men who lost a hand. "Saved my life using the very hand you took to wield a shovel and kill one of his superiors before he could attack me."

Saville didn't look at the workers and didn't reply.

"Therefore, I strip you of your rank."

"Excellency!" Saville's voice rose. "Please."

"I am sure these men begged for their hands. You didn't listen. I fear something must be done to you short of letting you hang."

Périer came forward, and Saville took off his hat and jacket with the lieutenant's insignia on it. His hands shook when he handed them to Périer, who brought them over to the table where Grégory sat.

"You are now a captain, Saville. You will receive a new jacket and hat later. Step aside."

"Périer," Jonathan said.

The man replaced Saville before the throne.

"I appoint you lieutenant. You will assume the duties that were Saville's along with a pay increase."

"Thank you, Excellency."

Jonathan tilted his head slightly, and Périer joined the other soldiers.

"Men of Shea-Talon, please step forward."

The workers glanced at each other and then obeyed. All of them knelt on the floor in a long line.

"Your names," Jonathan said.

They each answered.

"Grégory, give each man an *honor som.*"

It took Grégory a few minutes to pick up the pouch, open it and walk before the kneeling men, giving one to each. Once done, he returned to the desk and made a notation in the ledger, which he would fill in later.

"Kenshin and Ito. You both lost your right hand. This will limit your ability to work. Therefore, I grant you an additional *royal tlokel* each."

Grégory took the gold coins to the men and slipped them into their pouches since they didn't have their right hands.

"Thank you, Excellency, thank you." The men all said and started bowing once more.

Back at the table, Grégory watched Jonathan hold up his hand. The room became so quiet one wouldn't know it was full of Shea-Talonian nobles and Gil-Laelian soldiers.

"Men," Jonathan said. "Go to your families. Gather your things and return. Because of your loyalty to the crown and my person, I will find work for you here. Lieutenant Périer make a guard to accompany these men home and safely return them. We wouldn't want the Haranobu to try to kill them and rob them of their reward." Jonathan's gaze traveled over Grégory to the men behind him. He was almost sure it was Ose who received the emperor's stare.

The workers went to the side, and Grégory thought the meeting over. Then Jonathan surprised him and started speaking again.

"Natsu, please come before me."

The nobles seemed to all begin to whisper. There was some shuffling, and then Natsu walked past Grégory to stand before the throne. There was a great long pause. Jonathan watched Natsu in silence as he stood there.

At last, Natsu spoke. "Excellency." He bowed and sank to one knee.

"Natsu, before I was attacked by those men in charge of the workers in the cave, they mentioned your name. They indicated that *you* had hired them. What have you to say about this?"

Natsu lifted his eyes to Jonathan. "I know nothing about it, Excellency."

"Are you a member of the Haranobu? Their leader, perhaps?"

"I am not."

"Can you prove it?"

"I wouldn't know how to prove it, Excellency."

"Then I'm afraid that you must be detained until you can admit your guilt or prove your innocence." Jonathan lifted his arm. Lieutenant Périer, along with three soldiers, pulled Natsu to a standing position, tied his hands behind his back, and marched him out. Périer remained, however, and rejoined the soldiers to the side.

The nobles were talking. Some stood. Ose stepped forward. "Forgive Excellency, but Natsu is innocent."

"Can you prove that, Ose?"

"What can I show you as proof?"

"A written account of Natsu's dealings and activities."

"I can only provide what I know when I'm with him."

"Are you a member of the Haranobu?"

"No, Excellency. I would never oppose you."

"Perhaps I should have you join Natsu in Furuya Jun Prison."

"Excellency, I have done nothing wrong."

Grégory wanted to interrupt, to tell all he knew, but he really didn't have anything on either man.

"Take a seat, Ose, before I change my mind and arrest you." Jonathan shifted in his seat and lifted the sword, turning it over.

Ose said nothing else and sat.

Jonathan waited, and after a short time, the room grew quiet again.

"This unfortunate incident has brought my attention to the fact there is no one to replace me if I should die. No doubt, many of you hope for just that. In Gil-Lael, the crown prince chooses a friend to replace him should he not have an heir in the event of death. This person is known as friend-brother, and such a law assures that no war will break out and the power transfer is peaceful. I do not have a friend-brother. That changes today. Monsieur Grégory Mossé, please come and kneel before me."

Jonathan couldn't have surprised him more. He stood on shaking legs and stepped before the throne.

"Excellency, I must protest." A Shea-Talonian noble stood.

Grégory paused, turning to see who it was.

Terazawa Akii continued. "We have no such law."

"Now you do." Jonathan frowned.

"Excellency," Bito Arei said, standing as well. "He is a dwarf." He pointed at Grégory. "He cannot inherit the throne. Only a man of impeccable lineage may rule."

"Yes!" several shouted at once.

"No dwarf!" more yelled.

Jonathan stood and motioned to Umezawa, who stepped forward and slammed the staff down. The nobles quieted. Some sat while others remained standing.

Grégory didn't know what to do. He felt exposed.

Jonathan remained standing. "What would you have? A man of lineage full of selfish ambition and doesn't care for you or the people? A man of lineage who doesn't have a sharp mind and makes rash judgments? A man who goes to war every few years as Warwyk did? A man who increases your taxes until you can't survive and starve as a common man? Tell me, which kind of emperor would you choose?"

Silence followed.

"Master Mossé has a brilliant mind. He has proven that time and again. I can trust him, and that is more than I can say for most of you."

Grégory caught a look of calculated disgust from Ose and lowered his eyes.

"All of you sit. Come forward Master Mossé and kneel."

Grégory obeyed. Jonathan stood and stepped down from the throne, sword in hand.

"With this sword," Jonathan set the broadside down on Grégory's shoulder and then up and over to his next shoulder. "I appoint you friend-brother to me. Arise, Your Grace."

Grégory stood.

Jonathan smiled at him. "Friend-Brother is the highest title under the royal family. You will address my friend as Your Grace from here on."

Jonathan nodded to Umezawa, who stepped forward again and hit the floor with his staff. "The council meeting is adjourned."

The men behind Grégory made a lot of noise then, rising from their chairs and leaving. Once gone, Lieutenant Périer escorted the workers out, leaving only Jonathan and Grégory in the building.

"You have much to learn, my friend," Jonathan said, putting his hand on Grégory's shoulder.

Rumblings of War

Chapter 17

Jonathan pushed back from the desk. "This is unexpected." His finger tapped the ledger Grégory brought. "This amount in sales of my wine more than makes up for the tax cut I gave the people."

"Oui," Grégory spoke Gil-Laelian, as did Jonathan. He found it easier and assumed the same of the emperor.

"I'm looking forward to learning how I should invest the money."

"I will look into it." Grégory sat in one of the chairs placed before Jonathan's desk. "If I may, Excellency."

"Go on."

"You do realize that the nobles despise the idea I could inherit the throne."

Jonathan nodded. "Of course, they do."

"Then why?" Grégory pushed a stray hair out of his eyes.

"Why did I name you friend-brother?"

"Oui."

"You took charge when I was injured and unable to fulfill my duties, and you did an excellent job."

Grégory felt a rush travel through his body.

"And, I have no other friends here."

"That cannot be so." Grégory frowned.

Jonathan shut the ledger. "Indeed, it is. I am surrounded by enemies. Your appointment serves a dual purpose. First, you are my friend, and you are capable of taking over this position should I perish in the war."

"What war?" Grégory hid his hands below the desk and tapped his fingers together to ease the tension he felt.

"I hope to stir up the Haranobu to act before they become stronger. I suspect Ose Shigemori is their leader."

"Why?"

Jonathan lowered his gaze to Grégory's. "When I first met the Shigemoris, I had a strong reaction to them both. I'm sure you've noticed how I feel about Tamika."

"Oui."

"Soon after meeting them, I learned from Tamika herself that her grandmother was one of Warwyk's wives."

"Warwyk, the former emperor who fought with Renwyk in the war?"

"The same. Ose strikes me as a man who will do anything to achieve his goal. And that goal is to become emperor. Theirs was an arranged marriage. I sent a man down to Tamika's home in the south of Shea-Talon to investigate. He has recently returned."

Jonathan stood and went to the window overlooking a garden coming to life with flowers and budding leaves. Grégory joined him.

Without looking at Grégory, Jonathan continued. "Her parents and sister died in a fire. And before that, her brother died in a hunting accident. Ose was his best friend, and they were alone in the woods together. Within a few months of the fire, her uncle married her to Ose. Tamika being the only heir to her parent's fortune, the marriage transferred her wealth to Ose. He came from a minor noble family with little money. One must wonder about Ose."

"You think Ose was responsible for the deaths of Tamika's family."

"I do."

"Tamika is in danger."

"Oui. It eats at me. I asked her to leave him."

"What did she say?"

"By law, Ose owns her. Part of the marriage contract here."

"Owns! Like a slave?"

"My thoughts exactly."

"What will you do?" Grégory had been standing long enough and returned to the chair.

Jonathan continued to peer at the flowers. "I will change the law and give married women their freedom and their monies back."

Grégory whistled. "If my appointment to friend-brother doesn't start a war, that will."

Jonathan turned back to Grégory. "Oui, oui it will."

Silence fell between them. Jonathan returned to his desk.

"I have something I should tell you." Grégory lifted his eyes before dropping them again.

"Go on."

"I didn't just go to the geisha house alone. I met up with Ose and Natsu."

"You thought to act as my spy. I know."

"You know?"

Jonathan chuckled. "Oui, don't look so surprised. I have my own spies."

"Then you know about the soldier who has become an informant who reports to Ose."

"That, I didn't know."

Tamika knelt before the dining table. Clutching her hands so tight, her knuckles turned white. She kept her gaze lowered. Ose was angry. No…furious. He had already thrown the teapot and both cups. The small plants she brought into the room three days ago were yanked from their pots, dirt everywhere, and the buds pulled off. The paper walls were slit with Ose's hunting knife. A long sharp blade she hoped wouldn't end up across her throat.

"And you!"

She trembled. He was pointing the knife at her.

"You love him, don't you?"

"I am your wife." She spoke the words carefully as if every syllable made an impact. They didn't.

"You whore. You have slept with him!"

"I have not. I am faithful to you."

Ose dragged her from the cushion. His fingers bit into her arm. He still held the knife, which was flat against her arm. She met his gaze.

"I should kill you. I should kill you now and send your body as a gift to him."

Tamika held her breath. To speak may increase his anger. But, then again, not to speak may do the same. She couldn't control the trembling of her body and watched as a smile spread Ose's lips into an evil grin exposing his teeth.

"You can't hide the truth from me. Is he big?"

"What?"

"Big! I bet he is. You whore." He pushed her away. Tamika lost her balance, falling backward.

He loomed over her. "Do you know what he did today?"

Tamika watched as Ose swept the knife back and forth as if he were underlining each utterance.

"He made that dwarf his friend-brother. Do you know what that means?"

Tamika gagged and covered her mouth with one hand. He continued regardless. Fear engulfed every part of her, and she bit her finger to keep herself from vomiting. She shook her head no in answer to his question.

"If he dies, that dwarf will be emperor. Can you imagine all of us bowing to a dwarf!?"

This was the reason for Ose's temper. It suddenly struck her as funny. Unable to help herself, Tamika started to laugh. She held her side and laughed louder. Tears came to her eyes. And then…Ose struck her so hard across the face her entire body twisted. Her laughter died. He began kicking her. Once, twice, she coughed up blood. A third time. The room grew blurry. Four. Darkness sent her away from the beating.

Tamika opened her eyes. She lay in her bed. Light filtered through the curtains, and a breeze lifted the chiffon fabric and created a dance of shadow and sunlight. Someone had put a damp cloth on her forehead.

She tried to sit. Pain tightened her muscles, and she gave a cry before falling back into the mattress. There was little comfort in knowing she survived Ose's temper. He would beat her again when he wanted to hurt something or someone. He always did.

For a time, she thought he had changed. But when Jonathan arrived, Ose's temper resurfaced.

She thought about Jonathan's invitation to leave Ose and come to the palace. If she were brave, she'd do that. But she wasn't courageous. Instead, the thought of her friends shunning her filled her with dread.

The door slid open. Her maid, Enya, entered with a tray.

"I am so happy to see you awake." Enya set the tray down on the nightstand. She knelt before the mattress that rested on the floor.

"How long has it been?" Tamika almost added, *this time*.

"All night and most of the morning."

"I should go to the hot spring house."

"You must eat first, and then I will go with you in case you fall."

"I will eat, and you can walk with me, but I must be left alone in the bath, so I can think."

Enya poured tea into the cup. With assistance, Tamika sat. But her arms wouldn't work, and her fingers refused to hold the cup, so Enya pressed the cup to her lips. Neither spoke as Tamika ate. When she finished, she had Enya help her pull on a robe.

An hour later, she stood at the door to the bathhouse. Tamika turned to Enya. "I will see you later."

Enya bowed. "You must leave him."

"How can I? He owns me. He has all my wealth. Every piece of land and both houses. I will be nothing without him."

"The emperor will help you. You have told me so."

"But how can I impose on him? If I went to Jonathan…" tears filled her eyes. "If I went to him, Ose would start a war. You know it is so."

"The next time, he may kill you."

"Enya, I must think. My thoughts are jumbled. I must be alone." Tamika turned away and slid the door to the hot springs bathhouse open, and entered.

The bath was oval and hewn out of rock to catch the hot mineral spring water. Along both walls were potted bushes, but along the back were full-grown evergreen trees. The bathhouse roof was open above the trees, and several had grown so large their top limbs disappeared above the roofline. There were towels on a table near the rocky steps leading down into the water. Tamika removed her robe and set it over a chair.

The water burned her injuries but would cleanse them as well. She knelt in the water and submerged her face. Then she stood again.

"I am cursed, Honorable Ye Tai," she prayed. "Why did you give me such a husband? And my love, my heart is Jonathan. Impossible. I would be better off dead. Yes?"

She remained in the water with troubled thoughts. Her muscles had relaxed and no longer hurt. The light began to fade, and she knew it was close to sundown. Ose would expect her to come to dinner. But she couldn't bear to look at him. Leaving the water, she towel-dried and then wrapped her hair in the same towel. Slipping into her bathrobe, Tamika began to walk toward the door.

Voices. And a figure outside the door. Ose.

"Come in, come in." He pulled the screen open. Tamika turned and fled behind the tall evergreens. Would he see her watery footsteps?

The building had been constructed against the rocky hill. Those boulders were the fourth wall of the building. Bushes and trees grew out of the stone, and the hot mineral water flowed from within the earth, over the rocks, and into the pool. She climbed under the heavy pine limbs, closer to the trunk, pulling her body past it so she could peek through the thick needles and see the men. Her fingers came away, sticky from pine sap, and she wiped them on the damp towel, pulled off her head.

"Let us enjoy the bath." Ose held a wooden box. Tamika couldn't be sure, but she believed she'd seen that box before.

The men disrobed and entered the water, splashing as they found a spot. Watching them, she realized these were the nobles who sat at the council before Jonathan.

Ose set the box down on the same table that held the towels. "I have asked all of you here, so we might discuss what should be done with the new laws the emperor is introducing. He doesn't realize the amount of money it requires to give our old servants an income without receiving any benefit from them."

Many of the men spoke at the same time. "Yes, yes." "True." "No, he doesn't." "It cost a fortune."

"Not only that, but now he wants to give away food. What did he call it?" Ose lifted his voice above the sound of swishing water.

"Harvest Day." Tamika recognized that voice to be her friend's husband, Bito Arei.

"He did lower our taxes," Bito said.

"Yes, but is it enough?" Ose, still dressed while the others were naked, began to pace along the edge of the pool. "Now, I've learned he intends to change the laws of marriage, so our wives will retain their rights and their inheritance. These laws are a tradition! Our rights to sell our daughters into marriage will be banned."

"How do you know this?" Bito asked.

"I have a man who works there. He overheard that dwarf and the emperor talking."

So many men shouted that the echo of their displeasure hurt Tamika's ears, and she had to cover them. Her body sank all the way down to the ground.

The door opened, and dozens of men entered, dressed in gray Kimono. They came to stand along the three walls.

"I have asked you here, so you can join us to rid ourselves of this usurper. The Gil-Laelian imposter must die. He is not our emperor. He doesn't care about our traditions. Therefore, we need to appoint one of us as emperor."

Tamika's nose itched, and she inhaled sharply. *Oh Ye Tai, help me.* She used two fingers to press her nostrils close, and the other hand held her mouth.

Then, the men in the pool started shouting either "yes," or "no."

She sneezed into her robe. Looking at the men, back and forth, no one heard her. Not even Ose.

The room became quiet again though the movement of the water remained.

"I expect you have someone in mind?" Bito said.

Ose nodded. His hand rested on the box. "Yes, I do. But let me ask you first. What is the one thing Jonathan doesn't have? The one thing that proves him emperor?"

A prolonged silence followed. Tamika knew. Her eyes fell to the box. She remembered. Her grandmother had that box. She kept it hidden. But one time, when Tamika was small, her grandmother opened the box and showed it to her and…*her brother. Her brother knew. Her brother was Ose's friend.*

Bito answered. "The Bracelet of the Moon and Stars."

"Yes." Ose smiled.

"But it is lost, and no one knows where it is," one of the men said.

"Legend tells us our god, Ye Tai, arrived on the back of a dragon and gave the bracelet to our beloved emperor, Matsui. Therefore, only the man who has the bracelet may be emperor." Ose opened the box and pulled out something. He removed the covering to reveal the bracelet. He held it high and walked all the way around the pool, showing it as he went.

Tamika could barely see the bracelet, but she remembered. Gold wrought in five loops were connected by hammered gold symbols of the moon and stars. White opaque stones clouded by yellow were inset as the dragon's eyes and the head attached to the tail to form a clasp.

Ose stepped back at the table. "I am emperor." He slid the bracelet up his right arm to rest just above his elbow.

"It takes more than just the bracelet to be emperor," Bito said. "It takes blood."

Ose stared at Bito. Tamika knew that look well. Eyes narrowed, lips pushed into a thin line. She should warn the men Ose would soon lose his temper, but she didn't. She remained hidden.

"I am emperor by right of marriage and by the power of the Bracelet of the Moon and Stars. So I ask you, good men. Join me as a member of the Haranobu to oppose the usurper and bring about his death."

Oh…this is why, he wanted to marry her. Tamika wanted to throw something, but she held her fury close and remained hidden.

The men shouted. Some with approval and others with "no."

"Who will join me?" Ose pointed to one of the soldiers. He held up a paper and brought it to the table.

"Sign and pledge your allegiance to me."

No one moved for a moment, and then, Bito stepped out of the bath. Quiet settled over the men as Bito gazed at Ose. “I cannot sign.”

“Why?”

“Our lands were won legally by High King Healden in the war. Jonathan is his son. The age of our forefathers has passed. We now live in the present and must adjust ourselves to these times.”

Ose didn’t utter a word. Instead, he held up a hand, and the man who brought over the paper drew his sword and thrust it into Bito.

The men in the pool all yelled. Tamika sat back up and covered her mouth.

As Bito lay bleeding out at his feet, Ose turned back to the men. “Anyone else wish to refuse?”

One by one, the men left the pool and signed the paper, dressing afterward. They whispered softly to one another and gathered close to the door. Some of the soldiers stood before it and wouldn’t let them leave.

When all had signed, Ose met them at the door. “Welcome to the Haranobu. Each of you must recruit five hundred men and train them. You will receive word when we next meet and where.”

The men all left after that. Two soldiers lifted Bito’s body and carried him out.

Tamika couldn’t move. Her mind raced with terrible thoughts. If she knew anything at all, it was that Ose should never gain power. *I must warn Jonathan.*

She felt clear-headed as she watched the soldiers return and clean Bito’s blood from the paving stones. *Yes, she must tell Jonathan. And...she must leave Ose. Without her, he didn’t have right by marriage to claim the crown. Did this also mean he wouldn’t kill her?*

Afraid to leave the bath, she let hours pass. Hunger began to grow. When the candles started to sputter and go out, she came away from her hiding place. She reached the door as the last of the light died. Opening it only a crack, she peered out. No one was about.

She stepped onto the porch. Stars filled the night sky. A partial moon bathed the path with enough light that she wouldn't stumble. Stepping down, she began to walk, and her mind listed what needed to be done. She'd return to her room, eat, and then in the morning after Ose left for the council meeting, she'd find the bracelet and travel to the Ramoni camp. From there, she'd ride to Jonathan.

"There you are," Ose said from behind. He grabbed her arm and forced her to turn around. "I have something to show you."

Missing

Chapter 18

"Ose." Jonathan watched as the man turned back around to face him.

"Excellency." Ose bowed.

"A word."

The other council members filed out past the soldiers who stood guard around the throne room. Ose continued to stand next to his chair.

The room became still. The men were all gone, except for the soldiers.

"Come a little closer." Jonathan watched Ose step a few paces and stop before the throne. "Where is Tamika?"

"Excellency?"

"I haven't seen her all week. She is diligent and prompt, which makes me concerned about her absence."

"She has traveled south to visit her relatives."

"And they live?"

"In the province of Posong."

"I see." Jonathan stood and stepped down from the dais. "Does she often leave without notifying anyone?"

"I fear it is one of her shortcomings."

Jonathan frowned. *He's lying. How should I handle this?* "I know her family has perished."

Ose nodded. "Yes."

"What family is she visiting?"

"A cousin."

"And the cousin's name is?"

"Aihara Iyo."

Jonathan studied Ose carefully. "I don't suppose you know where Bito Arei is?"

Ose remained calm. His eyes didn't even flinch. But his left thumb began to tremor.

"No, I have no idea."

Jonathan nodded. "You may go."

Ose bowed and left. Jonathan waited a few minutes and then departed as well. "Have Lieutenant Périer meet me in my office," he told one of the soldiers.

Within an hour, Jonathan rode his stallion beside Périer. They traveled with six regiments numbering six hundred soldiers.

If he has done something to her...Jonathan forced his thoughts away from his fears.

They turned at a gallop toward the entrance of Wakisaka. No gate would deter Jonathan from his mission. Several men opened the wrought iron entrance.

Ose was walking along a path to a house pressed into the hillside. He turned when he heard them. Jonathan rode up to where he stood in a bathrobe and sandals.

"I'm sure you won't mind if we search the house for Tamika. Starting with that." He pointed to the building. If Ose was going to that house on the hillside, then perhaps Tamika was there.

"Excellency, she is visiting relatives–."

"Who are dead."

The top of Ose's ears turned red, and he lowered his eyes. "Not all are dead."

"My men will search your houses, your barn, your property, and I will start with that house." Jonathan pointed.

"As you wish." A brief smile passed Ose's lips to be replaced by a stoic expression.

Jonathan dismounted along with many others. He walked with Périer and a dozen men to the house, entering it. He felt the moist heat and smelled sulfur. He could hear water running from somewhere and assumed it had entered the massive pool, but he couldn't tell where. He walked the length of the pool toward the sound. In the back, behind the evergreens, he found the source of the sound. Water flowed out of the rocks and into a large pipe that must lead under the floor and spilled into the pool. Above, sunlight streamed through the opening in the roof.

The underground pipe must flow beneath the trees. Jonathan turned that way and studied the ground beneath several evergreens. Then he spotted something in the undergrowth. Kneeling, Jonathan picked up the small gold band. Tamika's wedding ring.

Standing, he peered along the line of trees. They're undergrowth thick. This unique feature inside the bathhouse would have made an excellent hiding spot. If someone concealed themselves here, they wouldn't be detected.

He pocketed the ring and left. Once outside, he looked around the property. A great expanse of land had grasses that were coming alive with green leaves. At the north end, midway between the house and forest was a stable and fenced pasture.

Jonathan stepped down the stairs to the path and walked to where Ose waited. Lieutenant Périer joined them.

"Search the house and property." Jonathan didn't take his eyes from Ose. If the man was upset, he hid it well.

"As you wish." Périer left. Several soldiers remained as Jonathan's personal guard.

"It is as I said, Excellency. Unfortunately, Tamika isn't here."

Jonathan began to walk back up to the main house. Ose hurried to catch up with his long strides. At the house, the soldiers swarmed all over the property, trampling flowers in their search.

"Your men are ruining my garden!" Ose ran toward the flowers. "Stop that, stop that!" His arms flying out at his side.

Jonathan paid little attention to Ose's frantic efforts. The servants all stood outside the building next to the drive. Jonathan studied them.

He had visited Wakisaka several times to enjoy tea with Tamika. Ose had been elsewhere. He knew some of the servants and recognized Tamika's personal maid. Why was she here if Tamika had traveled south?

Lieutenant Périer left the house and came to join him. "She isn't inside. Nor at the stables."

"Take the servants aside, away from Ose. I would speak to them without his interference."

Périer turned to obey and had several men join him. In the meantime, Ose stood in the garden. His sandals and legs were covered in mud. Anger etched his face as he peered at Jonathan.

"Excellency, look what they have done to my garden," Ose yelled.

When Ose noticed Périer and several others lead the servants away, Ose ran back out toward Jonathan. "What are you doing now? I need my servants."

"Of course." Jonathan nodded. "I will give you money for repairs, provided you're not a traitor. As for your servants, I wish to speak to them. You will remain here." With that, the soldiers circled Ose while Jonathan walked back down the path to where the servants waited.

He stood before the group of more than twenty men and women. "Tamika is missing."

Their reaction was immediate. Some lowered their heads, others trembled visibly, a few looked at one another.

"Well?" Jonathan glanced between the men.

"We cannot speak of it," one said.

"I am your emperor; I order you to tell me what you know."

With that, a young woman fainted. The others looked at her and then back at Jonathan, clearly unsure what they should do.

"I know you fear Ose. Anyone who speaks to me will have my protection."

Still, the most he got from them was trembling limbs.

"Enya."

The woman jumped.

"I know you are Tamika's personal maid. Ose claims she went to visit her cousin in the south. Is that true?"

Enya didn't lift her head.

"Why didn't you accompany her?"

Still, no response.

Périer joined his side. "There is no sign of her in the woodland either."

"A mystery." Jonathan looked at each servant, weighing his options. "Périer, that one is named Enya. She will come away with us."

Périer immediately went to Enya and held her arm.

Along with his men and Enya, Jonathan walked back up to the house where Ose stood, his temper still hot.

"What are you doing with her?" Ose's voice held an edge that made each word pronounced as if with a knife.

"Enya is Tamika's personal maid." Jonathan stood before the man while Périer directed the men to bring the horses.

"How do you know that?"

To answer him, Jonathan simply smiled. "You have no need of Enya since Tamika isn't here. So, she will come with me." Jonathan strode to his stallion and mounted. Enya sat before one of the soldiers. With that, the men headed back to the bluff where the palace was.

An hour later, Enya stood before Jonathan's desk with her head bowed. In fact, she hadn't looked up at him once. He folded his hands on top of the desk, glanced at Périer, who stood near the door and back at the woman. He judged her age to be somewhere around fifty.

"You are safe now, Enya. No harm will come to you, and you don't need to return. Please look at me and tell me what you know." Jonathan waited.

She lifted her gaze, though she continued to tremble. "If I don't return. Lord Shigemori will kill my family."

"Your husband serves him as well?"

She shook her head. "I am not married. No, he will kill my sister and her husband. He told us. He made us swear."

"Swear what?"

Her eyes studied the floor once more.

Jonathan frowned. "Where is your sister?"

"Her husband is a fisherman. They live along the side street to the docks."

"What are their names?"

"Sayame, my brother-in-law is Takeda Sayame, and my sister is Soi."

"Périer, bring them both here."

"Excellency." He bowed and left.

Jonathan returned his gaze to Enya. "You care for Tamika, don't you?"

Once again, her head was bowed. "Yes."

"Look at me. Tell me what happened."

She lifted her gaze only to drop her eyes to the floor again. Silence.

"I am your Emperor, Enya. I command you to tell me what happened."

Her eyes lifted to his. "You don't know him, Excellency. Tamika has told me of your kindness. But Lord Shigemori isn't kind. We were all told when we first arrived that we would not be allowed to marry. Some left after the first year. No one would employ them when they learned who it was they had served. Then my friend, Minagawa, met someone and wished to marry. A nobleman in another city hired her. He wasn't familiar with Lord Shigemori. Within the week, this nobleman's house burned down. All were lost, including my friend."

Another fire. It would seem Ose's calling card is fire. How many had there been?

"Is there proof of this?" Jonathan watched her closely. Her round cheeks had gone pale.

"I do not know. I only know, one must not anger Lord Shigemori. He takes pleasure in harming others."

"And Tamika?"

"He has beaten her."

It took every ounce of his will not to stand. Jonathan frowned once more. "What happened?"

Enya took a deep breath, shut her eyes, shook, and then looked at Jonathan again. "He had another meeting with the Lords who are on your council. Tamika was in the bathhouse; I was waiting outside. So, I hid and waited."

"Could you hear what was said?"

She shook her head. "No, I wasn't close enough. There's nowhere close to hide. They were in there for a long time, and then they came out. The men looked upset. A few were his soldiers, and they escorted the men to their carriages."

"He has soldiers?"

She nodded. "Yes, many. They don't live on the property. Then, finally, Lord Shigemori came out. He stood before the bathhouse, and…" she glanced around as if she expected to see Ose hovering nearby. "Several men carried out a dead man."

Jonathan stood and leaned against his knuckles on the desk. "Who?"

Tears filled Enya's eyes. "Lord Arei."

"Bito Arei?"

She nodded. Her tears began to slide down her cheeks. "They carried him off toward the forest. That is where Lord Shigemori buries those he has killed. No honorable burial for any of them."

"He has killed before?"

"Yes, I know of at least five servants who displeased him. I always feared for Tamika. She was careful how she spoke to him but still, he angered easily." She shuddered.

Jonathan walked around his desk and handed her a kerchief. Then he set his hands on her arms and helped her sit in one of the chairs before his desk. Next, he sat on the edge of the other chair and leaned forward. "Go on."

"Lord Shigemori walked toward the back of the bathhouse. I couldn't see him. Tamika didn't come out. And then, the candles inside began to flicker. I could see the light wane through the walls. The door slid open, and Tamika left. I almost ran to hug her, but…but… Lord Shigemori came around the building and took her arm. He said he had something to show her, and they walked toward the forest. She never came home."

Jonathan stood. He wanted to throw something. His fingers trembled. He stopped and turned toward Enya. "Thank you for telling me. A guard will come and show you to your room."

That was the last of what he could say without yelling at her, and Enya didn't deserve that. He left his office and took the stairs two at a time until he reached the flat roof. He walked to the telescope. He unlocked the cylinder, so he could swivel it toward Wakisaka. Then, he noticed smoke toward the southwest and swiveled it before looking through. Fire. An entire block of homes near the docks was on fire.

Found

Chapter 19

Tamika sat crossed-legged on the pad Ose had allowed her, looking up. She heard noises but couldn't tell what they were. She stood. The pit where Ose had thrown her was like a large box. The walls, floor, and ceiling, were lined in wood. The roof was, in fact, a trap door. The only light came through the slits between the trap door's wooden planks.

Still dressed only in her bathrobe, she was cold. Once a day, someone brought her soup, bread, and tea. Hunger made her stomach muscles tight. In one corner, there was a bucket for her to use when she needed to relieve herself. The same soldier who brought the food emptied the bucket, but he didn't wash it out. She would never get used to the smell. Even her robe held the stench.

She paced. Twenty-five steps in one direction and then back. The boredom was enough to drive her crazy. And the fear. Fear for Jonathan more than for herself. If Ose wanted her dead, he would have already killed her. But, no, he wanted her silent.

There was no way to measure time other than night and day. Now she was confined. She had too much time to think. Regret became her partner as if it were alive beside her, whispering. Always whispering. She should have taken Jonathan up on his offer and moved in with him.

Someone was at the trap door fiddling with the lock. Tamika backed up against the far wall and watched. When it opened, she had to shield her eyes from the bright light. Several of Ose's men stood around the opening. She expected one of them to put down the ladder and bring her food.

Then, Ose came and sat crossed-legged on the edge of her pit. "Have you learned your lesson?"

Tamika knew what he spoke of. In his mind, she deliberately spied on him. "I will not apologize for taking a bath."

"Anything else?"

She folded her arms and glared at him.

"Someone should have warned me about your stubborn will."

She continued to glare.

After a long moment, Ose tossed down a gray kimono such as men wear. "Dress." He stood and shut the trap door.

Tamika considered the clothes. It wasn't like Ose to put her in anything other than the tight and colorful kimonos in her closet. She dressed.

After a short time, the trap door opened again. Ose gazed at her once more. "I'm putting down the ladder. Climb up. We have somewhere to go."

Tamika backed up against the wall again. *What would he do? If he had plans to kill her, he didn't need to bring her a change of clothes. That couldn't be it.*

Ose stepped out of sight, and two of his men came to the edge with the ladder. It was cumbersome, and they struggled to maneuver it. Once they had it to the right angle, they began lowering it.

Yelling. The men with the ladder looked up, and one turned. He gave a cry, stumbled backward, and fell into the pit with the ladder following him. Tamika jumped away.

She looked at the injured man and saw his eyes open. At first, she thought he stared at her, and then, she realized…*he's dead.* An arrow was through his heart. The ladder landed partly on him. She clutched her own heart, which was beating so hard it was painful.

Horses. Looking up again, she saw the animals running past. The men were yelling. Words were flung about and overlapped, leaving her confused. She only understood one or two words. "Run!" "No!" and then "run" again.

What was going on? Had Ose started the war he promised in the bathhouse?

Her breath came quickly, and in that space, the noise was farther away. Silence settled around her. *What should she do? Stay with the dead body staring sightlessly at her? No!* The trap door was open, and the ladder was in her box.

To get the ladder, she had to touch the body. One of his arms was through the ladder rung. She stepped around him and pulled his arm through, and then lifted the heavy ladder. She pushed the ladder close enough to the wall that it stood, a little lopsided.

Catching her breath, she sidestepped the dead man and lifted the ladder at the center to push it up to the top, backing up as she went. No sooner had she done that than she heard more horses.

Ose came back. She'd missed her chance. Tears pooled in her eyes.

"Whoa." More than one person spoke. The sound of men dismounting and stepping on the old fallen leaves from last autumn did nothing to reassure her.

She backed up again. Then, an idea. She'd knock the ladder down. Out of reach, Ose wouldn't be able to get her. Two steps brought her closer, and then…

"Tamika."

A voice she knew. The man she loved. Looking up, she saw Jonathan and several others at the edge of the trap door. Her body shuddered as she gazed up at him. "Jonathan." Her whispered prayer had come true.

"Do you need help?" he asked.

"No." Tamika struggled to put the ladder back up. Her muscles trembled from weakness. She climbed up. At the top, Jonathan pulled her the rest of the way, and she immediately hugged him. His arms enveloped her, and then, to her utter horror, she started to cry.

War is Imminent

Chapter 20

Tamika stood alone in the dining room. This had been the first room to be restored. A fireplace was prominent on one wall, and opposite were the sliding walls that opened onto the garden. Now they were closed. A portrait of Jonathan decorated the far west wall. To either side of this were hanging baskets filled with red *tsubaki*. Their meaning, a noble death or love. With war imminent, Tamika prayed it didn't mean Jonathan's death.

"Do you like camellias?"

Tamika jumped. She hadn't heard Jonathan enter.

"You call them camellia? They are beautiful."

He smiled and walked to the sliding walls. As he opened them, he said. "The garden is coming along nicely."

Tamika joined his side to gaze at the lush display of budding trees and colorful flowers. There were benches along the path.

He led her to the table and pulled out a chair on the end. She sat. He also sat at the head of the table, next to her. Male servants entered, placing the emperor's fine china before them along with silverware. Both tableware and flatware had dragon motifs. The plates and silver hadn't been used on the first dinner when she met Jonathan along with her husband and other nobles.

Another servant brought in a soup tureen, and lifting the lid, took their bowls one at a time and ladled the steaming liquid into them. The smell of it brought back wonderful memories of her family. She gazed down at her favorite soup, *tori nanba udon* with chicken, noodles, and mushrooms.

She glanced at Jonathan. He dipped his spoon in the soup and moved it away from him, filling the spoon before sipping it. Tamika clutched the spoon. Her hands shook from hunger, and she couldn't control them. Jonathan put his hand over hers. Their eyes met. "Allow me."

She relinquished the spoon, and he began to feed her. The flavor filled her mouth with perfection. Between bites, she could feed herself the salted flatbread that was in a silver basket.

When they were both done, the servants returned, taking their bowls. Dinner was grilled salmon with a white wine sauce, vegetable sushi, and fluffy rolls with honey butter. Jonathan poured her a glass of wine before he poured his own. When she thought she could eat no more, a bowl of fresh strawberries was bought in.

At last, her hunger was abated, and her hand no longer shook. "How did you know?"

"What?" Jonathan lifted his second glass of wine and sipped it.

"All of this." Tamika indicated the meal with her hand. "Every dish is my favorite."

He smiled and sat back. "Enya told my chef. Did you enjoy it?"

Did she enjoy it? "Yes."

"I'm glad. You're feeling better?"

"Yes."

The differences between Jonathan and Ose struck her in the depths of her heart. When Ose learned she preferred something, he withheld it, while Jonathan made sure he provided what she wanted most. *What was she to do? She loved Jonathan so much and despised...yes, despised Ose.*

Jonathan stood and pulled back her chair. She joined him. Her blue silk dress fell in fabric pleats, hugging her upper body and flowing out at her waist.

"Shall we?" Jonathan motioned toward the garden with one hand.

Tamika nodded. She couldn't trust her voice. She wanted to cry again. This time from Jonathan's kindness.

He took her arm, and they strolled into the garden. A bouquet of scents greeted them as they wandered between blooms.

"You did all of this," he said. They reached a bench and sat. Someone had shut the dining room screen, and they were alone.

Yes, she had recommended each flower and bush. The dead trees had been replaced by partially grown specimens.

She took a breath and shut her eyes. *I must tell him.* There was no gentle way to say it. "Ose has the Bracelet of the Moon and Stars."

Jonathan frowned and turned sideways toward Tamika. "What bracelet?"

She lifted her gaze. "The Bracelet of the Moon and Stars."

Jonathan shook his head. "Ose has this bracelet, and it matters because?"

Tamika lowered her eyes. "You don't know of the bracelet?"

"No."

She took a deep breath. "When my people first came from across the great ocean to Shea-Talon, a man by the name of Matsui announced he was emperor. Others wanted to be emperor, and so there was a war. Then, amidst a great battle, wonder in the sky stopped the soldiers. It was the god Ye Tai, riding on a dragon. The men cowered, falling to their knees. The god Ye Tai landed in the middle of the battlefield. In appearance, he was terrible. Glowing eyes and skin a dark blue.

He looked from one man to another until he saw Matsui. Then

he raised his voice like a thundering boom and called Matsui to him. It is told thus."

"And?"

Tamika nodded and glanced at him before continuing. "Matsui approached and fell to his knees before Ye Tai, who took the Bracelet of the Moon and Stars off his own arm. It was huge. But when he put it on Matsui's upper arm, it conformed to his size. Then Ye Tai shouted that Matsui was the one true emperor."

"And Ose has this bracelet."

"Yes. The bracelet was lost from the time of Warwyk. I saw Ose put it on."

"Why was it lost? And how did Ose find it."

"It is my fault. I have brought this terrible thing down upon you."

Jonathan reached for her hand and folded her cold fingers into his palm. "Tamika, you can't possibly blame yourself."

"I forgot, Excellency."

"Jonathan." He corrected.

"By order of Ye Tai, the bracelet was to never leave Shea-Talon. Warwyk gave the bracelet to his favorite wife for safekeeping when he went to war in Gil-Lael. I speak of my grandmother. When I was little, my grandmother showed both my brother and me the bracelet. She said my brother would be emperor one day."

Jonathan nodded. "And then your brother died in a hunting accident, your family perished in a fire, and you were married to Ose."

"Yes. I'm afraid. I have long believed that my brother didn't die the way Ose claimed. I have long wondered how my family could perish simultaneously, leaving me the sole heir. I have wondered why, shortly after my marriage to Ose, my uncle died as well. It was all so Ose could become the head of my family as well as his own. By this, he became eligible to inherit the crown. With the bracelet, he will be able to convince many more to follow him. Your entire council has pledged an alliance to Ose. All but Bito Arei and Ose killed him."

"Is this bracelet magical?" Jonathan asked.

"Many legends surround it. Some say the emperor can walk on the clouds when wearing the bracelet and commune with the gods. Others say the bracelet causes your enemies to fall at your feet, trembling with fear. It is said the sea will rise to swallow any challenger. Yet, another story tells of the mountains opening to bury enemies alive. And then there is the story of the trees coming to life and fighting alongside the true emperor." Tamika watched as Jonathan turned toward a fountain.

"Regardless of the truth, there is power in belief. Ose must be stopped," he said and turned back toward her.

Later, after dropping Tamika off at her room, Jonathan hurried to his office and called for Lieutenant Périer. He paced his chamber, thinking. He couldn't blame his council. Tamika had gone into detail about what she saw. They had all been unarmed and faced with Ose's men. *No! I will never call him Ose again. Shigemori.*

I'll write to father and Eamon. Send for men and arms. I have close to ten thousand men, but a war will require more. Has Shigemori had time to build up his army. I hope not.

When at last Périer arrived, Jonathan said, "You must gather men and go to the estates of my councilmen. Arrest them and take them to Furuya Jun Prison. There isn't much time. Send at least two hundred to each estate under your best command."

"Excellency." Périer nodded.

"We are at war. Before you go, who is your best longbowman?"

"Claude Coulomb."

"I require his services."

"Tonight?"

"Oui, tonight."

Assignment

Chapter 21

Claude Coulomb stood before Jonathan's desk in the emperor's new palace office. Claude's military uniform was fresh from the laundry. Black pants over polished boots. Red jacket with a single row of brass buttons and his steel sword with a simple, unadorned handle. There were no golden tassels off his shoulders. No double-breasted brass buttons. No ribbons of valor or a single medal, not even one for long service. *And his service had been long. Fifteen years long.*

He'd seen others promoted who had unremarkable histories. Some friends, still in Gil-Lael. He'd come to Shea-Talon five years ago in hopes of changing that. But instead, he found a corrupted governor who had no mercy for the people. That had changed Claude.

Bookshelves lined two walls in the emperor's office. An intricately carved mantel of wisteria trees and cherry blossoms depicting the god Ye Tai in the center was behind Jonathan, where he sat his desk.

I wonder how the high priest feels about that?

"Longbowman Coulomb."

He dropped his eyes to see Jonathan sitting back in his chair studying him. Claude threw his shoulders back, clicked his heels, and bowed. "Excellency."

"I have been told you are the best bowman in service to me."

"I like to think so."

"Good. I have a job for you." Jonathan tapped a single finger on the report before him. "You are aware Ishikawa Natsu is a prisoner at Furuya Jun Prison. And he has ties to the Haranobu."

"Oui," he answered in Gil-Laelian.

"It has become apparent that Shigemori is their leader. War is upon us. I've sent Périer to arrest my council. I believe Shigemori will attempt to free his friend and the other councilmen in prison this night. They all support his claim to be emperor."

"Furuya Jun Prison is secure."

"Perhaps, but I don't want to take any chances. Therefore, I am sending you and fifteen additional bowmen to guard the prison. You are to command them. I want you to take the night shift. An attack will most likely come at night."

Jonathan pulled out a drawer in his desk and stood with a brass medal in his hand. He walked around the desk and pinned the medal on Claude's jacket. "You are now First Bowman."

At last. First Bowman means more money. I'll put it all in a bank, earn interest. But not enough. "I am honored."

"Hand select your *comrades* and report there before the night is through." Jonathan handed him his orders.

"As you wish." Claude bowed and turned to leave. Glancing back before he shut the door, he saw Jonathan standing at a window gazing out at the stars.

Fatigue gnawed at Claude. He needed to sleep if he was to be effective this evening. The guardrooms in prison were sparse and small. As First Bowman, he had his own room. He smiled. No more listening to the snores of the other men. Still, sleep must come later. It was time to head into Aya and purchase his usual bottle of wine. Maybe more than one this time.

He went alone. Some of his friends argued the current conditions made going solo dangerous. Claude laughed at their concern. “I always go alone.”

Aya was growing. An entire city block had been added since Jonathan’s arrival. The streets were clean. There used to be hundreds of beggars, but Jonathan’s edict to care for older workers provided those poor with food and housing. Claude couldn’t imagine these people rebelling against Jonathan. However, the nobles were a different story. The same policies which gave the common men and women hope, angered the aristocracy.

His destination was a wine and spirits merchant two blocks off the main thoroughfare. He brought his horse to a stand before the store, dismounted, and looped the reins around the pole. Then, adjusting his jacket, he stepped up onto the boardwalk. A whistle made him stop. He glanced around until he saw a man leaning against a building opposite from where he stood.

Changing course, Claude walked across the street and headed south. He turned into an alley three blocks down and stepped into a doorway, becoming invisible to those who walked by. The interior was dark.

“Are you alone?”

“Yes.” Claude wasn’t surprised by the stealth of the speaker. This wasn’t the first time they met.

The man left the inner room and stood before Claude.

“What do you want?” Claude gazed down at the angular eyes of the man.

“You have been assigned to Furuya Jun Prison.”

That was fast. “Yes. Who is your spy?”

"Our leader requires you to free Ishikawa Natsu."

"That will take some doing." Claude studied the man. His gray kimono needed cleaning. He'd always been impeccable in the past, but they were in hiding now.

"I have funds."

"Let me see."

The man passed a pouch, and Claude opened it, dropping coins into the palm of his hand. "More."

"This is a fortune."

"You're asking for more than information this time. You want me to free the man I've been assigned to keep in prison. There's a considerable risk. I will need to search out how to do it, and I'll need to distract several hundred people as well."

"Our leader requires it to be done tonight."

"Impossible. I've only just arrived at the prison. I need to investigate and find a weakness. We will meet in a week."

"Our leader won't be happy."

"Tell Shigemori it can't be helped."

The man took a step back.

"Don't be so surprised." Claude waited. "And a thousand royal tlokel for the job."

"Royal tlokel?! A thousand gold coins."

"Exactly."

"A million. You want a million?" The man began to tremble.

"We meet back here in a week. Same time." Claude whistled a tune and left.

Jonathan gazed at Périer. He was unshaven and mud-spattered his pant legs while blood stained his jacket and brass buttons a dirty brown.

"We've been met with small skirmishes at most of the estates south of Aya. They knew we were coming. Thus far, we've only captured five of the nobles who sat on your council. Two of them didn't fight or resist. Both would like an audience with you."

"Sit, Périer, you look exhausted." Jonathon waved Périer to a seat.

"Thank you, Excellency," he sighed.

"Are there any casualties?"

"A few serious injuries on our side, the enemy lost close to seventy."

"Who are the two nobles who wish to speak with me?"

"Terazawa Akii and Sugi Sawako. Neither had an army."

"Where are they now?" Jonathan held a quill pen and took notes.

"Furuya Jun Prison."

"Get some rest, Périer."

He stood, clicked his heels, and bowed. "Excellency."

Jonathan watched him leave. A servant entered with his breakfast, eggs, bacon, and toast with blueberry jam. Jonathan scooped two forks full before drinking some tea. A knock.

"Come." He sipped the hot tea.

Grégory entered.

"Have you eaten?" Jonathan lifted a piece of bacon.

"Oui." Grégory waddled toward the desk and set papers on it before he climbed into a chair. "I have sent the falcons. The royal blacksmith requested help since he must make a thousand swords and twice as many arrows."

"Bring as many blacksmiths as you can to the plateau. We don't need them kidnapped or killed." Jonathan pushed away his empty plate.

"I've also sent falcons to all our outposts throughout Shea-Talon."

"Good." Jonathan sat back.

"You look tired," Grégory observed.

"I haven't slept."

"You should get some rest."

"I will tonight. Now, I must gather the men we have here and encourage them. Who besides Périer can lead the men?" He knew this, but his thoughts were jumbled, and he needed the reminder.

Grégory cleared his throat. "Besides Périer, we have Desmarais, Émilien, Lionel and Cazal."

"We will need more."

"If I may, Excellency." Grégory's brow was furrowed.

Jonathan lifted his hand.

"Ose Shigemori is a dangerous man who will stop at nothing."

"This I know."

"You shouldn't leave the plateau."

"I won't for some time, but when a true battle commences, I must."

Claude counted his steps as he walked the length of Furuya Jun Prison. Four days passed since he'd been contacted. Enough time for him to get excited. His mind spun with imaginings of his future life. He'd be rich. Perhaps his wealth would exceed the emperor's treasure. Then, he'd have to move. But he didn't know where yet. Not Gil-Lael. Someplace where the House of Calimar couldn't find him. Shea-Eoforwic was out. Jonathan's brother Eamon was emperor there.

Perhaps Telaneasse. No, Marlon had gone there, and Jonathan's friendship with their king made it a dangerous choice. But Caerleon was a viable option. He could blend in because, in appearance, the Caerleonians were like his own countrymen of Gil-Lael. Oui, and once there, he could live like a king.

He rubbed his hands together from the chilly spring air and stopped at the corner. A moat of fetid, stinking water circled the prison. The only entrance was the front, and a drawbridge must be lowered to allow entry. But, at certain times of the day, it was kept open.

The water in the moat was low. Winter still held firm in the mountains. Spring wouldn't awaken for another month, and then the runoff would fill the canal to the brim.

As Claude stared, he thought he saw an opening. He walked closer and then slid down the incline to inspect a gap in the earth. A stench far worse than the moat greeted him, and he knew this was the sewage system for the prison.

He grinned. To show the proud Ishikawa Natsu, this exit would be entertaining. By the time he joined his fellow conspirators, he'd smell so bad he'd never live it down.

Claude climbed back up and continued his walk. Perhaps there was another way. He reached the northeast tower and stared up at the structure. Tonight, he'd guard that same turret. He made his way back inside and retired to his room. A little sleep was in order.

Refreshed the following day, Jonathan found Tamika in one of his gardens. She'd been cutting flowers, and her arms were laden with blooms.

He stuck both hands in his pockets. Work had kept them apart. "How are you?"

Tamika looked up and smiled. "I should ask that of you."

"Much has happened. I'm sorry I missed having dinner with you. I trust you found Grégory and Umezawa good company." He had both men move into the palace. He needed the manor homes to house an increasing number of Shea-Talonians he'd given sanctuary to.

"Yes. Grégory is entertaining with many stories about Gil-Lael. Umezawa is serious."

"That is true."

A soldier ran up to them, bowed, and said, "Excellency, we have received falcons." He passed two small, folded papers to Jonathan.

Opening the notes, he scanned them. "I fear duty calls." He noticed Tamika's worried gaze.

"You deserve more of an explanation. Perhaps I will be free later to talk with you. As it is, I beg your indulgence."

She set a hand on his arm. "I will light a candle for you."

"You're not going into town to the temple, are you?"

"No, I have brought several gods to my room and made a shrine to them on my table so I can worship and pray."

He nodded. "I see." He kissed the back of her hand and hurried away with the soldier beside him.

Once in his office, he called for Lieutenant Périer, Grégory, and Umezawa. He had all his books brought over, and on an enormous table was displayed an equally huge map of Shea-Talon. On the map were figurines and buildings he could move to give reference to the multiple locations. He pushed the figures now in response to his messages.

"Excellency," Grégory said.

Umezawa entered.

"This map should help." Jonathan motioned for the two to come forward. "Shigemori has been planning this for some time, I think. There have been skirmishes around Xuqihar, Guihar, and Soutsukawa." He used a pointer to indicate each city. "We've had a few casualties."

Jonathan lifted his gaze to Umezawa. "Why didn't you tell me about the Bracelet of the Moon and Stars?"

"The bracelet…" Umezawa folded his fingers together. "It's a legend. I didn't think it mattered."

"It's more than legend, Umezawa. Shigemori has it and has laid claim to the throne. The question is, how many will follow him because of it?"

Umezawa unfolded his fingers. "Many. Many will see it as a legitimate claim. The bracelet and his marriage."

"Why his marriage?"

"Lady Shigemori is granddaughter to Warwyk."

"How does he communicate with his men?"

"The same as you, Excellency. He may have falcons or pigeons."

"Grégory, send word; each of our falcons must wear a red

choker. Once this command is carried out, all birds without this choker will be shot out of the sky."

"As you wish." Grégory scribbled a note.

"Umezawa, tell me about this bracelet. Lady Shigemori seems to believe it has powers."

"If the reports are true, it does. Magic emanates from the stones laid within."

"How does it work?"

"When the true emperor wears the Bracelet of the Moon and Stars, whatever he commands will come to pass."

"Whatever he commands? Does this mean Shigemori can order the ground beneath my feet to part and swallow me?"

"Yes."

Jonathan transferred the pointer to his other hand and frowned. *If that were true, why hasn't Shigemori already done it?*

Three days passed since Claude first walked the prison grounds. He only had one day left. It was beginning to look as if Ishikawa Natsu was going to have to tread through sewage. Or climb over the turret and swim across the moat that also had waste floating in it. He'd rather not do the turret since it would be hard to explain if asked why he had a rope.

He walked into the basement of the building. No prisoner was kept here. Instead, there were rooms filled with storage containing jars of food and dried food as well as uniforms, weapons, and many other items. On the east end was the laundry room. Claude was alone on the west side. His excuse for these walks was to be sure the prison was secure. No one questioned him.

As he went, he pondered the difficulty of his mission. But, he wasn't one to give up, especially when there was money to be had.

The hall joined an empty one that ran east and west. He held his torch first one way and then the other as he walked the windowless corridor. The air was stale. He continued until he met a door. Turning the handle, he entered the empty room. Like the rest of the basement, the walls and floor were brick. His search found torches in iron holders on the walls, and he lit them. In the center of the floor was a trap door. There wasn't a latch locking it. He'd seen a map of the prison and this room and trap door wasn't on it.

Claude opened the door and peered down a deep shaft into darkness. A stench rose from the depths. Not the smell of human waste, but something else. Lowering the torch, he could see a ladder attached to the opening. He set the torch down, pulled out his kerchief, and tied it around his nose. Then, holding the torch again, he climbed down the ladder.

The room below was once again like the rest of the rooms. He wasn't sure what made the smell. He couldn't see anything that might contribute to it.

A hallway led further in, and Claude walked it. Soon, he saw cells to either side with a solid iron door for each and a small, barred window in the door. Three, four, he stopped at number five. Curiosity made him try one of the doors. It was locked. When he peeked through the window, he couldn't make anything out because of the darkness.

Returning to the main room, he found keys on a hook in the wall. Once more, he stood before a cell door. The lock took a little effort, but soon, he had the door open and entered the room. A cot was pushed into a corner, and a skeleton lay on it.

Claude backed up. The clothes the man had been wearing were rotted away. *How long has this man been here?* He left and checked the remainder of the rooms. Twelve in all and all but one had the remains of some poor soul. Two lay on cots, three were chained to the wall, and the rest were sprawled on the floor. *Who did this? Barbaric.*

At the end of the hall was a round hole close to the floor. Iron bars were over the opening. Claude knelt. The air in the shaft was fresh, and he knew immediately it served the purpose to provide oxygen.

Claude tried the bars and found one side loose from age. Rust came off on his hands, and he wiped them on his pants. He managed to pull the bars away from the opening and proceeded to crawl through, keeping his torch ahead of him. As he went, he counted the length. After a while, he pushed aside debris. A leaf caught fire, and he put it out quickly with his hand.

This tunnel must run beneath the moat.

Now that he was some distance from the lower cells, he pulled his kerchief down and breathed in the cool fresh air. Not long after, he came to an end and found more bars over the opening. Past the bars, he could make out the forest. He didn't trouble with the bars this time. Shigemori could do that. He'd found the escape route.

Troubles, Details, and Plans

Chapter 22

Jonathan gazed at the volcano peak. Snow-covered the top. Then…it exploded. A gray cloud shot up filled with ash. Billowing out, it raced toward him. He woke, sat, and clutched his heart. A dream. He rolled on his side, and stared at the dark interior, and then slept.

The volcano spit lava from the top, back down, and up again. It curled down the side of the mountain. When he looked, the river of hot molten fire cut through the rock around where he was standing. Surrounded, there was no escape.

Jonathan sat up. He was hot. The dreams robbed him of enough sleep every night. Never quite the same but the feelings they left were hard to deal with. He longed for his family. Here, isolation cut deep.

He stood and walked to the window. Opening it, he welcomed the cool breeze. He dressed. A few hours of broken sleep weren't enough. He took breakfast alone in his office. Only a few servants were up. He re-read the message from his brother. The island nation of Shea-

Eoforwic was two weeks by ship. Eamon would send a thousand men at a time. In total, he had pledged seven thousand men.

His father's missive informed him that twenty thousand men would come over the mountain pass as soon as the weather allowed. According to Umezawa, that wouldn't happen for two months. But it would take longer by ship, and the open sea held many hazards.

Jonathan set the paper down and rubbed his eyes. He stood, threw on his jacket, and left the palace to walk in the garden. A dove called out and was answered by several others. He made his way to the overlook and peered west. The ocean crashed against the shore, and the biting taste of ocean salt filled his mouth. He turned back and saw a line of orange brilliance touch the top of the mountains in the distance.

Jonathan turned back toward the ocean. Soon, the eastern sunrise would meet the sea, and he could soak up the brilliance.

Tamika smiled, hugged herself, and twirled. She danced to the window and opened it. Jonathan stood alone in the early morning light on the rock slab near the bluff edge. She dressed and hurried out her door.

She stopped just before the rock hewn stairs. "Excellency."

He turned. His face was etched in concern. "Tamika, it is good to see you. Come."

She climbed the three steps and joined him. He put his arm around her shoulders when she did, and his hand squeezed her upper arm. Warmth filled her heart.

"It's beautiful." She smiled.

"Yes, it is. The ocean clears my head, and I can think things through."

"I wish I could do more to help you."

"Your presence here is enough. One less concern."

"I'm sorry I made you worry."

He was still for a long time. Tamika began to think he would leave. But his thumb continued to rub her upper arm.

Jonathan turned. He made her face him and put both hands on her arms. She gazed into his eyes and perceived his doubt. *Was it fear? Or worry? Or both?*

He lifted his hand to her face and rubbed her cheek past her ear with his thumb. Then, so quickly it caught her breath, Jonathan pulled her against him and kissed her. The sensation ran through her like hot honeyed tea. She put her arms around his neck, and her fingers caressed his hair.

"I love you," he said.

"I love you as well."

"What are we to do?"

A question that plagued her. She welcomed his second kiss and marveled at her joy. Ose had only left her in sorrow. Sorrow, she'd never love him or be loved by him. Now there was Jonathan. A wonderful man. A man who would protect her from her husband. And that was the problem. She was married.

Claude leaned against the wine merchant's building, waiting. Shadows played on the wooden structure. The bilious clouds above promised rain. Men and women walked by, but only a few peered into the alley. No doubt they wondered what a royal guard was doing alone. He kept his head angled away from the opening of the alley. It wouldn't do for Jonathan to get a good description of him.

He'd been here a long time. If the Shea-Talonian didn't show soon, he'd go. He folded his arms and pushed his head back, looking at the sky between the two buildings. The door next to him opened.

Claude turned. "It's about time."

"Forgive, there are many soldiers between here and there."

Claude couldn't dispute that. He entered the building and shut the door. Only a little light came through from a window above the door.

"Do you have a plan?"

"I do. Do you have the money?"

"Emperor Shigemori says, for 100 royal tlokel, you must do more than bring him Natsu."

Claude nodded. "What else does he want?"

"He wants all the lords."

That's extreme. Claude shifted his weight. "I told you I can't do that…but perhaps once Natsu is free, you can enter the prison and free the others yourself."

"And how would we do such a thing? Furuya Jun Prison is fortified. Why else would we come to you for help?" Sweat beaded his forehead.

"Turns out it isn't as secure as one would expect." Claude then outlined his plan in detail. "I will include a map of the prison with Natsu. All I ask is that you wait a few days."

"When will you do this?"

"I will buy wine, enough for every guard and bowman. I need you to bring me crushed S*ilverleaf Haldi*. I'm adding it to the wine to put the men into a deep slumber. I need you to bring it to me, so it can't be traced back to me. And I need enough for twenty bottles of wine."

"That doesn't seem enough for all the guards."

"It's enough for the night shift. We will meet again in two days. Don't forget the *Silverleaf Haldi* and my money."

Several days later, Jonathan stood on one side of the map while Grégory, Périer, and Umezawa stood opposite.

"There has been a major battle between the Province of Posog and that of Hashiba. The cities of Guihar in Posog and Kangjin in Hashiba are burning. It was well planned out, and many have died.

"Your thoughts, Périer." Jonathan watched him.

Périer stepped closer. Lifting one of the clay soldiers, he moved it along with several others. “We need to march on Hashiba before they reach Yuuki. Let us outnumber them by the thousand.”

“What of the palace?” Umezawa asked.

“We can send that many and still leave men here.” Périer turned toward the Shea-Talonian scholar.

“I should lead them.” Jonathan moved several clay towers to the Province of Yuuki, representing thousands of soldiers.

“No!” Grégory stepped up onto a small footboard. “You can’t risk it. They fight under the cover of trees and from the rooftops of buildings. Your height would make you an easy target.”

“I can’t remain here forever.” Jonathan frowned.

“Not forever,” Umezawa said. “Just long enough for more troops to arrive.”

Jonathan tapped one of the figures. He wanted to crush Shigemori. He envisioned a confrontation between them. Then, once Shigemori was dead, and the country was secure, he would marry Tamika.

Claude took the finely ground powder from the man with no name who bargained for his help. “And the money?”

The man handed him the pouch. Opening it, Claude poured four royal tlokel into his hand. He dropped the purse and lifted the man by the collar, turned and pressed him into the wall.

“This is but a fraction of what I asked for.”

The Shea-Talonian coughed. “It is the first installment.”

Claude put him down again while keeping his fingers locked in his kimono.

“Bring us Ishikawa Natsu, and we will give you more. Then we will pay still more once we free our friends. After that, we will meet again to discuss the next task.”

“Bring half of what I asked for, or I will alert the prison officials, and you will find a battle you can't win greet you."

The man paled. "Half. When should we meet again?"

"Three weeks."

"One."

"Two. No sooner. And not here,"Claude said.

"Where then?"

"I'll think on it and give my answer tonight." Claude hadn't intended to crawl through the air shaft. He'd envisioned Natsu crawling forward alone while he joined the men he'd be gambling with that night, drink his wine and fall asleep. Now he had to change his plans. He couldn't blame Shigemori. He'd asked for a lot of money, and the man probably didn't have it all. He'd better get it.

"Come take a walk with me, Grégory." Jonathan stood from his chair and walked around his desk. He needed to find a solution to the question of Tamika's marriage and his rampant desire.

Grégory joined him, and they left the palace together. The evening was cloudless, and the sky glistened with the last rays of sunlight. A guard walked between lamp posts lighting them. Pools of light spread between shadowed images of flowers, bushes, and trees.

Jonathan matched Grégory's smaller stride. They reached the stone patio overlooking the sea, and Jonathan went to his favorite spot by the stone wall. A half-moon glowed.

"Since the time of King Julian, the law of the land has been clear. The king must marry by twenty-nine. I am thirty-two. No man may rob a virgin of her prize, her virginity. If they do, they will lose their title, or their money, or both." He glanced down at Grégory to see his troubled eyes looking back.

Jonathan nodded. "My father raised me to respect this law, and he added to it, saying I must not have an affair. Never. When I marry, I must be faithful to my wife even if I fall out of love with her." He turned his gaze back to the ocean in time to see a whale break the waters.

"I suppose that is why it has taken me so long to marry. But, the truth is, I haven't fallen in love…until now."

Grégory said nothing. Jonathan turned away and found a bench. Grégory sat near him. Time was punctuated by the sound of the ocean waves breaking on the rocks far below.

"What am I to do, Grégory? I love Tamika. She is married. And married to my enemy."

"Would it be easier if Ose was a friend?"

"Shigemori."

"Shigemori." Grégory corrected.

Jonathan shut his eyes. "No."

"Excellency…" Grégory's words thinned until he spoke just above a whisper. "We are not in Gil-Lael. You aren't governed by the laws of Gil-Lael. You are the emperor, which means you can make new laws."

"I had intended to make the law of Julian effective here too." A gentle breeze touched his cheek.

"Tamika isn't a virgin."

"True."

"If you want her, issue a divorce and marry her."

"But she is the wife of Shigemori. Wouldn't that give him more justification?"

"It would."

Jonathan squeezed his eyes closed and lowered his head in his hands.

"I take it she feels the same."

"She does." Jonathan didn't lift his head.

"Whatever you decide, Excellency, I will stand beside you."

Jonathan lifted his head then and gazed at the little man. "What of you? Do you fancy any woman?"

Grégory shifted his weight and studied the stones of the patio. "Oui."

"And who is she? May I assist you somehow?"

Grégory took a deep breath and turned his gaze to Jonathan. "Isabella of the Romani."

Jonathan kept his lips tight and refused to grin. "She is beautiful."

"Oui, that she is. I know she'd never entertain the idea of being with me."

"We will see." Jonathan stood again and went to the wall that kept him safe from falling off the edge.

Claude's laughter echoed.

"Come, Coulomb, take a seat and throw in some coins," a thin, dark-haired man said.

"No, no. There isn't time. I'm due at the northwest tower. But I brought you all a bottle of wine as a gift." He uncorked the tampered wine and poured all five men a glass.

"Excellent wine, Claude." Another man lifted his glass in a toast.

"Damn strong."

Claude smiled. "That it is."

Two of the men slumped over. Another fell on the floor.

The fourth said, "What did you put in it?"

"Nothing, I bought it from that vendor…" no need to finish. All five men were snoring.

Claude walked out and climbed the stairs to the third floor. Every guardroom he passed had men sleeping in it with bottles of wine on the tables.

He came to the room where they kept the keys and snatched them. Once he reached Natsu's cell, he unlocked it. The man sat up in bed.

"Come with me," Claude said.

"Why?" Natsu stood but made no attempt to join Claude at the cell door.

"Come on, man. Someone to see you."

He didn't move.

"Must I prod you with my sword?"

Natsu followed him then. Claude glanced around as he led the way toward the stairs. Several prisoners watched. *Witnesses*. He noted which cells they were in. *I'll take care of them later.*

"Say nothing," he whispered to Natsu.

They reached the stairs and descended the steps to the basement. Walking past the room where his friends snored, he glanced in to be sure they all slept. They did.

"Where are you taking me?" Natsu kept glancing around at the windowless brick walls.

Claude grinned. "You'll see."

Natsu turned and began running back the way they'd come.

Claude was taller, leaner, and fast. He grabbed Natsu by his prison garb and shoved him against a wall. "Damn. Can't you see I'm trying to free you?"

"You're not going to kill me?"

Claude pulled his sword. "See this? If I wanted you dead, I would have killed you while you cowered in your cell."

On the move again, they reached the room with the trap door. Earlier, Claude lit the wall sconces in the room and below as well. The trap door was already open.

"Climb down."

"What is that awful smell?" Natsu raised his eyes.

Claude shrugged. "Who knows." He nodded and pointed to the ladder.

Natsu knelt and put one leg over and then the next. Claude followed. Just before reaching the bottom, he felt a burning against his backside. *"Putain de bordel de merde." Fucking hell!* Claude turned quickly and punched Natsu in the face. Then he ripped off his buttons and shed his jacket, stamping out the flames.

"You tried to burn me alive. Just how did you think you'd find your way out?" Claude asked. "Get up, you bastard." He managed to return to Shea-Talonian though he really wanted to continue in Gil-Laelian and punch Natsu unconscious. *He's worth a million.* Claude shrugged off his anger. *In a future battle, my arrow will pierce your heart.*

Natsu stood. Claude shoved him forward. "Who has the torch now?" Claude put it close to Natsu's backside, and the man ran toward the long hall.

"What's that smell?" Natsu asked again and glanced back with his hand over his nose.

"It's your friends, rotting away." Claude brought the flame close again. "On your knees, fool. Crawl through the tunnel."

They both continued. The rivets in the steel tunnel scraped his knees. Dry leaves soon turned to damp mush mingled with mud and soaked his pants. Rats squeaked and ran around. Claude grunted. *I'll have to change my clothes.* By the time they reached the end, his knees were protesting. The iron latch had been removed, and Natsu passed through to the other side.

A cheer sounded. Claude managed to emerge. He stood and pressed against his lower back, popping it. Ose was hugging Natsu. A stupid grin spread across both their faces. A moment later, Ose's eyes rested on Claude.

He watched as another man handed Ose a pouch. Shigemori tested the weight of the bag before approaching.

"It's good to have friends." Shigemori handed the money to him.

He opened the pouch. Royal tlokel gleamed, and he poured a few coins into his palm. Then, calculating the amount by the weight, Claude looked up at Shigemori. "You trying to rob me?"

"Not at all. I have one more task, and then you will receive the full amount." Ose lifted his fingers and inspected his nails.

"What is it?"

"Bring me, my wife."

"Tamika!" Claude couldn't believe his ears. "You had her in a pit."

"Only for her own safety."

"I believe that as much as I would believe the sun rising in the west. What could you want with her?"

"She is my wife."

"It will be hard to do."

"You have riches awaiting you."

True. Claude stepped backward and looked at the gathered men. He frowned. There were close to a thousand men. He couldn't force more money from Ose at this time.

"You'll have to wait until I'm assigned back at the palace."

"Of course."

"Very well. I'll meet your man at the new location."

Shigemori nodded.

"Don't follow me inside. You'll have to wait a little while for the others. Otherwise, you may compromise me. I'll be suspect as it is."

"Of course." Shigemori bowed.

Claude grunted and turned his back.

"The map."

"Oh, yes." Claude turned back and pulled the map from an inner pocket.

Ose opened it. "This isn't a good map."

"I had to make a copy. It gives you the basics."

"And should they not be enough?" Ose let the map hang from one hand.

"The prison isn't intricate. It will be enough. Just wait a few days, as I said."

With that, Claude left. He crawled through the tunnel and out, glanced at his burned jacket on the floor, left it, put out the torches, and climbed the ladder. Once he dispatched the few prisoners who'd seen him leave with Natsu, he went to his room for clean clothes. Afterward, he climbed the stairs to the top of the northwest turret, stepped over the sleeping longbowmen, and drank his own wine.

Price

Chapter 23

Jonathan kissed Tamika in the garden across from the dining room. He pulled back, cupped her face in his hands, and watched the smile spread across her face.

She lifted her eyes to his. "I love you."

"And I you."

"Why must we wait? I am not a virgin."

Jonathan broke contact and backed up. "We are not married."

"You are emperor. Emperors may do as they please. Warwyk had nineteen wives and ninety concubines. And still, he took many of his councilmen's wives to himself for as long as he wished before giving them back."

"I'm not Warwyk. He was an offense to all men. I read that some men even mutilated their wife's faces so he wouldn't take them."

Tamika frowned and looked down. "Yes, it is so. None are still alive to give testimony."

He approached again and took both her hands. "When I

marry…no, when *we* marry, you will be the only one in my bed. I won't be intimate with any other. I love you and will treasure you. In Gil-Lael, we marry for love and remain with the one we love all our lives."

"You really love me?" Tears swam in her eyes.

She needed constant reassurance, and he gave it. "With all my heart." He brushed the tears away from her cheeks with his thumb and tilted her head up for a kiss. Hunger for more consumed him, and he pulled her close, holding her against his body.

"I love you," Tamika whispered between his demanding kisses. "Why can't we enjoy each other?" She held him and stood on tiptoe to run her fingers through his hair.

The sweet taste of her filled him, and he groaned. "I want you," he whispered.

She stepped back, breaking his embrace.

He knew he needed to leave, to send her to her room, but he couldn't bring himself to do it.

She smiled, stepped close to him, and rubbed his rigid member.

Jonathan groaned in pleasure.

"I want you to touch every place that Ose touched. I want you to erase his memory from my body. I never want to think of him again or be… afraid."

"We should marry—"

"When you love me, completely. When you enter me and take away his foul touch. The memory of him will be expunged from my body forever." She took his hand, kissed his palm, and pressed it to her breast.

"Please," she whispered.

His lips brushed against hers, and he kissed her deeply. She smelled like cherry blossoms. Her hand was liquid fire on his penis, and he groaned. Everything his father taught him slipped through the passion that surged within him. He pulled her to the ground. She giggled, lifted her skirt, and removed her panties.

His entry was smooth. Their bodies blended despite the clothes.

Their passion soared, each gasping from the contact. She was his, and he hers. He loved her more than his own life and kissed her tenderly just before his essence surged into her.

Afterward, he adjusted his clothes and chided himself in silence for his lack of control.

"I want to share your bed." Tamika sat and put her hands around his arm.

Jonathan shut his eyes for a moment. There were many reasons why this was a bad idea, and only one argued it to be good. A necessity in his life. *Were the rules different enough? Different because she wasn't a virgin? Or was it something else?*

Then, she provided the answer. "This isn't Gil-Lael. This is Shea-Talon, you are the emperor, and I'm not a virgin."

Jonathan woke. This had been the first night in weeks he slept through the night, and it was all thanks to…he rolled over. Tamika lay next to him, still asleep. Her long black hair showered her shoulder. He pushed it back from her face, and she opened her eyes.

"Good morning, my love." Jonathan eased closer and kissed the corners of her eyes, then her mouth. She responded.

"We must find a way to divorce you from Shigemori."

Tamika answered him in his native tongue. "I know of some law defenders who can help."

"I'll send for them…" he pushed the blankets away from her naked body. "After breakfast."

Claude heard something from far away. He took a gasp and continued to sleep.

"Get up!"

Pain in his side where the man had kicked him woke Claude. Light filtered through the glassless turret windows.

"Up!"

He recognized the man, but he was too groggy to recall his name. The other guards were sitting or standing. Claude managed to join them.

"There's been a break-in."

He knew it would seem that way to them.

"All the lords of this God-forsaken country have been freed, and some of the guardsmen were killed. While asleep, I might add."

Damn Ose, he didn't wait.

Jonathan read the *communiqué*. "Bring Longbowman Coulomb to me." He threw the note down on his desk.

The soldier bowed and left.

How could this happen? All the lords. Even the two who surrendered peacefully. *I should have sent for them sooner.*

A knock. "Excellency, Master Yaginuma." A short, fat Shea-Talonian entered. His black hair was pulled back in the traditional bun. A single gold earring graced his left lobe. His kimono was black and had a gold chain around the waist.

"Yaginuma."

"Excellency." He bowed.

"Take a seat." Jonathan waved his hand to indicate the chairs and then sat as well.

"How may I serve you?" Yaginuma sat.

"I know a woman who wants to divorce her husband. I need you to tell me what she must do?"

"I'm afraid the law says a husband owns his wife and may do as he pleases to her."

"I changed that law." Jonathan sat back and ran the quill between two fingers.

"I hadn't heard that."

"I changed it months ago."

"Is there another grievance? One her husband would accept. And the other nobility too." Yaginuma's dark eyes rested on him.

"Why are you concerned with that?"

"There are rumors, Excellency."

"Please, enlighten me."

Yaginuma shifted his weight. He glanced at the bookshelves, then the fireplace, the windows.

"Yaginuma," Jonathan said.

"It is said that one has risen to challenge you."

"Yes. Why would that make a difference to my inquiry?"

"Because…" Yaginuma cleared his throat again and shifted in his chair. "All depends on who becomes–."

"Emperor."

"Yes."

"I am emperor."

"Yes, but it is said this one has the Bracelet of the Moon and Stars."

"I have heard the same. So far, the ground hasn't swallowed me. I am emperor now, and I will continue to be emperor. Answer my question."

"As I said, the law–."

"I grow tired, Yaginuma. Her husband murdered her family to become head and sole heir of their riches and titles."

"If he has committed such a crime, she can leave him. But we must have proof. Who is this woman?"

Jonathan studied the man. He heard birds chirping out the window. A shovel turned over the earth, and the scent of it reached him as he noted the folds in Yaginuma's clothes. "Lady Shigemori."

"Ose Shigemoris wife?" His voice quavered at the end.

"The same."

Yaginuma pushed the chair backward. Sweat beaded his brow, and he removed a kerchief to wipe it away.

"You fear him."

Yaginuma's hands were shaking. "I would be a fool not to. He is powerful, and many follow him."

"But not all."

"No."

"Do you know who follows?"

"I only know rumors." Yaginuma set the kerchief in his lap.

"Grant the divorce."

"I must have proof of these charges. Especially since it is Lord Shigemori."

Jonathan lifted the bell on the corner of his desk. A guard opened the door. "Bring me Friend-Brother Mossé."

They didn't have long to wait since Grégory's office was across the hall. He entered carrying files, approached the desk, and set them down. Yaginuma stood and bowed. Grégory returned the greeting and sat along with the Master of Law.

"Master Yaginuma requires proof of Shigemoris crimes," Jonathan said.

Grégory reached for the top file, opened it, and handed it to the man. "This is the report the doctor submitted after the death of Lady Shigemoris brother. His name is Maniwa Ietsuna, indicated at the top of the file."

Yaginuma read.

"As you can see, his head was bashed in with a rock while hunting alone with Shigemori. The doctor clearly states the injury was too severe for a simple fall from his horse, as Shigemori claimed." Grégory leaned close and pointed to the statement.

"This is not proof," Yaginuma said.

Grégory pulled the following file and exchanged them. "Here is the report on the fire that swept through the Ietsuna family home. All were lost. Authorities said the fire was started outside. Every corner of the home had evidence of brambles being stacked against it. Several stable hands claimed they saw Shigemori running away. He denied this."

Grégory didn't wait and pulled the next file. "This is a report on the fire that killed Lady Shigemoris uncle and his family. His name was Bando Koetsu. Her grandmother's son. The son of Warwyk, not yet born when the former emperor fought in the war."

"I didn't know Warwyk had a living son." Yaginuma turned his gaze on Grégory.

"It was hidden. Only a few knew. As you can see, the telltale signs of the fire are the same."

"But how do you know he was Warwyk's son?"

"His mother knew. She passed the information down to the family." Jonathan leaned forward and took the file he'd already read from Yaginuma.

"Even so, how do you come by this knowledge?"

"Lady Shigemori," Jonathan said.

"I will need to speak with her."

"Before I send for her, is this enough?"

"Yes."

"Then, I command you to issue the divorce and make it known publicly."

Sweat ran down the side of Yaginuma's forehead. "You ask the impossible."

"Why is it impossible?"

"He has the bracelet–."

"Of the moon and stars. I know. Aside from superstition, tell me why it is impossible."

Yaginuma squirmed in his chair. He glanced at Jonathan, then Grégory, and abruptly stood. "Because I want to live."

Jonathan used the bell again. "Sit."

Yaginuma plotted back down in the chair.

"Bring Lady Shigemori." Jonathan directed the guard at the door.

Much later that day, Jonathan paced before his throne. He had donned the crown and royal robe over his uniform. More than a dozen soldiers stood along the side walls. Since Shigemoris uprising, no nobles attended his council meetings. However, Grégory and Umezawa were there.

"It is time, Excellency," Grégory said.

Jonathan climbed the dais stair and sat on his throne.

Grégory readied his quill and paper. Umezawa stood before the throne. His staff in hand. The throne was high enough, so Jonathan could see the soldiers enter with Longbowman Coulomb. His hands were secured behind his back. He had a slight limp, and his face showed signs of bruising around his eyes and jaw.

Umezawa slammed his staff on the ground. "Kneel before his Excellency, Servant of the Most Excellent God, Judge of the Land and the Seas, Emperor of the People, His Royal Majesty, Jonathan Eoin Healden Calimar I."

Umezawa stepped aside, and Jonathan had a clear view of Coulomb. "You served wine to the guards. Wine that was drugged with a sleeping potion."

"I didn't drug the wine. I was a victim too."

"Twenty bottles."

"Yes."

"If one or two bottles were drugged, I'd believe your story. But twenty?"

Coulomb didn't respond. His head was bowed.

"Look at me."

He turned his head to the side, eyes on the floor, and then lifted his head to look at him.

"Explain."

"I needed to find a wine merchant that I could afford. So, I didn't go to the usual establishment."

"Which one is that?"

"My preference is Moon and Stars Wine, but as I said, I needed a lower cost, and so I went to Bottom Liquors. He is known to water down his goods, so he can sell at a reduced price."

"The bottles were unsealed?"

"No, he can re-seal them. The poor are stupid enough to think they're getting quality."

"Stupid or just poor." Jonathan shifted his weight. The throne was far too hard and upright.

"Maybe Shigemori had someone taint the bottles."

"How? How would he know you'd go to that merchant?"

Coulomb shook his head. "I don't know. I purchased the wine and made arrangements to pick it up later."

"Your defense is that Shigemori had men follow you and add a sleeping potion to the wine. They guessed all the guards and bowmen would drink the wine and fall asleep. This doesn't seem plausible. Why not poison the wine?"

"Shigemori is careless. He thinks he's smarter than everyone…ah, well, who can guess his motivation?"

Jonathan looked toward Grégory, who had stopped writing to peer at Coulomb. "How did Shigemori manage to breach the security, enter the prison, murder guards who drank your wine, and vanish with all the imprisoned nobles?" Jonathan turned his attention back to Coulomb.

"I don't know."

"You don't know. Try and speculate."

"Speculate, Excellency? I can only surmise Shigemori must know the prison."

"And how would he know the prison?"

Claude shrugged. "He is Shea-Talonian."

"I see. Why did you buy so many bottles?"

"I wanted to celebrate my promotion."

"A promotion you have lost." Jonathan waved one hand, and a

guard next to Coulomb removed his ribbon. Coulomb let his head fall for a moment before lifting his eyes to Jonathan.

"How much did Shigemori pay you?"

Coulomb's mouth twitched, lifting in one corner for a moment before he smoothed his face. "Pay me? No one paid me."

"You betrayed me for free?"

Jonathan stood. Coulomb eased back on his legs.

"Return him to Furuya Jun Prison and provide him with the most secure cell you can find."

The guards pulled Coulomb to his feet and left. Jonathan shed his crown and robe before stepping down. "Bring me, Lieutenant Périer."

Possibilities

Chapter 24

Claude Coulomb paced his cell. It was small, damp, and cold. He had a single blanket and pillow on his cot and a bucket in the corner for his waste.

Damn! *Baise Moi*, fuck me, I should have found a better hiding place for my money. Idiot! The basement cells would have worked. Ghosts have no need for money, and they wouldn't turn him in. Instead, he'd hidden the money in his room under the mattress. Someone else had that room now, and he was stuck in this God-forsaken cell.

I should have found a horse and rode to the docks and boarded the first ship out of here. Baise Moi!

All it would take would be for his replacement to discover the money and turn it in. It would be the gallows for him if that happened. *Maybe my replacement is greedy and will keep the money.* If he were anyone else, perhaps that thought would have been comforting, but not Claude. It angered him. He'd worked hard for that money. *Baise Moi.*

It took all seven steps for Claude to reach the bars from the back wall. He turned and marched back. *Damn Shigemori, couldn't he have waited? And killing his friends at the card table. Damn.*

"Dinner, you traitor." A soldier he didn't know shoved the tray under the bars on the floor toward him.

"I'm innocent." Claude picked up the tray and sat on his cot to eat. Upon inspection, he had no idea what the meal was. Perhaps gruel.

Tamika moved her hand across the table toward Jonathan. "You look tired tonight."

Grégory sat close by.

"I am. A long day, following a long week." He took her hand and smiled at her. "It is good to be with you at the end of each day."

Tamika smiled as well. *Jonathan was so much easier to be with than Ose ever had been.*

The servants entered with their meal. He ate as if he hadn't eaten in a long time while Tamika chewed slower. Watching him.

He pushed his plate away, sat back, and took a sip of his wine.

Tamika hadn't eaten even half her meal when she did the same.

"Are you well?" Jonathan turned his eyes from her to the plate and back.

"Yes. I'm not very hungry, that's all."

He set his wine down and took her hand with both of his. "Yaginuma will grant the divorce, and we shall wed the next day."

Yaginuma. She frowned. "I must tell you something." *She'd meant to earlier when he interviewed by her.*

"What?"

"Yaginuma is Ose's personal law master. I have seen him many times at the house."

Jonathan sat back in his chair. "I gave you several names Grégory, why did you contact this man?"

"Umezawa assured me that Yaginuma was the best."

"He is favored by many of our…Ose's friends." She looked away from Jonathan at the flowers in the garden. "I'm not sure you can trust him."

"Not to worry. Trust is a luxury. I learned that years ago."

"But…you have this way of…of expecting people to obey you."

Jonathan smiled. "I know it appears I trust everyone. I do expect people to obey my commands. I'm emperor. But I don't simply trust them. Not always."

Why doesn't he see the danger? "He is expensive," she said instead.

"I shall drain my coffers for you." Jonathan lifted her hand and kissed it. "I will never beat you, Tamika. If you know something you think I should know, tell me."

Tamika pulled her hand away. "I…I fear for your life. He has the bracelet."

Jonathan stood and pulled her from her chair. "I can't promise a future for you, my love. But I can promise you I'll do all I can to be sure you are safe." He kissed her.

Grégory cleared his throat and left.

Tamika lifted her arms over Jonathan's shoulders. Her body pressed against his. "I love you," she said when the kiss ended.

"Shall we retire?"

He would kiss her, touch that secret place. "Yes."

After breakfast the next day, Jonathan took Tamika riding. Along the northern and eastern expanse of the plateau, pine and oak grew tall. Their scent filled the air. The forest had pathways meandering through the undergrowth. Squirrels chittered at them as they rode. A few rabbits scampered past. A family of red-breasted quail took flight.

Ten soldiers rode close but not so close to overhear what Jonathan said.

He eased his horse beside hers and smiled. "I wish time would stop. Then we could spend it without a thought."

She laughed.

Toward the edge of the bluff, the forest gave way to rock and dirt with a few bushes clustered near the drop-off. The cliff wall fell straight down. An occasional tree grew sideways and spread spindly branches devoid of leaves twisting this way or that.

Jonathan dismounted, tying their horses' reins to a bramble. The soldiers on either side also dismounted. Bowmen readied their arrows.

Jonathan helped Tamika from her saddle. They walked toward the western edge. Below them, the forest continued its span broken only by the clearing holding Furuya Jun Prison. Seeing the prison reminded Jonathan of the escape. *How did it happen?*

A soldier approached. "Excellency, please step back. A marksman may be hiding in the trees below."

Jonathan did as the man said. He reached for Tamika's hand, and the two of them viewed the forest below from a safe distance.

"Ever since I discovered the guardhouse with stairs descending to the ocean, I've wondered if there are any other hidden passages up to the top."

"This site was chosen hundreds of years ago for its security."

"Security can be an illusion." He frowned as he scanned the clearing around the prison. "There was a break-in at the prison. No one can tell me how it happened. I think I need to clear the forest several hundred yards away from the building. That would make it harder for someone unseen to break in as well as escape."

Tamika brushed a strand of wayward hair from her eyes. "The original purpose of the prison was to torture, friend or foe, that the emperor deemed untrustworthy."

"A gruesome thought." *Torture. Was there a hidden room or more than one in the basement of the prison?* Jonathan studied the structure. *I should have brought binoculars.* Once, while visiting his mother's homeworld, they each got a set of binoculars with night vision. He'd send a missive and ask his father to send them with the soldiers he'd promised.

At the palace once more, Jonathan took Tamika to his office. He ordered tea and biscuits before showing her the map of Shea-Talon, spread across a vast table. The three-dimensional map showed hills and valleys to rise and fall and the eastern mountains to separate this country from his homeland of Gil-Lael.

Tamika smiled and pointed to the Province of Posong. "This is where I was raised."

Jonathan came around the table to stand beside her.

"Here." She indicated a place close to the mountains. "Bando spent many hours exploring the caves along with Ose."

"Caves? Your brother and Shigemori?"

Jonathan turned his eyes on her to see her brow crinkled.

"Oui, Ose." She spoke Gil-Laelian.

"I will not say his first name."

Her expression didn't change.

"Not since he hurt you and made himself known as a traitor."

Tamika smiled and put her arm around his. "You are such a good man." She stood on tiptoe and kissed his cheek. "And big."

"Taller than most."

"Oui, and big here too." She reached for his crotch.

Jonathan chuckled. "You like it."

"Yes."

He would have thrown her down and made love to her if someone hadn't knocked on the door. Instead, he gave her a quick kiss on the cheek. "Enter."

Lieutenant Périer opened the door. "Excellency."

"Come."

Périer looked at Tamika and then back to Jonathan.

"Go ahead."

"The two lords who didn't fight us and were freed as well…" he looked at Tamika again.

"Go on." Jonathan frowned.

"They were hanged in the middle of the night just outside the lower guardhouse."

Unknown Forts

Chapter 25

Ose Shigemori leaned back against the tree. Soon, he'd leave Aya for the Province of Xuqihar. Those men who pledged their support had made it to the cave system in the mountains. The time had come for him to abandon hope of having Tamika returned. Coulomb was out of his reach as well. It wasn't worth the death of good men to help him escape.

Shiho knelt at his side, cleaning his fingernails. She wasn't a madam to the onsen anymore. He arrived with his men, raided the geisha house, and forced the women to come with them. Now, Shiho attended to his needs, and right now, that meant his fingernails.

Natsu had other needs. Ose glanced at the man, naked with his onsen geisha and grunting. *I should have saved my money. All he's done is to argue and stick it to his onsen.*

Shiho was polishing his nails now with a brush. She'd given him a hard time until he beat her senseless. The bruises were still visible. *I might just do it again soon.* He smiled.

Captain Chikusa entered. "Excellency." He bowed. "The traitors have been hanged as instructed."

"Good. Did the usurper notice?"

"Yes. The usurper's men cut them down."

Shiho finished. Ose brought up his hand to admire his fingernails. "Gather the men. We leave in an hour."

Chikusa bowed. After he left, Ose stood and walked to where Natsu lay naked. He wrinkled his nose at the scent of sweat-dampened skin. "Get dressed."

Natsu rolled his eyes and stood.

"You need to stop fornicating and make yourself available to me."

"But my little geisha is so much fun."

"We are at war. Anyone not giving me their full attention may end up hanging from a tree."

"Ose, I'm your friend, not just your minion."

"I have no time for friendship." Ose turned and walked away.

Jonathan gathered his men. The various *chef de brigade's* and *capitaine's* along with Umezawa and Grégory. *If only there were more I could trust.*

They gathered around the map.

"I have learned there are caves, all along the southern mountains from the tip to the far north. There are also extensive mining operations Shigemori might hide in and exploit." He pointed to several areas of the map. "My guess is he will utilize these caves and mines to gather his men.

"My brother's men will be here in a few days. When they arrive, we will pursue the traitor. Give me your thoughts."

Émilien stepped closer to the map. He was a short man with raven black hair and a large nose. "We should send falcons and inform the post along the mountains."

"How many posts do we have?" Jonathan frowned.

"How many?" Émilien asked and looked around.

The others spoke at the same time. "Do you know?"

"No."

"How many?"

"Where?"

Jonathan held up his hand. "No one knows? You've all been here for ten or more years, and you don't know where the forts are?"

Grégory pushed through the men. He climbed the stool Jonathan provided. "Here is the record among your books, Excellency."

He put the book down on the map and opened it about a third way through. Jonathan took the volume, turned it, and scanned the page. A miniature map indicated with dots and in small print a series of forts. Fifteen in all.

"Some are no longer there," Umezawa said.

"Which ones are gone?" Jonathan set the book down, and Périer lifted it.

Umezawa shrugged. "I don't know."

"Périer, ready the falcons."

"None of the falcons are trained to go to these locations."

"Then how close can we send them?" Jonathan took several small flags and handed them to Périer since he held the volume. Then, setting the tome down, Périer began putting the flags in every place where the book showed a fort. The larger fortified châteaus that contained several thousand men each were already indicated with other colored flags.

"There are falcons trained to fly to every château ."

"Then send them and instruct the officers to seek out these forts." Jonathan waved his hand, and the men prepared to leave.

"Umezawa."

The older man stopped and turned. Jonathan had never been bothered that this man was the only Shea-Talonian in his private councils. But now… "Once again, you have failed to give me information."

"Excellency." Umezawa bowed lower than usual. "Forgive me. I will try to do better. I will pull the volumes and search."

"Make sure you do." He waved, and Umezawa left.

Jonathan tapped the pointer stick against the map. He needed someone who wasn't afraid. Someone he could trust. But trust seemed scarce these days. After Coulomb, he wasn't sure if he could trust his own men.

He walked to his desk and rang the bell. "Bring me, Lieutenant Périer." While he waited, he contemplated the garden outside his window. When at last the man entered, Jonathan turned.

"Excellency."

"I want you to assign men to follow Umezawa. Discretion is needed. Don't let him know. Is that clear?"

"Oui."

Jonathan nodded and waved him away.

Divorce

Chapter 26

Tamika rested her head against Jonathan's shoulder and ran her fingers over his muscular chest. Making love with him was wonderful. His thumb rubbed her shoulder, and he turned his head to kiss her forehead.

"Warwyk had many wives and concubines." As emperor, he was entitled to do so, though she hoped he wouldn't. *Did he want multiple wives and concubines?*

"So, you have said."

She moved her head, so she could look up at him.

He smiled down at her. "That is not our custom. One wife is enough for me."

Tamika snuggled her head in his shoulder and smiled. He'd said this before but she needed reassurance.

"Umezawa is a problem."

She glanced back up at him.

"He isn't informing me of things as he should be."

"What things?"

"The bracelet for one, the caves and mines."

"Umezawa is a wise scholar. He has an extraordinary reputation. I can understand about the bracelet. I had forgotten it until Ose showed it off to the nobility. Most thought it was lost. But the caves and the mines would have been my first concern after Ose's rebellion. I don't know why Umezawa didn't tell you."

"You told me." Jonathan rolled over on his side, and Tamika settled her head into the pillow.

"Should he have told me of the guardhouse built into the rock with stairs leading to the ocean below?"

Her eyes widened. "There's a guardhouse? Where?"

"Up here. I discovered it. That is how I became injured. No one told you?"

"No. I thought you must have been attacked when traveling into town."

Jonathan became quiet. Running his fingers along her arm.

"Your uncle was Warwyk's grandson. Why didn't your grandmother give the bracelet to him?"

"I don't know. Perhaps because he didn't have any sons. Or maybe she just loved my brother more."

Silence settled between them. Tamika lifted her hand to run her fingers through his hair. She loved his hair. Light brown. And soft.

"I must replace Umezawa soon. The problem is, who can I trust? Who won't be so afraid of Shigemori that they will tell me the truth? I need absolute loyalty."

Tamika frowned. *Who could he trust? What were their credentials?* No one came to mind. Maybe in the morning, she'd think of someone.

The minutes ticked by. Neither spoke. When she lifted her eyes to Jonathan's face, she found he had fallen asleep. She smiled and rolled over.

February arrived with rain morning, noon, and night. Tamika missed the horse rides with Jonathan but didn't miss getting drenched. At present, he was holed up in his office with Grégory and his *chef de brigades*. Generals. He had recently appointed three men to that position, including Périer. She liked him. His brown hair covered his head in tight curls. He was always kind to her and soft-spoken. Because of this, she doubted whether he'd make a good *chef de brigade*, but then, Jonathan was a kind man, and he made an excellent emperor.

Over the last week, she'd begun bringing Jonathan his afternoon tea. She stood at the door with the tray now, and the guard knocked before opening the door.

"Lady Shigemori," he announced.

"Enter." Jonathan's voice called.

Tamika walked in and immediately saw Grégory standing on his step stool before the map. The other men had already left.

Jonathan came around from the other side and took her tray. Bending, he gave her a quick kiss on the lips. "Good afternoon, my Love."

She smiled and followed him to his desk, where he set the tray down.

"I'm sorry, Friend-Brother Mossé, I didn't bring a cup for you."

Grégory climbed down the stool and bowed to her. "I was just leaving."

She watched him go. Mossé didn't speak to her often. *Did he hate her?* She turned and poured the tea. Cream for Jonathan and a little sugar to hers. He was back at the map. She walked there with their tea.

She'd seen the map, but beyond noticing the movements of Jonathan's symbols for cities, provinces, and men, she hadn't really looked at the terrain. It was a three-dimensional map, and she admired how majestic the mountains appeared.

"My brother's army has arrived, and I have sent them to all the châteaus as reinforcements. Two thousand each of my own men have already set out to these forts, located here and here."

Tamika looked up and set the teacup down. "Who made this map?"

"It was a gift from Umezawa."

Tamika nodded and then lifted the pointer stick from the end of the table. "Do you see this area here?" She indicated a large strip of land that had no name attached to it. The property began almost flush with their province of Gusanke and spread west past the mountains, a river meandered west as it flowed in a southern direction. It traveled to Xuqihar and even had access to the sea between Gusanke and Yuuki.

"When my people first came here from our lands across the ocean, a group of people not native to us came as well. In appearance, they are similar but very tall. Emperor Matsui I, gave them all this land and granted them the freedom to govern themselves. But they chose to be governed by Matsui. They are Shea-Talonian, and yet don't involve themselves in our business. This province is named Cao Zhen.

"And do you see this little blue line starting in the mountains of Cao Zhen? This is a major river that begins in the mountains with many lakes and a huge waterfall. It is big enough for ships to sail and continues to the Southern Ocean. Here in the Province of Yuuki, it forks and flows to the southwestern Port of Kangjin, in the Province of Hashiba.

"If I'm not mistaken, this river should appear three times its size."

"And the caves you told me about?"

"Yes, the caves are a short ride along the mountains from the river."

"And the name for the river?"

"It is called Quan Kun. Here where it turns west, it is called Du Zhi. There is much commerce along this river."

She lifted her eyes to Jonathan. He smiled, set the teacup down, and walked around the table to her. Then lifted her and twirled her around. The warmth of his body and his kiss turned her to jelly. Laughter bubbled up and escaped her lips as soon as he removed his mouth.

"I love you."

She smiled.

"I'm making you the Royal Advisor." He set her down.

"Oh…" Tamika stepped back a little and studied his face. "I am honored, but I don't want to slam the stick down and announce you in the throne room."

Jonathan chuckled and swept her off her feet again. "I shall have someone else do that."

Much later that afternoon, Jonathan held a meeting with Grégory and Périer.

"Tamika has pointed out a few flaws in our map." Jonathan loosened his collar, removed his jacket, and walked to the windows, opening both. "I need a trustworthy man to go as ambassador to the Cao Zhen people." Back at the map, he used the pointer stick and explained all Tamika had shown him in detail.

"There is a Shea-Talonian teacher who you may trust." Périer lifted his eyes to Jonathan.

"A teacher?"

"Oui, he teaches the children of our married soldiers."

"How do you know this man?"

"I am married to a Shea-Talonian woman. She has borne me a son. They live with her parents in Aya."

Immediately Jonathan thought about housing for these men and their families. *But where? The plateau was getting crowded.* "What is his name?"

"Ikehata."

"Bring him to me."

Périer bowed and left.

Only a few moments later, a knock followed by the wooden pocket doors sliding open. "Master Yaginuma to see you, Excellency."

"Thank you, Nathanaël, show him in."

Yaginuma's black kimono was ankle length and exposed his wooden sandals. He bowed. "Excellency, as you commanded, a legal and binding divorce for Lady Shigemori."

Jonathan walked to the law master. "Thank you." He took the paper written in the delicate symbols of the Shea-Talonian people.

"May I be of service in another matter?"

Jonathan looked up from his study of the document. "Has Shigemori been told?"

"No one knows where he is. I had a copy posted on his door and another sent to his southern estate."

Jonathan frowned at the paper once more. "Nathanaël, send for Lady Shigemori." Unable to read the writing on the paper, he wouldn't trust Yaginuma's word. The room had become chilly, and he walked to the windows and shut them. Without the need to be told, Grégory sat at the small desk opposite the table with the map and prepared ink, quill, and paper.

Jonathan glanced at the mantel clock as he returned to the map.

Yaginuma fidgeted, shifting his weight from one foot to the other. Grégory sat quietly with his hands folded in front of him.

Tamika lifted her hand and turned to acknowledge Nathanaël.

"Pardon, my Lady. His excellency has called for you."

Tamika set the brush down and stood away from the painting. A depiction of the flower Jonathan had given her. She followed Nathanaël out. When they reached Jonathan's office, Nathanaël slid the door open and announced her. Upon entering, she bowed first to Jonathan and then to Master Yaginuma, who returned her greeting.

Jonathan waved his hand, and Nathanaël left. "Master Yaginuma has brought the divorce papers. I'd like you to read it for approval."

She took the paper from him and sat at Jonathan's desk to read. After a short time, she turned, leaving one finger on a symbol. "Why does it say 'With Lord Shigemoris approval'?"

"The law requires it."

"We've been through this, Yaginuma." Jonathan took several steps toward the man. Yaginuma backed up.

"I told you!"

"I cannot change the law."

"No. I can. And I already have." Jonathan stepped away, his back to Tamika. He turned abruptly and marched to the wooden pocket doors. Opening them, he left.

Oh! What should I do? Tamika glanced from the door to Grégory.

"I should go," Master Yaginuma said.

Grégory stood. "You haven't been dismissed."

"I have work to do." Yaginuma moved toward the door.

Tamika had never seen Grégory run and was surprised when he did so now. He positioned himself between Yaginuma and the door.

"Move out of my way, Dwarf."

"I am Friend-Brother Mossé to you." Grégory folded his arms and remained.

The pocket doors opened, and Jonathan walked in accompanied by three soldiers. He glanced between Grégory and the Master of Law.

"Yaginuma," Jonathan said. "You disobeyed a direct command from your emperor. Therefore, these men will escort you to Furuya Jun Prison, where a nice room awaits."

"Excellency, forgive."

Jonathan lifted his hand, and two guards took Yaginuma's arms and pulled him out the door. They could hear him yell, "Excellency," over and over until the distance swallowed his voice.

"Grégory, inform my *chef de brigades* that I require every judge and law master to attend me tomorrow in the throne room at nine in the morning."

Grégory nodded and left.

Jonathan then turned to Tamika. "I am sorry, my Love."
She went to him, stood on tiptoe, to kiss his cheek.

Fear

Chapter 27

The next morning, Jonathan paced from one end of the small room he had built behind the throne to the next. He glanced at Tamika and Grégory. They sat at a small table with wine poured in three glasses. One for Jonathan, but instead, he marched.

He wore his official uniform, black pants, red jacket with a gold sash from shoulder to the opposite hip. Laying across a chair was the royal robe he must put on before going out, and the crown was on the table.

The walls were lined with thick fabric in a dragon design and backed with wool to make the room as soundproof as possible. He reached the end and turned again.

"I have studied this damn country since I was nine. But so much of the history and customs were left out that I feel as if I'm wandering at night in a dark forest." He turned and passed the two watching him on the way to the other side.

"Stubborn! That's what these people are." He turned again.

The door opened. Not a Shea-Talonian pocket door, but a Gil-Laelian door, thick, heavy, and carved with the likeness of a dragon. Nathanaël stood there. "Excellency, the men have arrived."

Tamika lifted his cape. Jonathan walked toward her. He had to crouch down a little so she could fasten it around his neck. Then, standing, he watched Grégory grab the staff and leave with Tamika. She paused long enough at the door to look back at him, and he nodded to her, then picked up the heavy crown and put it on his head.

At the door, he heard Grégory hit the floor with the staff and announce. "Bow before your Emperor, Servant of the Most Excellent God, Judge of the Land and the Seas, Emperor of the People, His Royal Majesty, Jonathan Eoin Healden Calimar the I."

Jonathan walked out into a room filled with men all standing. As he passed, they bowed. He climbed the dais stairs, and turned. The men still stood, watching him.

Seeing how they used to grovel on the floor, this is one change they didn't have any trouble with. Jonathan motioned with his hand for them to sit. He sat as well.

Grégory joined Tamika and the Shea-Talonian scribe. She would read what the native scribe wrote to ensure he was accurate.

"Welcome, Law Masters of Aya. Last autumn, I decreed that married women need not lose their property, monies, or possessions to their husbands and that if they wished to divorce and it was granted, they would retain their goods. But, it has come to my attention, this new law has not been recorded or honored.

"Who among you keeps the law records?"

The men looked at each other, and a murmur filled the room as they spoke soft back-and-forth.

"If you keep the records, stand."

The men quieted to a heavy silence. No one stood.

"Must I ask again?" Jonathan frowned.

A chair slid on the wooden floor, then another until three men at the same table stood.

"Excellency," one of them said. "We are charged with maintaining the law books. I record property laws, Haga records business laws, and Chino records family laws." He turned to indicate each man.

"And you are?"

"I am Iwamoto."

"Am I correct that the law I changed concerning women is under family law, Chino?"

"Yes, Excellency." Chino bowed his head.

"Is my change in your book?"

"No."

"Why?"

Chino kept his head bowed and didn't answer.

"Sit." The three men did so.

"Come, Chino, join my scribe at the table and sit between him and Lady Shigemori."

Chino left the table. He was an average man, black hair, a small nose, angular eyes. Once he sat, Jonathan nodded, and his scribe passed him paper, a fine bristled paintbrush, and put the ink bottle between them.

"Record this." Jonathan stood and walked down from his throne. "No man, no woman, no child, no servant, no wife or husband is property. Each is their own person with certain rights. A wife will retain her property, monies, and possessions. If a husband or a wife is found to have beaten or murdered family members of their spouse or tried to control their partner in any way, that husband or wife may seek a divorce, and it will be granted. She or he will retain their property, monies, and possessions."

Jonathan moved slowly before Chino as he wrote in the symbols of the Shea-Talonian language.

"That is now law. I will expect you to present me with the law record book tomorrow."

Chino glanced up at Jonathan. His frown gathered the lines

around his eyes and caused him to appear as if he were squinting. Jonathan turned and walked back to his throne. He sat.

"I have proof that Lord Shigemori murdered Lady Shigemoris family to secure their lands, monies, and possessions for himself. He has beaten her and starved her. "He glanced at Tamika. Her eyes were shut, and her lips quivered. *Damn.*

"I brought Law Master Yaginuma to me to present him with the proof and demanded he grants her a divorce. When he returned with the divorce decree, he included at the bottom. 'Upon Lord Shigemoris approval.'

"No! Shigemori has no say in this matter. He has committed crimes against Lady Shigemori. Who among you will write and submit the document granting her divorce?"

The room grew small for Jonathan as if the walls had shrunk in on him. The men once more began to speak among themselves in hushed tones that sounded like birds cawing in the distance. Heads bobbed back and forth. Eyes occasionally glanced his way. Jonathan's heart kept rhythm as the minutes ticked by. The room became heavy with the scent of perspiration despite the rose oil added to burners throughout the chamber. He could almost taste the odor.

"I am your emperor," Jonathan shot from his chair. "I demand that this be done." He waited again, but no one offered to write the needed document.

He stepped down from his throne chair and began to pace in front of the men. "I have studied your history. I know about your former emperors." He passed the table where Tamika sat. Her hands were on the table, and her fingers folded together while she gazed at him.

"In the beginning, they were good men, but before long, they each brought to the monarchy self-serving attitudes. First in how to treat women, then the poor, then servants and working people. Until the end." He reached the other wall and turned. His cape flowed out with his long strides.

"The last three emperors had outrageous habits of stealing wives and children for their own pleasure. They robbed even the elite. They pillaged towns within their own country. They murdered men and women if they didn't like the look on their faces." He stopped before the throne but didn't climb the dais.

"And then you had Warwyk, not the name he was born with. Warwyk's adoptive name matched his lust for war, trying to gain lands and peoples. He gained some and lost others but wasn't held accountable until he met my father." Jonathan glared at the men. All of them were watching him as if they'd never witnessed anyone losing their temper before.

"Would you have me become like them? A tyrant? Would you have me travel Shea-Talon and randomly select innocent people and have them murdered for my pleasure?"

Silence. Jonathan's heart raced against his chest. "Answer me!"

The men dropped their gaze. Some tried to conceal shaky hands. At last, a short man stood at a table nearest the door. He was so small, Jonathan thought him a dwarf until he stepped away from the table and he could see his limbs.

"Excellency," he bowed. "May I?"

"Come forward and tell me your name."

The man strode his way with delicate ease. "I am Koide Morihiro. We are afraid, Excellency. Lord Shigemori has the Bracelet of the Moon and Stars. All know the legend. He has declared himself emperor by right of the bracelet and his marriage. Lady Shigemori is the granddaughter of our last emperor, Warwyk. As her husband, Lord Shigemori has the right to claim the throne."

"I know this," Jonathan said. "My father won the throne through war, and I am his appointed heir. The old laws no longer apply."

"Forgive me. Lord Shigemori came to Aya in the dark of night. His men called out the town to the center. He rode his horse around and declared himself rightful emperor showing off the bracelet. Then he selected three men, two older and one young. He brought them to the raised obelisks and beheaded each himself. He said the same would happen to any who disobeyed him."

The air rushed out from Jonathan. Damn Shigemori, murdering his people. Recovered, he said, "When did this happen?"

"It has been a month now."

"Are you married?"

Koide's mouth opened for a moment before he spoke. "Yes."

"Children?"

"Yes."

"You're afraid Shigemori will do the same to you."

"Yes."

Jonathan looked past him at the others. "You're all afraid." He didn't need an answer.

Looking back at Koide, he said, "will you write the document I require?"

The man lowered his gaze, frowning. Then, after a moment, he peered once more at Jonathan. "I will."

Jonathan smiled and set his hand on Koide's shoulder, turning him to look at the others. "This is a brave man who stands beside me. He is now the royal law master." Then, turning back to Koide, he continued, "Bring your wife and children to the plateau. Warn any other family members or friends to find a safe place to hide.

"For the rest of you." Jonathan stepped away from Koide. "I am your emperor. Shigemori will not prevail. You would do well to model Koide's behavior. If you do not, I will consider you traitors and will have you locked up in Furuya Jun Prison, and from there, you will be publicly hanged." He turned, climbed the dais stairs, and sat on his throne. "Dismissed."

Announcement

Chapter 28

Much later, after sparring with his swordmaster, Jonathan stood in the stables, staring at the saddle Shigemori had given him. He had changed into his cotton shirt, dark brown pants, and leather jerkin.

"The saddle was my idea." Tamika stood beside him.

Jonathan glanced down at her.

"I knew the Romani were giving you one of their prized stallions for your birthday, and I told Ose the perfect gift would be a saddle. Don't ride it for him. Ride it for me."

He grinned at her and kissed her cheek. "You are ever in my thoughts."

She wrapped both hands around his arm and leaned her head close to his shoulder. "Be careful. There are enemies everywhere."

"I ride with two hundred men into Aya. I'll be safe. There's a telescope on the roof of the first manor house. You can watch from there. But I must do something this afternoon to address what

Shigemori has done. He murdered *my people,* and I want them to know I will punish him for the crime."

"I fear for you." Her lips trembled.

He patted her hand and stepped toward the horse. Once mounted, he gazed at her again. "I'm not sure how long this will take." Then he urged Quickflame into a trot. Just past the stables, the horse gave a panicked whinny, beating the air back down. He bucked, twisting in a circle. Jonathan grasped the reins and soothed the animal as much as possible, but Quickflame would have none of it.

A stable hand ran toward him and tried to grab the reins. The stallion rose on his hind legs once more, beating the air. The man took a blow to the head and fell. Then the steed bucked violently. After five times, Jonathan lost his balance and fell. On the ground, he rolled away from the stallion. Quickflame whinnied again. Several more men came at a run, lifted their arms, and yelled. Périer reached Jonathan and helped him up.

Tamika joined them. "What happened?"

Jonathan took a deep breath. "Bring me a different horse and saddle." He looked at Tamika. "Apparently, something is wrong with the saddle." *I've ridden with it in the past. Why now? Did Shigemoris reach extend to his groomsmen?*

His black Norman Cob thoroughbred was being led to him at a trot by Stablemaster Munemori.

"Excellency." He bowed.

"I expect a report on Quickflame and the saddle when I return."

"As you wish."

Jonathan took the reins and mounted the horse. His leg was sore from the fall, but he ignored the pain. "Shall we, Périer?"

"Oui."

The soldiers waited for them at the bottom of the bluff. Jonathan urged his horse forward, and Périer did the same. They joined the center of the men. The soldiers flanked them both giving them the best security possible. The ride to Aya took them less than half an hour. The people quickly hurried out of the way and bowed when they saw Jonathan.

A few of the men in Jonathan's military were Shea-Talonian, and they called out. "Our emperor requests you come to the center of town."

As the horses trotted along the street, they soon passed the port where almost a year earlier, Jonathan had arrived on a Gil-Laelian vessel named after his mother. It seemed so long ago, yet less than a year.

When they reached the center, the paving stones circled a giant obelisk situated around a series of steps leading up to it. Farther back from this, many small shops lined the road, and multiple lanes forked off in different directions. Everything was wet from earlier rain, and the air was chilly. *I can smell the ocean, and somewhere, fish are frying.*

Some of the soldiers rode their horses down the various lanes, and many of them dismounted. Jonathan also dismounted. His leg muscles were tight from the earlier fall. He walked a little, giving the reins to a soldier, and climbed the steps to the grand pillar in the center, Périer beside him.

The Shea-Talonian people were running toward the town square. Others were riding in carts. The clip-clop of their wooden sandals hit the pavement. Horses' hooves added to the noise, and many of them whinnied. The wheels on carts creaked. Fabrics swished in the air. Mothers called for their children. Fathers encouraged their families to be silent. Close to half an hour passed before the people were gathered all around the center. Jonathan waited, watching the controlled chaos while the people gathered. A sea of men and women. *His people.*

As he turned, he saw they had their heads bowed. None looked up. The tension came toward him like an ocean wave, and he remembered the last time these people were gathered here Shigemori murdered three men and threatened them. *I must be strong and yet reassure them at the same time.*

As directed earlier, the Shea-Talonian soldiers came toward the center and yelled in unison. "Quiet, His Excellency, Emperor Jonathan wishes to speak to you."

An instant change settled over everyone. Men, women, and children lifted their heads. Jonathan took a breath. It was time.

"My people, I am your emperor by right of conquest." Jonathan walked slowly around the obelisk so he could address everyone. "I have recently learned of your loss by the hands of the traitor, Lord Shigemori. His claim to the throne is an illegal one. The Bracelet of the Moon and Stars may be in his possession, but it is not his. He is not of the blood of your previous emperors. His marriage to Lady Tamika Ietsuna, the granddaughter of Warwyk, was coerced. Shigemori murdered her family to gain the bracelet," Jonathan spoke to them in their own language.

"War is upon us. Shigemori and those who follow him will be captured, imprisoned, and hanged. You are all now on alert. Should you see any of them, notify your sheriffs. They will, in turn, notify my men. If any of you think to join with Shigemori, they will be considered a traitor and duly punished.

"More importantly, you are my people now. I will not tolerate anyone coming among you to murder or pillage. I will give you protection. I will assign two hundred soldiers, night, and day to patrol your streets and shops from this day on. They are ordered to protect you. They will break up fights, question arguments, and seize anyone threatening harm. You will be safe.

Tamika pulled away from the telescope. "He's on his way home."

Grégory stood next to her on several crates to make him tall enough to see out the telescope. "We will hear what happened soon enough." He jumped off the boxes.

Tamika turned away. "I'm so happy no one tried to harm him."

"Too many soldiers."

Tamika glanced at Grégory and found him studying her.

"Someone will eventually. War is imminent," Grégory said.

"I wish I could change that."

"You do realize that there is a price to pay for your relationship with Jonathan? A price he will have to pay."

Tamika frowned and teetered. With effort, she took a deep breath and tried to stand taller.

"You don't look well."

"I'm well enough." She pushed against her stomach and smiled. Severe cramps stretched long, cruel fingers across her lower abdomen. Tamika bent, and tears came to her eyes. It had been months now, and she needed the peach pit removed. *Where were the Romani? Where was Mariyam, the old healer?* Périer told her that they had vanished.

Grégory put a hand on her arm. "My Lady."

The flat roof came up too close as she fell and struck her hard in the face before things went black.

Sickness

Chapter 29

Grégory sat across from Tamika and next to Jonathan at the dining table. He lifted the chicken, sautéed in something or other, and bit into the tender meat. Jonathan hadn't said much. Tamika sat stoically like some Shea-Talonian obsidian goddess. She wore a yellow kimono with an enormous peony imprinted across the material. Her black hair was coiffed in a bun with a fan to match her dress. Thank the Great Créateur she hadn't painted her face white. *Why did she feel the need to remind them that she was Shea-Talonian?* Grégory peered between Jonathan and Tamika. *Lover's quarrel?*

"Aren't you hungry?" Jonathan glanced at Tamika.

She lifted her eyes to his. *Bloodshot from crying?* Grégory frowned.

"I'm not well." Tamika lowered her gaze once more.

"What's wrong?" Jonathan set his fork down and covered her hand with his. "You're cold."

"I need to see Mariyam of the Romani."

"Last I heard, they left. Could someone else help you?"

Tamika lowered her gaze and shook her head. "No."

She is a master manipulator. Grégory took another bite of his chicken. *Although, of course, she did faint. Perhaps he was wrong about her. Whatever the cause, she remained Shigemoris wife, and he didn't trust her.*

Jonathan stood and pulled her up. "Get some rest, my love. I'll send someone out to look for them." He hugged her.

"But, do you know what happened with your horse?"

"A torn in the saddle."+

"How?"

"We will find out. Now go and rest," Jonathan said.

Tamika shuffled off once Jonathan released her.

"You have any idea where the Romani went?" Jonathan sat once more.

Grégory shrugged. "No idea."

They returned to eating and said little else. When dinner was over, they walked to Jonathan's office. Grégory appreciated how he took care to match his pace. That couldn't be easy for him because he was so tall.

"Anything happen while I was gone?" They entered, and Jonathan went to the map.

Grégory climbed the steps to the platform where he stood on the opposite side of his friend. "We received a falcon."

"Where's the message?"

"On your desk." Jonathan went to the desk and opened the note, then returned to the map. "Ikehata says the Cao Zhen leader is willing to meet but requests we go to him.Citing the recent skirmishes."

"Will you go?"

"I must, and you're coming with me."

Tamika lay on the bed, rolled to the side, and clutched her abdomen. A large hand covered her forehead. She opened her eyes to find Jonathan gazing at her with a frown pulling his eyebrows together. Light filtered past her window and caused shadows to linger around the edges of her furniture. She was in her room.

"How are you feeling?" Jonathan moved his hand, and Tamika captured it between her own.

"A little better, I think." She remembered laying down for a short nap last night. Unfortunately, her nap lengthened into an entire night.

"Good, I have sent *Chef de Brigade* Émilien with a contingent of men to find the Romani. In the meantime, I sent for a doctor."

Should I tell him about the peach pit? Would he think less of me? A woman who won't carry her husband's child. Tamika's lips trembled a little as she smiled. She scooted back so she could sit. "You are such a kind man. It worries me. Ose will use it against you."

"Not to fear, I will do what I must." He smiled. "I'm leaving to meet with the leader of the Cao Zhen people. When I'm done, I intend to travel to all the Provinces of Shea-Talon. The people need to see me, and I need to gather their hearts."

This was terrifying news. "How long will you be?"

"Months."

"Several months, maybe a year," Tamika predicted.

"Oui, several months."

"I should come."

"It's not safe."

"If it's not safe for me, it can't be safe for you."

"Shigemori will try to kidnap you. He'll just try to kill me."

"Just…" she put her hands across her heart. "It would kill me to lose you."

He smiled again. "I would die if I lost you. It can't be helped. I will gain no allies sitting on my perch. I must engage the people. You, however, must remain safe. Send me falcons, so I know how you fare, and I will return them to you with my own news."

He stood then and bent, giving her a kiss on her forehead. "I must leave now."

"Jonathan…" *she wanted to make him stay, but what argument could she give?* "I love you."

He turned back and bent down again, this time giving her a long kiss on her lips. "I love you, too."

Then, he was gone.

Oh no, she must stop him. Had she dozed off? Tamika hurried to dress and then ran outside despite her pain. She couldn't find Jonathan. Making a dash for the manor house, she climbed the stairs and gasped. Bent at the waist, she whispered, "Breathe in, breathe out." Once her lungs didn't hurt, she went to the telescope and peered through it. At the bottom of the plateau, a line of soldiers road from the mountain pass and headed toward Aya. There were so many of them. Jonathan should be safe.

Then she saw him, riding in the center. His robe fell across the rear of his Romani Vanner stallion, and his crown adorned his head. Grégory rode a pony beside him. Tamika laughed at the absurdity of it, a magnificent stallion and little pony side-by-side. "Ye Tai, keep him safe."

The men continued to trot forward. Soon Jonathan was swallowed by distance and hundreds of men following him. She wondered if any soldiers remained behind. At the end of the line came twenty or more wagons filled with supplies, and after that, men drove cattle. She lost count of the number and stopped watching them at all.

He is safe.

Five days! Tamika forced herself to rise from her bed. Her face was moist from perspiration, and she took the cloth next to her bed and wiped it. She didn't tell the doctor that came about the peach pit. That was private and illegal.

Enya helped her dress in a brown skirt with a cream-colored blouse all the while chattering about Tamika's fever. Like a fly in her ear, she heard Enya, but she didn't understand half of what she said. Nor did she have the energy to respond. Once dressed, she moped around the palace, entered the dining room, and sat. Creamed rice with berries made it past her mouth twice before she shoved the bowl away. Now cold, she shivered. The cup of tea brought warmth, and she sipped it.

Finished, she stood and walked toward the main door to go into the garden. The flowers were beautiful, but she found no pleasure in them this fine March day. She stepped away from the garden and followed the path to Jonathan's patio.

I miss him. Where was Émilien? Why hadn't he returned with Mariyam? If he doesn't come soon...I will leave and find them myself.

Jonathan promised to write every day, and he did. She received the brief missive at dinner and had her short note ready to hand the falconer when he came. She never talked about her fever. Instead, she just told him she loved him and to be careful. She included petals of the flower she picked that day and rolled it in the note. Earlier, she returned to the garden and selected a peony to include.

Each night after reading Jonathan's note, she could hear Grégory say there was a price to pay for loving Jonathan. A price *he* would have to pay.

She retired to bed early and sat on the edge thinking about the recurring nightmare she had. It was always the same. She was running from Ose. Jonathan appeared, and she hid behind him. Ose lifted his sword and commanded the Bracelet of the Moon and Stars to kill Jonathan. The end differed. Either a tree swallowed him, or the mountains, or the ocean, and then the time when the earth opened and

Jonathan fell in, yelling until his voice disappeared along with him into the darkness.

Tamika shuddered. She prayed to the god Ye Tai. "Lift my fever. Please don't let me have the nightmare and keep my beloved safe."

When morning came, Tamika couldn't lift her head. She threw off the sheets. Enya hurried to her and began to wipe the perspiration off Tamika's body.

"Don't you worry about getting up." Enya's hand wrung out the towel in a bowl of cool water. "You rest."

Tamika let her head slip back down on the pillow and shut her eyes. Then, the nightmare began once more.

Tamika heard singing. She turned her head aside on the pillow. She knew this song, something about a young man, his love, and a wisteria tree. The person singing sat on the edge of the bed, and the noise of water being wrung out interrupted the song. Tamika opened her eyes.

Enya was there. "My Lady." She wiped the perspiration from Tamika's face.

"Have they found Mariyam yet?"

"No. But his excellency has written. Do you want to see it?"

"Read it to me."

Enya put the cloth down, stood, and retrieved the missive from the table. Then, sitting on the edge of the bed again, she unrolled the small note.

"My Lady, it is written in Gil-Laelian. I can't read this."

Tamika pulled her arm out of the covers and held out her hand for the letter with considerable effort. "We make camp just outside of the city of Wei Yan. Talking with Long Tai tomorrow. I love you."

Tamika smiled. "You must write him back. I always send a single leaf from a flower I pick in the morning." *Should she tell him about her illness?* Tamika hesitated, staring at Enya.

“What is it?” Enya came to the bed and wrung the towel before tapping Tamika’s forehead with it.

“I thought about telling him?”

“Telling him what?”

“About my sickness.”

“You should.”

Tamika pushed her hand away. “No, no, he has so many troubles laid on him from Ose. I will spare him this worry.” Her eyes dropped.

The Cao Zhen

Chapter 30

Jonathan took the lead with Grégory beside him and entered the City of Wei Yan. When he reached the center, tall spikes held the heads of three men. The place where they lost their heads was still stained with their blood.

Jonathan pulled on the reins of Quickflame, and the stallion came to a stop. "My people," he shouted so all those nearby could hear. "I see Lord Shigemoris idea of justice before me. But he is not your emperor. I am Emperor Jonathan." He signaled several men, and they, dismounted taking down the spikes.

"I promise you. I will never ride through your province and demand the innocent be killed. Together, we will defeat Shigemori and bring about prosperity. Take these men and give them an honorable burial."

The people continuously bowed low. Jonathan turned his horse.

"Excellency, Long Tai's shop is there." Grégory pointed toward a building with a sign attached to the wall. An older man stood outside the shop along with a woman. He was almost as tall as Jonathan.

Jonathan dismounted, gave Quickflame to one of his guards, and walked toward the shop with Grégory beside him.

The man and woman bowed. "Excellency," he said. "Welcome to Wei Yan City. Please come in." He motioned to the door.

"Are you Long Tai?"

"Yes."

Jonathan entered the shop along with Grégory, Long Tai, and the woman. Display cases lined the walls and stood in places in the center filled with delicate figurines, vases, and china decorated with flowers or symbols.

"This is my wife, Lin Lim."

"My Lady." Jonathan lifted her hand and kissed the back. Lin Lim giggled and hurried toward the rear of the shop.

"Come, we have prepared tea." Long Tai followed his wife past a set of pocket doors.

Jonathan walked behind. Long Tai wore a robe without any adornment. His single braid had streaks of grey entwined with his black hair. They passed several doors in a hallway and entered a small but clean room with a low table and cushions all around. Here and there were tall pedestals with flower-filled vases. The scent was sweet and spicy.

They came to a stand, and the leader of the Cao Zhen waved his hand to indicate Jonathan should sit on one of the cushions before the table.

"Did you make the pottery in the shop?"

"It is china, and yes, I crafted it."

"Impressive. It is beautiful. When this war is over, I will order a set."

"You honor me, Excellency." Long Tai bowed again. "Shall we?"

Jonathan pulled his sword, knelt, and put the weapon across his legs. Grégory, Périer, and the guard had come along and stood a little off. Long Tai knelt on a cushion across from Jonathan. Lin Lim entered and approached with a tray holding a teapot and cups. She set it down, lifted her dark eyes to Jonathan, and then lowered them. Then, pouring the tea, she left.

After taking a sip, Long Tai set the cup down, folded his hands in his lap, and said. "You have come to ask for our help in the coming war."

Jonathan put his cup down as well. "Indeed."

"The people of Cao Zhen have always honored the emperor of the Shea-Talonian people. We trade goods with your people, we obey your laws, but we don't fight in your wars."

"This war is different."

"How?"

"Lord Shigemori has committed treason and declared himself emperor. He is a dangerous man and will make a dangerous emperor, as you must realize based on the heads of many we have seen in Cao Zhen. Including those outside your door. I believe he won't allow your people to remain isolated and governed by their own leader. Governed by you."

"But you will."

"I have no reason to change an age-old agreement your people made with Emperor Matsui I." Jonathan watched Long Tai's expression. His eyebrows drew together for a moment.

"Yet, you have changed many things."

"For the better, I hope."

"We appreciate the new tax laws."

"A benefit Shigemori will take away."

"Yet, Shigemori has the Bracelet of the Moon and Stars, and you don't."

"He stole the bracelet by murdering his wife's family."

"We have heard that as well." Long Tai unfolded his hands and let his fingers stretch along his legs.

"Then you realize that murder doesn't make you emperor."

"There have been many emperors that rose to power through

murder."

"Perhaps, but if given a choice, do you want to be ruled by one?"

Long Tai sipped his tea and then lifted the teapot to pour more. He offered it to Jonathan, but he shook his head and put his hand over the cup. After filling his cup, Long Tai set the pot down and put his hands in his lap once more.

"Shigemori claims you have kidnapped his wife."

"He dug a pit in the forest next to his property and threw her in. I freed her."

"Where is she now?"

"My personal guard keeps her safe at Katatsune Palace."

"He claims you have relations with her."

Jonathan frowned. "Shigemori claims many things."

Long Tai drummed the tip of his fingers together before lifting his tea and taking a long swallow. "I like you." He set the cup down.

Jonathan smiled and nodded.

"When Shigemori rode through our town, beheading our men and proclaiming himself emperor, he showed off the bracelet. I invited him to tea, as I have you. While he talked of you, I examined the bracelet he wore on his upper arm. I've read much about it. The yellow stones set for eyes in the dragon were dull. But, in every account, it is said that they glow amber when the emperor wears the bracelet." Long Tai shut his eyes for a moment. Jonathan waited.

"In all the many years we have lived under the rule of the Shea-Talonian emperor, we have never been so disgraced as when Lord Shigemori passed through our lands. So, many have risen and traveled to speak to me. You have our pledge, Jonathan. There is already an army of 40,000 men waiting for your orders."

"That is good news, Long Tai." Jonathan smiled.

"A toast." Long Tai clapped his hands.

This time his wife returned from another room with a bottle and two glasses with painted vines along their pristine porcelain. She poured a dark substance into the glasses.

Long Tai lifted his glass. “May we win this war and bring peace to the people.” Then he drank.

Jonathan coughed after swallowing the strong liquor.

“Now, it is time for me to take you to our army.” Long Tai stood, and Jonathan followed.

That night when Jonathan entered his tent, he sat in a chair before the small circular table. Exhaustion stretched along every muscle of his body. The review of the soldiers went well. He found them disciplined and ready for battle. The Cao Zhen people supplied him with additional wagons and food, as well as cattle. In addition, he was instructed to stop at every village along the river for fresh fish.

His falconer entered. Jonathan waved him closer, and the man handed him the missive from Tamika.

He yanked his boots off and his socks, extending his toes, then opened the letter. A red tulip petal fell on the table. He ignored it as he read.

She had written in the Shea-Talonian symbols. ‘My love, I picked the tulip today. Tamika.’

He frowned, re-read the note while lifting the petal to his nose. There was something off about the letter. The symbols were written with the same flowery script that Tamika used, but the lines wobbled. The note was shorter, too, with less information about her day.

He stood and went to the tent flap. “Bring me, Périer.”

While waiting, Jonathan shed his clothes and put on his nightdress.

“Excellency.”

Jonathan turned to find Périer inside the tent flap. “I’ve received a note from Lady Shigemori. Something is wrong. Send a hundred men back to check and have them send word to me. Also, send birds to my falconer Henri and have him contact me about Tamika’s condition.”

Once Périer was gone, Jonathan laid down and stared at the tent ceiling. Images of Tamika being held hostage by Shigemori floated before his eyes.

Incense burned somewhere in her room and woke Tamika. She felt much better, but days with no food left her weak and hungry. Then, a groan and rustling noise made her turn her head to look. Mariyam stood up from a chair and made her way toward her.

She smiled. "You have come."

"Yes, child." Mariyam sat on the edge of the bed and took her hand. "The pit caused an infection. You almost died."

"How long has it been?"

"I arrived four days ago and took it out right away. Unfortunately, your fever took longer to mend. I'm afraid I can't give you another pit for at least six months."

"No need to ever do that again."

"Oh?"

Tamika couldn't help the smile that caused her dry lips to crack.

"You are in love with the emperor, just as I saw in my cards."

"Yes, but I also fear."

Mariyam patted her hand. "Do not trouble your heart. You must continue to rest, for the danger to your health is still a concern. But for now, you must eat, then you can tell me all about your love."

The next day, Tamika sat across from Mariyam at the small table in her room.

"I'm glad you can eat," Mariyam said, indicating their breakfast dishes.

"I'm eating enough for three people. I will have to slow that down, or I will look like the Cao Zhen's god, Buddha."

Mariyam laughed. "I can't imagine that."

Enya slipped in and took their breakfast dishes.

"Come, let us walk in the beautiful garden." Mariyam took Tamika's arm.

Neither spoke until they reached the solitude of the gardens. The magnolias were blooming, and Tamika stopped to smell the heady scent. She picked several for her room.

"It is time for us to leave."

Mariyam accepted one of the flowers Tamika gave her. They found a bench and sat.

"Don't go just yet," Tamika said.

"You are well, child, and I must return to my people."

"Then take me with you."

Mariyam's face took on a frown that made the wrinkles on her forehead double. "Why would you wish it when you have the love of our emperor?"

"I must leave him." A tear touched Tamika's cheek.

"What?" Mariyam took her hand. "Why would you do that after telling me how wonderful he is?"

"I am Ose's wife. I wish I weren't, but I am. I will bring shame to Jonathan. The people will never accept me. I will be a constant reminder for everyone that Jonathan stole me from Ose."

"No, child, I don't think that is true. His star chart is a clear indication that the two of you are meant to be together."

"But it is, Mariyam, it is. I am a curse, and I must be removed before I tarnish the throne and all the good Jonathan is trying to achieve." Grégory's words rang in her mind. She'd thought of little else on the days her fever permitted any thought. *Jonathan would pay a heavy price for loving her, and she loved him too much to allow that to happen. She'd sacrifice herself for him.*

Traveling

Chapter 31

Jonathan stood on the shores of the Du Zhi river that flowed west, cutting a wide swath through the land. When he peered across the waters, he could just make out the bluffs beyond. There wasn't a bridge. Instead, long barges gave passage to the other side. And there were only two. It would take them days, maybe a month, to ferry so many men, cattle, and wagons.

The 40,000 Cao Zhen army had tripled the size of his own. His plan was to travel to all the forts in Shea-Talon, meet with many local people, and continue to spread the word that Shigemori was a traitor and had no legal right to the bracelet or the throne. All the while, Jonathan had doubts about the bracelet. *Could it really do all that folklore claimed?*

Chef de Brigade Tian Xia of the Cao Zhen army approached and bowed deeply. His uniform was like the Shea-Talonians, but he had a dog-like creature on a blue and brown background instead of a red dragon.

"Chef de Brigade." Jonathan nodded. He spoke Shea-Talonian.

"Excellency, the men are building more barges per your order and have prepared the animals and wagons for transport."

"Very good. Begin the conveyance."

Tian Xia bowed once more and left. Jonathan watched as the first barge was loaded with approximately one hundred, and the other held a wagon along with the animals and men.

Yet another Cao Zhen *chef de brigade* approached and bowed. "Excellency, we have received word that many bargemen within thirty leagues are on their way to help."

"That is good news indeed, Wan Qing."

Once more, Jonathan was alone when one of his falconers came. He was a man of few words. Bowing, he handed Jonathan the missive.

Opening it, he read:

My love.

I have been ill, but Mariyam has come.

My prayers are always with you.

He turned it over to keep reading:

Forgive that Enya wrote instead at my bequest.

Tamika.

It held a magnolia petal.

Jonathan frowned. *Enya wrote it. Why?*

Tamika held out the small missive already rolled in the container. "Give this to the falconer tomorrow."

Enya took it. "I should come with you. You will have need of me."

Tamika shook her head. "No, it would look odd for a member of the Romani to have a servant. Not even Maryam has one." She was dressed in the clothing of the Romani, and Maryam had given her a black wig with enormous curls, some of which fell into her eyes.

Tamika brushed them away. "After tomorrow, go to your family. Then, when this is over, I'll send for you."

"You will be empress."

"Maybe." Tamika turned her head to glance toward the window. Dusk had fallen. She loved to walk in the garden this time of night when the dim light changed the hues of everything.

"You shouldn't go. What will his excellency think?"

"I must leave. I will bring him shame." Her heart was heavy, and she thought it might break. "The Romani will keep me safe from Ose. He'll never guess where I am."

"But their camp is so close to your home."

"No longer, they have moved further east to avoid the coming war." She smiled and pulled Enya to her. "I will miss you."

Enya rubbed her hands along Tamika's back. "I love you too."

Mariyam interrupted them. "We must go."

Tamika pulled away from Enya and smiled at her before turning toward the older woman. As they walked along the hall, her thoughts worried her. Guards stood at the entrance to the palace, and she averted her eyes from them.

She stumbled. Her shoes were a little too big. Kourken jumped from the wagon. He grabbed her arm to keep her steady. The Romani wagon was as close to the palace doors as he could get it.

They hurried toward the back of the wagon. She climbed up the three steps leading to the door of the decorated coach and entered. Then, before shutting the door, she watched as Kourken lift the steps that collapsed in on themselves, folded them, and latched them to the underbelly of the wagon.

"I will ride with Kourken. If you need us, just knock on the wall behind the driver seat." Maryam turned then and walked with Kourken to the front.

Tamika shut the door and then hurried toward the bed to sit down so she wouldn't fall as the horses moved them forward.

She could hear Maryam and Kouken talking. Then the wagon lurched forward, taking them along the road toward the bottom of the bluff. She felt every bump, every movement. Her heart thudded within her chest. Then they stopped. Tamika hurried toward the wall separating her from the driver's seat, pressed her ear against the wood, and listened.

"Good day, Madam. We must inspect the inside of the wagon," One of the guards said.

"Why would you want to look at the possessions of an old woman?" Maryam asked.

"Orders." The soldier answered.

"If you don't mind, I will wait here, and Kourken will open the door for you."

"No need, my men will make quick work of it."

Tamika jumped away. *I must hide.*

The wagon was filled with oddities. Books, glass containers, the bed she'd been sitting on. A wardrobe. *A wardrobe.* She could hide in...*that is the first place they'd look.*

Tamika grabbed all the clothes in the closet, dumped them in a heap on the floor, and...she heard men struggling with the steps Kourken had tied. Then, just before she laid down, she threw some of the clothes around to make it appear no one cared about them. Once done, she knelt, curled her body on the floor, and covered herself with Maryam's clothes.

The door opened. Boots stomped into the room. Tamika put her hand over her mouth to still any noise she might make.

One soldier kicked a skirt next to Tamika's head. "What a mess."

She could see him through a gap in the clothes.

"Nothing here," another man said.

Both men left. The door shut. Tamika didn't move, not until the wagon lurched forward once more.

Strategy

Chapter 32

Claude Coulomb mopped the basement floor of Furuya Jun Prison along with twenty-three other men. The smell of vinegar burned his nose, and he rubbed the tip. He glanced up. Five guards huddled together at the opposite end. He continued to mop, moving from one side to the next while making his way slowly toward the long hall that led to the room with the trap door.

Shouts made him jump. He glanced toward the others. The guards were beating someone with their clubs. He couldn't tell who since all the other men had gathered close and blocked his vision. All he could see were several clubs rising over all those heads and coming down fast. Then, several of the prisoners started shoving the guards. Somehow, many of them were able to grab the clubs and the guards were on the defensive.

Claude left his mop against the wall with the bucket beside it. Then he ran. Glancing back, the circle around the guards had increased and from what he could tell, the beatings continued. The echo of his prison slippers dulled as soon as he entered the back hall. At the end, he looked back. Good! He hadn't been missed.

He continued to run all the way to the western door, opened it, and struggled to lift the lid of the trap door. It'd been months since his imprisonment. By his calculation, it was now the end of April. All this time, his only food had been gruel. His muscles ached from the effort to open the door.

At last, he managed it. He climbed down the ladder and made sure to close the trap door as well. He wasn't going back.

The moment the door was shut, the little light there had been, vanished. He didn't have any means to make light and climbed down with care. He turned and stumbled over something, then fell. "*Putain de merde!*"

Now his knees and palms burned. He reached for whatever it was and felt material and buttons. His burned jacket. He pulled it on over his prison garb.

Standing, he reached forward until he could feel the smooth tile wall, then he inched along and found the hall of cells. Time hadn't improved the smell. As he walked, he counted the doors on one side. Four, five, the wall connected with another facing north. Inching, inching, there. Finally, the rounded top of the air vent told him he was right where he wanted to be. He knelt. The rusted iron gate had been left open.

Something scurried past him. Then another, he grabbed it. The creature screeched. It had a long tail and… "Ouch." The rat bit him. He threw it hard against the wall and smiled at the thud.

The air vent must be full of them, not a happy prospect. He continued on his hands and knees. Rats darted past him, and a few climbed on him. He killed as many as he could. *Disgusting creatures.*

As he crept, light began to filter through the open vent at the other end. That gate was off its hinges too. *Have I been missed yet? I need time, time, and good fortune to distance myself from this place.* He'd thought about this escape for a long time. He had friends in Aya.

Significantly few soldiers were ever in town. At least that was the case before he was locked up.

At last, he emerged from the vent and stood. He stretched and looked around at the green landscape. Moss covered most of the trees except for the southern side. Grass and weeds vied for position, wildflowers poked delicate blooms of yellow and orange toward the sun. The smell of earth and green things filled his nose. Claude shut his eyes. *Heaven!*

A noise made him turn. Out of the forest walked a dozen Shea-Talonian soldiers dressed in the garb that Ose had selected. Copper scale armor breastplates and helmets with a neck guard.

"Emperor Shigemori wants you to bring him his wife," one of them said.

"You've been waiting here on the off chance I'd escape?"

"We are here to watch the activity on this road." He pointed toward a group of trees and just beyond the road leading away from the prison toward Aya was visible. "If any of our men are captured, we rescue them."

Claude shook his head. "How do you know he wants me to bring his wife?"

"He gave that order should you escape."

"I don't think I'll be admitted to the palace grounds."

"She isn't there."

"Where then?" Claude asked.

"She's with the healers."

"The Romani?" Claude scratched his forehead. "If she's not under guard at the palace and is with the Romani, why didn't you grab her?"

"We are watching the road."

This conversation made no sense to Claude. "I'm not interested."

All three men pulled their swords. "Then you will die."

Claude backed up. “Wait, wait, wait. I’ll do it, but I need a few things first.”

The soldiers glared at him.

“Clothes for one and a horse. I’m starving, so good food to gain my strength back.”

The month of May sprang upon Jonathan like a cat in hiding. He wanted nothing more than to return to the palace, eat a good meal and make love to Tamika.

It had taken more than two weeks to cross the river. A necessary delay but one that made Jonathan anxious. Now they had left the banks of the river to head southwest, stopping at one fort after the other until they’d reached the Province of Posong, Tamika’s homeland and Shigemoris as well. He believed it would be there where Shigemori would encamp. He must know the area better than the rest.

“Riders!” A man shouted.

Jonathan looked around until he saw them. He’d sent out three men to scan the landscape for danger. They were only a few days away from a fort.

One of the men jumped from his horse and bowed. “Excellency, men are marching on Fort Miki.”

“How many?” They’d traveled by Fort Miki, located in the Province of Guihar on the other side of the river Du Zhi. Shigemori was behind him. He needed to turn around.

“Two or three thousand.” Jonathan studied the man, and then he said to a different soldier. “Bring me Périer with Tian Xia.

While they waited, he said, “How soon will they arrive at the fort?”

“A few hours.”

Jonathan began to pace. Shigemori had proven to be slyer than he'd given him credit for. When Périer arrived with Tian Xia on his heels, Jonathan gave them the news.

"Suggestions?" He gazed at the two.

"We must send men to intercept," Périer said.

"Impossible, we are too far. But men are stationed close. We should send a falcon to Castle Zi Yun." Tian Xia added.

"See that it it done, Périer." Jonathan made his way back to the tent and called a meeting. They must prepare. After months of traveling, they'd only seen small engagements, a few raids, nothing that did much damage. *Now, would this be war at last? How close was Shigemori to the palace? And...to Tamika?*

Claude Coulomb finished eating the fish the men had prepared. "How do you propose I gain access to the Romani and steal the lady? It's not as if I can dance into their camp."

"There will be no dancing."

"Then what?" Several choice curse words came to mind, but Claude held his tongue.

"We will spy on the Romani. Then in the darkness, you will enter the camp and take her."

"All for free!"

"I received a note from the true emperor. He will pay you when you bring her to his camp."

Claude smiled. *Money!* "Where's the camp?"

"It is several days ride. We will travel through the forest."

Doi and Umeda brought the horses. Claude stood along with Himi. They mounted and rode off leaving the remainder of the men behind.

Kidnap

Chapter 33

Jonathan took the message his falconer brought.

Out of the mountains in two weeks.

Papa.

His father was with the Gil-Laelian troops. Another reason to head back. Sitting, he prepared to eat his breakfast of eggs, bacon, and toast. He had ordered that whatever he ate, his men should eat as well. That had resulted in eggs and bacon once a week. The rest of the time it was gruel in the mornings. He didn't mind. Honey made oatmeal sweet.

When he left his tent, the men were taking all the others down and started on his. He joined Wan Qing, Périer, and Grégory by the horses. Once they were again across the river, the news of victory at Fort Miki had encouraged everyone.

"Any problems?"

"We are running low on water," Wan Qing said.

"We are by a river," Jonathan said.

"It is not suitable to drink that water."

"Several of the men have started to fight among themselves." Périer pointed toward camp.

"Shigemori has stolen all the Emperor's Wine in every town he came to. As a result, we are losing money," Grégory said.

"How serious is this loss?"

"It is minor at the moment, but if it continues–."

"We may run out of funds." Jonathan frowned.

"Yes."

Before Jonathan could respond further, the falconer brought him a second message. "Pardon."

He opened the message, read it, and then read it aloud so others could hear. "Shigemori is massing his troops outside Aya."

Tamika, Shigemori thinks she is unguarded.

Jonathan continued. "We head north along the banks of Quan Kun. Périer, select a thousand men to ride ahead and lead them back to the palace. The rest of us will come as one from the east once we reach Gosanke. I will send word." He signaled the falconer who opened his pouch to produce paper, ink, and quill.

"Wan Qing, speed is of the essence. We will split into groups of four. The wagons and animals will take the longest. Therefore, we must leave them behind and forage for food along the way. Once in Gosanke, we will rejoin just outside of Aya on the east side."

"As you say." Wan Qing nodded.

"Périer, bring me Captain's Toneyo, Moïse and André."

"As you wish." Périer bowed.

Jonathan turned and wrote a quick note to give to the falconer. "Send this to the palace."

Within the hour, all the men were ready, and their journey back to Aya began.

Five days later, Claude Coulomb crouched against the forest floor. Himi was next to him, and the other two lay behind their trees just outside the meadow where the Romani were camped. Several enormous black iron pots were over the same number of fires. Women stirred the contents and the smell…Claude's stomach rumbled. He'd eaten nothing but fish, and now, he'd welcome a bowl of beef stew.

Children were playing with sticks, pretending to fight each other when…a stick came flying and struck the tree just above Claude's head. He crouched lower and shimmied back. A child ran toward the tree. Himi pulled out a knife. Claude set his hand over the Shea-Talonian's. The little boy grabbed the stick and ran back.

Women walked about the camp and gossiped with each other. Several men were adjusting the strings on their musical instruments. Even more, tended the horses that were behind a makeshift corral. Half a dozen had set up a target attached to a tree and were practicing archery.

Try as he might, Claude didn't see any sign of Tamika. "You sure this is the right Romani camp?" He whispered to Himi.

The man glanced his way and then looked back without answering him. Himi did this a lot, and Claude's patience with him was weakening. He'd like nothing more than to beat the man senseless. But then, he saw her. She wore Romani clothing, but her long straight black hair gave her away. If she had curls, he might have never known.

Lady Shigemori walked with grace, each step a gentle stride. Most of the Romani women tended to bounce a little as they moved.

"There she is," Claude whispered. "I hope you don't intend to charge in and grab her."

"I won't charge anywhere."

Claude's fist began to hurt. He'd held it tight for several minutes now.

"We wait until dark. Learn where she sleeps. Then Doi and I will kill the watch while Umeda frees the horses. After that, you will enter the place where she sleeps and get her."

Claude awoke. His side hurt where Himi had poked him. He sat up before remembering where he was and almost cursed Himi.

"There are more guards than I had anticipated. We will need your help."

Claude rubbed his eyes, turned to look, and said, "Where is she?"

"In the third wagon from us. The one that has three men guarding it. There are five others posted around the camp." Himi pointed to the wagon and then the guards.

"How am I to kill them, and which ones?"

Himi handed him a knife. "Doi will go with you. You'll both take care of the guards before her wagon. Umeda and I will handle the other five and bring the horses."

Claude took the knife and then crawled deeper into the forest. He'd escape now if it hadn't been for the promise of money. Instead, he stood, looked at Doi, and together they ran from tree to tree. Doi's knife caught the light of the moon, Claude hid his knife. No need to alert the men before their necks were sliced open.

They left the forest at the same time. Coming up from behind the men. Claude reached around, grabbed the guard's mouth, pulled back, and slid his knife across the man's neck. Blood squirted out, and the man fell dead as he wiped off the blade and tucked it away. While Doi took care of both the second and third guard, Claude climbed the three steps to the wagon's door and entered.

For a moment, he stood inside the wagon, trying to adjust his sight to the darkness. Everything was shadow. Then, a movement. Lady Shigemori sat up. He rushed her before she could scream and yanked her from the bed. Using the hilt of his knife, he hit her on the top of the head, and she slumped forward.

Claude lifted her over his shoulder and left the wagon. Himi and Doi were already on their horses.

"Give her to me," Himi said.

Claude lifted the woman to Himi.

"What, you fool. This isn't the lady. Go back and get her." Himi shoved the unconscious girl from him, and she fell.

Claude watched and realized she was a child. He grunted, turned, and climbed the steps to the wagon's door again.

Tamika waited next to the door, iron skillet at the ready. She knew the soldier was coming since she heard the conversation. The door opened, and she swung the skillet as hard as she could with both hands into the face of the man. A dull thud. His breath escaped, and he stumbled backward.

She recognized a Romani man speak. "Get off your horses."

Tamika stepped over the man and stood in the doorway. "You'd better do what they say, Himi."

Himi pulled back his shoulders. "We have come to return you to your husband."

"He isn't my husband anymore. I divorced him."

Romani Justice

Chapter 34

Jonathan was saddle sore and weary. They'd ridden hard for nine days and now found himself in the Province of Yuuki and a day's ride from Fort Dayu with his men. He dismounted and stomped his legs to bring back the circulation. He smelled of horse sweat and his own overwhelming stink. The scent even left a nasty taste on his tongue. Whiskers darkened his face. He needed a bath and shave. He took the water skin from a man and drank deep to quench his constant thirst.

At noon when they stopped to eat, they would each exchange horses to assure their beasts wouldn't perish from the near-constant gallop that drove them to cover the distance. An hour, then a walk for half and resume the gallop again. Jonathan would like to exchange himself, but since that was impossible, he needed to keep going.

Today, Jonathan was too exhausted to wonder how Tamika was or if he'd left enough men behind. The minutes stretched long while he waited for his tent. They'd eaten the last of their food supplies at breakfast. He was too tired to eat anyway. His men needed the rest.

They'd stay for a day or two. Some would hunt for food, and some would travel to the nearest town to buy food, exchanging it all with a promissory note. He was out of money.

As soon as his tent was ready, he entered. While several men brought in his fur pelt, he considered the wisdom of charging toward Aya. They'd be worthless in battle with Shigemori if he and his men weren't well rested and well feed. Perhaps he should have them rest for a week. The Great *Créateur* knew they needed it.

The men left his tent. Jonathan stripped off his clothes and fell on his fur pelt wearing only his loincloth.

In the morning, Jonathan managed a quick sponge bath by the river, joining numerous men there. When finished, he joined several others to eat breakfast with the new supplies. Afterward, he joined Captain André to inspect the horses.

"We need new horses." André ran a hand along the animal's knee before him and lifted his leg to inspect the hooves. "I've had to order over a hundred put down."

Jonathan frowned. He loved his horses. War destroyed so much of what he treasured.

"Rider!"

The man jumped from his saddle and approached. He had come from Fort Dayu. "Excellency." He bowed and handed him the note.

Jonathan pulled it from the small container, and unrolled it.

Lady Shigemori is missing. We think she left
with the Romani. What would you have us do?

Jonathan shut his eyes and crumpled the note. *Tamika!*

Claude awoke to a massive headache. He was tied to a tree. Rain pelted his body. Smoke battled the rain, swirling from a fire close by and leaving a pungent scent. Several Romani men hunkered down in the shower with bows across their legs. Himi and Doi were tied to the trees beside his, but where was Umeda?

"Get me out of this downpour."

The Romani looked at him then but didn't trouble getting up.

"You have no voice here, traitor."

"For the love of the Créateur, get me something to ward off the rain." His hair was drenched, droplets ran down his face and into his eyes. This was torture.

"What have you to do with the Créateur? You are nothing in His eyes." The Romani man stood and approached. "Your judgment will be swift, but your death will take a long time."

The man left, leaving Claude to ponder the meaning of his words.

The rain stopped just before dawn. Claude shivered in the early morning darkness. The prison would have been better than this. At least there, he'd be dry, and he'd have a bed.

"What's for breakfast," he yelled.

The Romani still sat together around what had been a fire and now was smoldering wood.

"Nothing for you, traitor," the same man said.

"Have a heart, I'm starving."

"Did you have a heart when you killed our brother?"

Claude looked over at Himi, who was staring at him. "Where's Umeda? Did he get away? Will he bring help?"

"He's dead. Now shut up before the men decide to kill us all."

The activity in camp picked up when the sun rose. Areas were cleared, and fires started. Several women began to cook over iron skillets. The smell of bacon made Claude's mouth water.

The Ramoni guards had left, replaced by three other men.

"Can I get some of that bacon," Claude said.

The three men looked at him.

"Some water then?"

"You're not wet enough?" One of them said.

"To drink, you piece of…" he thought better of his words and stopped speaking.

While Claude watched the Romani stand in line with plates and cups in hand, he realized that a man could be tortured without being strapped to a gruesome device. Every one of them received bacon, cheese, and bread. Their cups steamed with whatever liquid they drank.

His stomach protested. "Come on, give me something."

The three guards looked at him. Then one of them picked up his cup and approached. Claude couldn't wait to taste the drink. But the guard stood before him, drinking.

"What is it?" He asked.

"Tea." When the man finished, he picked up a small rock and tossed it in the air. "One more word from you, and the three of us will play a game of toss the rock. You'll be the target."

"Come on, have mercy."

The man turned toward his companions, and they all picked up several rocks. Then, taking aim, they threw them. Claude was hit in the chest, the arms, and his face. The last drew blood that ran down his cheek.

"Stop, stop, I promise to be quiet."

Lady Shigemori came soon afterward accompanied by a man and young girl. The child's arm was in a sling. They stopped before the three of them, and the man stepped toward Himi.

"You pushed this girl off your horse."

Claude wasn't surprised when Himi didn't answer.

"You broke her arm. Now we will break yours."

The three guards approached, untied Himi, and made him stand between them. Then tied him to the tree again except for his right arm. The men moved to Himi's side and blocked Claude's vision. A moment later, Himi screamed. The men left him, and Claude saw the horrible angle at which his arm dangled, useless from his body.

The men came to Claude next. "No, no, I didn't throw her."

"Shut up." They untied Claude as well. He'd been sitting, now he pushed one man who stumbled backward. The others shoved him against the tree and tied him to it while he stood.

"I didn't hurt her, I didn't–."

"Shut up," the same man said and slugged Claude in the gut. He'd have doubled over if he weren't tied so well. After they did the same with Doi, they left.

Hours slipped along at the pace of a tortoise. From time to time, he glanced at Himi. He didn't like the man, but he wouldn't wish his fate on anyone. Well, except for Ose, he wouldn't mind seeing him tortured.

Another meal came and went. Claude's stomach no longer growled. Now it cramped with hunger. Their position in the trees was a little to the side of the meadow. His neck hurt from holding up his head and from turning it at an angle to watch the Romani. He needed to sleep.

Seven men approached from the campsite. They had bows at the ready and quivers slung behind their backs. They took a stance before the three of them and pulled an arrow, notching it.

"What are you doing?" *Great Créateur, spare me!*

"Target practice," one of them said.

The twang of the bow and whistle of the arrow as it flew was followed by the thwack noise the tree made when the arrow slammed into it next to his ear. Three more times and Claude screamed at the men. "Stop!"

"Final shot," the man said. "Make it count."

Seven men, the three of them. Two arrows hit Claude through his arms, pinning them to the tree. Claude yelped like a feral dog. Himi and Doi took the arrows without a sound. The Romani turned and left.

Claude's vision blurred. Not far from him, several men were skinning a deer. The women came to get the meat and exchanged greetings with the men. One man stood, pulled a woman close, and kissed her. She laughed as she left, her hips swaying.

Claude had imagined having a wife in his grand house once he left Shea-Talon with all his money. Now that life had slipped from his grasp. He glanced at Doi. Like him, his arms were held against the tree with two arrows. Himi, on his left, was slumped forward.

The group's laughter followed by music and dancing once supper was over brought tears to Claude's eyes. He wanted to belong. He wanted to be part of the Romani instead of a traitor, despised by all. He shut his eyes and let his head fall forward. He pushed with his legs against the tree to remain standing, but no matter how hard he tried to ease his pain, the arrows in his arms tore at his flesh.

A hand on his forehead pushed his head back. The sudden movement woke Claude and brought back the throbbing pain.

A Romani man stood before him. "Target practice." He smiled.

"No, no, it's dark."

"All the more reason, we need our skills sharp in case an enemy tries to kidnap the Lady Shigemori." He turned and joined the others. Eight this time.

The men readied their bows. Claude winced at the first two arrows, slipping past his face. The third one sliced into his right leg and the fourth into the left. Himi and Doi were hit too. This time, it was Doi who received the most arrows and began to scream.

Sunlight spread between the trees and bathed the meadow. The Romani went about their daily life with friendly banter. Claude's vision blurred. Once again, he couldn't sleep for the pain. A glance in either direction told him that both Himi and Doi were dead. The smell coming from them confirmed it.

He remembered his youth. His pride when he learned he'd been accepted to the army. Then the post in Shea-Talon. *When had he become disillusioned?*

Flies were buzzing around him. Some landing on his body. He needed to kill them. He needed–. Men approached, bows at the ready, arrows notched. The same men stood before him.

"You're stubborn," the same Romani said.

He didn't smile. "What is your name?" Claude waited.

"Your friends are dead, but here you are, still breathing."

"Your name?"

"You have no need of my name. You and your friends have defiled our campsite. We must move. But I want you to know. You and your friends will receive no burial, no honor. We will leave you for the crows." He turned then saying. "Target practice."

Claude no longer flinched with the practice arrows that hit his tree. "Forgive me, my *Créateur*."

Claude Coulomb slumped forward, an arrow through his heart. Kourken returned to him and pulled all the arrows from his body. Two others did the same with the Shea-Talonians. Romani justice was hard and final.

Dragon

Chapter 35

July promised to be hot with little rain. Jonathan eased forward on his stallion and lifted his spyglass. Before him was a vast prairie. Tall grass spread over small hills and low valleys. His own flag of a twisting red and green dragon on a blue background flew on the western side where his men camped. Far in the distance was the Gil-Laelian flag of a tree with three falcons and three stars. He could just make out the top of a few tents in the distance.

"Father…" it was a whisper, a breath on his tongue, a prayer. "Don't use the Carmelidrium Scepter." He knew the tale, having heard it his entire life. How his grandfather, King Llewelyn, rode forth on the battlefield with the scepter to kill Renwyk, Lord of the Symberveen, by the power of God. Both had died when the scepter issued forth lightning.

They would win the war the old-fashioned way, by their numbers and the strength and will of the fighting men. He rode out onto the valley. Long Tai rode beside him. Their armies joined those already there.

When he dismounted, soldiers took his horse. The fresh air of the prairie was replaced by the smoke of a hundred campfires.

"Excellency." Chef de Brigade Périer bowed. "All those who separated have come together. The Gil-Laelian camp is–."

"*Oui*, I saw. What news?"

"We have a map in yonder tent."

Jonathan nodded and removed his leather gloves as he walked. Dusk was upon them. Crickets began to chirp, and a few grasshoppers landed on the tent as they approached.

"Grégory." The little man hurried to keep up and began to cough. Jonathan stopped. "I don't like the sound of that. Find your bed and rest and send for the healer." *I must import the Tandlewood bush.* He reminded himself of the healing plant.

The Tandlewood bush grew in Gil-Lael and had green-purple leaves. When applied to an injury or the sap added to boiling water and drunk, it would heal almost anything.

Grégory stopped and bowed. "*Oui*–" his cough interfered with anything else he might have said.

Jonathan turned back and entered the tent. Within, he found a large table that displayed a map with markers to indicate the position of the armies.

Several Romani turned and bowed.

"Kourken, have you traded in your guitar for a sword?" Jonathan smiled.

"It would seem so."

"How many did you bring?" Jonathan hadn't ever seen more than fifty men in the Romani camp.

"My grandmother sent word to all our people throughout Shea-Talon. We have gathered five thousand men at your command."

"This is good news." Jonathan steadied his hand on Kourken's shoulder. "What of the Lady Shigemori?"

"She is well and prays for you daily."

Out of the corner of his eye, Jonathan noted a short Shea-Talonian soldier in metal armor and helmet. “Who is this?” He didn’t wear the colors of either the Cao Zhen people or of Shigemori.

“We came upon this soldier who wished to travel with us here.” Kourken nodded.

“Remove your helmet so I might–.”

A man entered in a Gil-Laelian uniform. “Highness.” He bowed and handed a missive to Jonathan.

“Excellency,” Périer corrected.

Jonathan took the note. “My father wishes me to come to their camp. Be quick, Périer. I didn’t see any sign of Shigemori when I arrived though the map shows him here.”

Périer lifted the pointer stick and used it as he spoke. “Beyond our camp, there are a series of hills. After this one, we arrive at a low valley many leagues wide. Here, just this side of the Quan Kun River is the enemy’s camp.”

“They chose a valley. I’d think Shigemori would be smarter than that.” He removed his jacket and threw it over a chair.

Périer continued, “They are spread as far south as the Province of Cao Zhen and north to the edge of Matsunaga Province.”

Matsunaga, where they were now, was directly east of Gosanke Province, where the palace was located. Matsunaga was farmland. Only one major city served the people here. And it was far to the west of their location.

“How many?”

“They outnumber us at seventy thousand strong.”

Jonathan wiped his brow with a kerchief. The heat of the day would soon cool, and he looked forward to that small comfort.

“Long Tai, take your men and make camp south of here so we surround Shigemori except for the eastern side where the river will do our bidding and keep him from retreat. My men and I will be here on the west, and my father with Gil-Lael are to the north. We ride forth to do battle tomorrow morning. You will hear our battle horn proclaiming the advance with a series of three long blasts."

He glanced around the tent and frowned. The short Shea-Talonian had vanished. Leaving his jacket, Jonathan left to ride to the Gil-Laelian campsite.

Night concealed them as they rode toward the Gil-Laelian camp. Jonathan took only a few men with him to confer with his father, including Périer.

The horn of Gil-Lael announced them. It was deeper than the Shea-Talonian horn in sounded with a profound resonance. Jonathan hadn't realized how much he missed the sound. As a child, he and his brothers had often tried to hide from trained scouts. When found, the men blew the horn. His memories made him smile.

They entered the encampment and eased their horses into a trot. When the soldiers saw him, they began to cheer. It took time to reach the center of camp and the large, oversized tent that was his father's. Jonathan jumped from his horse to find his mother nearby.

"Oh, my son. It is good to see you."

"You are here as well, Mama." He embraced her. The sheer warmth of her body and the familiar smell of her perfume sent a wave of comfort over him. He kissed her cheek.

"Father." He clasped hands with Healden, and the two embraced.

"Son, let us take refreshment together."

They entered the tent. A small table held wine and goblets. His stomach rumbled. Almost at the same time, several soldiers brought in their meal. Venison, with wild asparagus and dandelion buds along with flatbread.

Jonathan began to eat.

"You've lost weight," Michelle said.

He nodded. "And you look as beautiful as I remember." He

glanced at his father and decided not to point out that his hair had gone completely gray.

When their meal ended, they each remained at the table sipping Gil-Laelian red wine.

"When will you attack?" Healden ran a finger along the wood grain in the table.

"In the morning."

His father nodded. A frown creased his brow.

"I know you brought the Treasures of Carmelidrium. I must implore you, don't use the scepter." Just the thought of it twisted Jonathan's gut.

Healden smiled. "I won't use the scepter unless there is no other choice."

Michelle reached across the table and took Jonathan's hand. "He won't use the scepter. But I will play the flute, and you must wield the sword and wear the ring."

Jonathan knew the sword would be invincible when his mother played the flute. And, the ring would bring him wisdom. He didn't know how wisdom would help in a battle, but he wouldn't argue the point.

"What can you tell us of this man, Shigemori?"

Jonathan pulled his hand away from his mother's grasp and turned to his father. "He is a nobleman who has murdered to reach his current position. There is a legend here of a bracelet, and he has it. The people believe that possessing this token gives him legitimacy in his claim to be emperor. It used to belong to Warwyk. Shigemori married into the family that kept it hidden and safe."

"What sort of legend?" Michelle asked.

"The sort that gives one nightmares."

Shigemori gathered his army before him. Since there wasn't a tent large enough to hold so many, they met outside. Stars shone down on them along with the moon. Small fires dotted the landscape and stretched as far as the eye could see.

"Report your positions." Shigemori sat in an elaborate chair before them, which had been placed on a wide table.

Each man gave the details of their location. Finally, after an hour, one nobleman stepped forward. He dropped to his knees before Shigemori and kissed the ground. "Excellency, if I may?"

"Go on, Yujiro." Shigemori waved his hand.

The nobleman sat back on his legs. "The enemy has arrived. More than we anticipated, and yet you haven't given us your strategy."

"Not to fear." Ose stood and began to march along the top of the table, which wasn't long. "I have the Bracelet of the Moon and Stars."

"But, if it doesn't work, what shall we do?" Yujiro asked.

"I claim the throne by right of marriage to Warwyk's granddaughter and by the possession of the bracelet. Therefore, whatever I command will come to pass."

"And yet, Jonathan has arrived and sits in his camp. You have cursed him three times, and no ill has come his way." Having spoken, Natsu stepped forward. He didn't bow or kiss the ground but stood before Ose as a man of equal worth.

"Kneel." Natsu had become too big a problem. "The battle will be short once I set eyes on the usurper. He will die."

Another nobleman stepped forward, sank to his knees before Ose, and kissed the ground. Then, sitting back, he said. "High King Healden has come with the queen. They have the Treasures of Carmelidrium with them, and the queen has her flute."

"I know this, and I assure you when Jonathan comes before me, I will kill him, and then I'll turn my power on the king and queen of that God-forsaken land. The bracelet came to us by the god Ye Tai, not by elves. It is greater. Once they are all dead, I will be emperor of both Shea-Talon and Gil-Lael."

Horse's hooves announced the rider. He jumped down and paid obeyance to Ose. "Excellency, I have ridden hard to bring you this news. Himi and his men have perished along with the Gil-Laelian. They were tortured."

"My wife?"

"The Romani fled, and there is no sign of her."

Anger surged through Ose. He jumped off the table and charged the messenger hitting him and then kicking him. The man curled, covering his head. Ose continued to kick him. Natsu grabbed his arm to prevent him from killing the man.

Ose yanked his arm away, turned, and glared at his former friend. "You have become a problem." Then, pulling his sword, Ose thrust it through Natsu's belly. He gasped, bent forward, and fell to the ground. Ose drew his sword free and smiled.

He turned. "Does anyone else wish to question me?"

In the morning, Jonathan stood alone in his camp between tents sipping strong tea. The blue haze of the mountains kissed the skyline. The sun spread rays of brilliant light, turning the sky from crimson to purple with pink wisps across the horizon as it lifted above tall peaks. This was the day that would mark the beginning of his reign reborn or the end of his life. He must prevail for his people. Ose would be a tyrant.

His thoughts strayed to his love. Somewhere beyond those hills was Tamika. *Keep her safe, my Créateur.*

There was no point in delaying. He turned and walked back to his tent. There he found Périer, along with Moïse and André.

"The men are ready," Périer said.

Jonathan pulled on his gloves and the ring of Carmelidrium over them. Two men put armor breastplates on over his shoulders. He hated the extra weight of it. Half an hour later, they rode out. Three blasts of the horn advertised their advance. Within the hour, they reached the summit of the hills.

Shigemoris camp spread like a plague on the grassland as far as he could see. The wide river licked the shore behind the tents. Jonathan still wondered why Shigemori left himself so vulnerable. The fresh scent of tall grass was replaced by the body odor of thousands of men.

The activity in the enemy camp increased. Men were running, grabbing horses, putting their swords in their sheaths, and saddling their mounts. Jonathan put the spyglass away. He eased his horse forward and began to gallop back and forth before his men.

"Today, we gather to fight an enemy that would destroy all that we believe in. We fight for those we love. We fight for our right to live in peace. We fight for our very lives. May each of you be empowered by our Great Créateur. May He reside in you, a mighty sword, a shield from harm, and a light in the darkness."

Jonathan pulled Quickflame to a halt just in front of his men and looked toward Shigemoris camp. On his right, the Gil-Laelian armies had crested a hill and stood poised. On his left, Long Tai's men did the same.

Kourken joined him. "We are ready."

Beside him was the same Shea-Talonian soldier he'd seen in the tent. Jonathan nodded. Another three blasts from the war horns made him stiffen. He held up his hand to stall the charge and kept it there, turning his stallion around to view Shigemoris camp. A lone rider left the enemy camp as they too lined up before their tents. He pulled the spyglass out. *Did his eyes deceive him?*

Shigemori pulled his horse to a stop midway between the armies and remained in the saddle.

"Jonathan Calimar, I call for single combat! There is no need for our men to die when the argument is between us." Shigemori pulled out his sword. He wished he had eyesight strong enough to see the usurper's face and imagined his fear. A cruel smile pressed his lips over his teeth.

The emperor rode out alone toward Ose before stopping a short distance away. "Are you mad?"

To that, Ose burst out laughing. He couldn't wait to see the usurper die.

Jonathan waited, watching Shigemori double over with his insane mirth.

"So, Shigemori, you have gathered all these men only to challenge me to single combat. Seems a little strange."

"They are here to witness my glory."

Jonathan drew out the great sword of Carmelidrium. "Then, I shall give you a glorious death." Clutching the sword, Jonathan could feel the power of it strengthen his arm. From a distance, he heard several strains from his mother's flute. Quickflame sidestepped.

Behind him, a single rider advanced. He turned to see the small Shea-Talonian soldier. The young man pulled his horse to a stop beside him.

"I gave no order for your company. Return to the others, lest someone kills you."

The man didn't respond but sat his animal across from Jonathan. Then he turned his gaze toward Shigemori.

"I said single combat, and you have brought another! Unfair!" Shigemori shouted.

The young rider pulled off his helmet. Glorious long black hair caught the breeze and flowed past her shoulders toward Jonathan.

"Tamika, no!" *What was she thinking?* "It's not safe! Return to the tent. Please, I beg you."

"I will be fine," she said and turned back to Shigemori.

Jonathan's heartbeat increased, anxiety tightened his muscles. He started to reach for her horse's reins. He'd escort her back himself if need be.

"I command you to come to me, my wife," Shigemori said, his

laughter disappeared along with his smile. He frowned.

Tamika's horse took several steps forward.

She called out. "I have divorced Lord Shigemori! He has told you I am his justification for claiming the crown. I am not! Join our true emperor, Jonathan Calimar, before it's too late!" As she yelled, she set her horse in a trot before Shigemori's men, riding close enough for them to hear her.

Ose's anger burned in his heart. He turned his eyes from Tamika to his men. Most lowered their weapons. They spoke to each other, gazing from Tamika to himself. He turned back to Jonathan, who still held the mighty sword of Carmelidrium.

Tamika turned her horse around and was coming back. *How dare she oppose him.*

Raising his scimitar over his head, he kicked the stallion and charged toward his wife.

Jonathan nudged Quickflame, and his horse shot out toward Shigemori. Out of his peripheral vision, he saw the two armies gallop toward each other. An arch of arrows whizzed overhead. Tamika turned her horse's head and was fleeing her husband. The shouts of men and clang of weapons reached Jonathan. Quickflame leapt over several men coming together to kill each other. A third Shea-Talonian traitor was trampled under the Romani Vanner's hooves.

Shigemori gained on Tamika.

Oh, Great Créateur, keep her safe.

Tamika's horse stumbled and fell forward, causing her to fall over its head.

"Yah!" Jonathan leaned forward and kicked his stallion.

Shigemori had reached Tamika. He dismounted and lifted the sword over his head. Quickflame leapt between them, and Jonathan jumped from the saddle. Shigemori back stepped, Jonathan advanced. Their swords met. The metal clanging in his ears. His breath came in a burst and his lungs hurt, but Jonathan pressed the shorter man back.

"You cannot win, usurper. I have the bracelet."

"Let's see you use it." Jonathan took two large steps and bore down on him.

Shigemori backed up, turned, and slammed his sword at Jonathan, who bent in. The blade missed Jonathan's stomach. His own powerful thrust nearly cut Shigemori open, but the man dodged at the last moment, and he wasn't cut. Shigemori's men came closer, and he turned and ran away.

Jonathan paused to look for Tamika. Périer stood by her, fighting off those that came near. He turned back, but Shigemori had disappeared behind his men. The sun beat down on him, and Jonathan glanced at the cloudless sky. Sweat ran along every muscle in his body. And then he heard it.

Ose thrust his sword back in its sheath, adjusted his stance with his legs apart, and commanded his men to give him a wide berth. "Calimar!"

Jonathan heard his name. He held up a hand, and the horns blew. The battle seemed to freeze. Men looked from Shigemori to Jonathan. Even the enemy paused in their bloodlust.

Ose shouted as soon as he met Jonathan's stare. "This day, you die by the hand of our god!" He laughed once more. He'd had dreams of this moment. This glorious moment.

Pointing with his right arm, he yelled, "Ye Tai, by the power of the Bracelet of the Moon and Stars, swallow the usurper up into the ground."

A tremendous rumbling began. Billowing mists rolled in from every direction covering the bright sun. Then, the white cumulus clouds turned dark purple and crashed into each other just above their heads.

Ose grinned before laughter exploded within him. Then a tremendous ache began in his arm where the bracelet hugged him. He still held his arm out though now it trembled as he pointed at Jonathan.

"Swallow him up. Swallow the usurper. Bury him in the ground."

The Bracelet of the Moon and Stars vibrated against Ose's flesh, and then…it shot out from his arm and flew toward Jonathan. "No, come back! I am emperor!"

Jonathan bent down and lifted the bracelet from the grass where it landed after hitting him. Immediately, the cloudy yellow stones in the dragon's eyes started to glow amber. He thrust the sword into the ground and put the bracelet on. It hugged his upper arm, twisting around, so the snake-like body stretched down to his elbow. The eyes still glowed. The golden cutouts of a moon and stars seemed to come alive and changed color. When he lifted the sword once more, his fingers vibrated with the power of both the bracelet and his mother's music.

Then, out of the clouds came a snaking dragon. Its enormous body was the size of two vessels undulating as it flew back and forth. The color of it was green and blue. No god sat on its back as had been told in legend. It reached Shigemori, and circled him, rising, and looking into his face. Then, like a serpent, it slithered just above the ground toward Jonathan. Occasionally the creature lifted its head to peer this way or that.

“Oh, Great Créateur!” Fear overwhelmed Jonathan. It took every ounce of strength for him to remain where he was. The massive dragon curled around him three times before rising to peer into Jonathan’s eyes. His throat went dry.

Ose grinned. Even better. The dragon would swallow Jonathan whole. He rubbed his hands together, waiting for it to happen, and then…the dragon circled around Jonathan’s body and lifted its head, so it hovered above the usurper. Flame leapt from his nostrils, and Ose perceived that it looked at *him.*

“I command you–.” A great rumbling began to shake Ose to the core. The ground beneath his feet crumbled, tossing him down like a flapping fish taking its last breath of the air that would kill it.

“No, I am the emperor!”

Earth crumbled. The ground slipped and rotated this way and that. Ose fell and rolled back and forth. He tried to stand but couldn’t. Jonathan disappeared from his view to be replaced by a dirt wall, and then a final rumble and the earth opened underneath him. Ose screamed as he fell to his death.

The earth continued to shake after Shigemori disappeared until it lifted and filled back in, leaving a round desolate mound devoid of grass where the man had stood. The dragon moved from around Jonathan and flew into the clouds above. As he watched, the clouds turned white once more before dissipating.

The men in Shigemori’s camp all knelt and shouted. “Long live Emperor Jonathan!.”

Tamika ran to him, and he caught her up in a hug and gave her a long kiss.

"Ye Tai's dragon has honored you." She gazed up at him. "My Emperor."

"I must ask you, why did you leave the protection of the palace?"

Tamika looked down for a moment. "I was foolish. I feared that if I stayed, I would be the cause of your death. Mariyam counseled me, and I eventually saw her wisdom. Then four men tried to kidnap me, and afterward, all I wanted was to return to you."

"They tried to kidnap you?" Jonathan would find these men, and they'd never see the outside of Furuya Jun Prison again.

"Not to worry, my Emperor. The Ramoni have their own justice, and the men are all dead."

Then he hugged her tight and set his cheek on the top of her head. "You are precious to me."

Tamika moved her head so she could look up at him. Jonathan ran his fingers through her hair and kissed her.

Chapter 36

The news of Shigemoris death spread throughout Shea-Talon. Ten days later, when Jonathan rode into Aya with Tamika at his side, the people lined the streets with the nation's flag cheering. Unlike his first arrival when they were silent.

At the palace, his chef put on an elaborate meal featuring salmon and crab. Jonathan ate with his parents, officers, Long Tai with his colonels, Grégory, and Tamika.

When the earth swallowed Shigemori before all gathered, and his men surrendered, he pardoned them all, knowing they joined Shigemori out of fear of the bracelet. He didn't trust the nobility, however, and set a watch on them.

"What you've done with the palace is beautiful." Michelle smiled and waved a hand to indicate the dining room.

"I have Tamika to thank for that." Jonathan gave her a wink. She sat next to him in powder blue cotton.

"You must give me a tour," Michelle said.

"I will be honored." Tamika nodded and glanced at Jonathan. He shook his head just a little, passing on their secret code. *No, I haven't told them yet.*

When finished, the men all went into the library while Tamika and Michelle began their tour.

"Ah, Grégory Mossé." Healden put a hand on the little man's shoulder. "I'm pleased that you have been such a help to my son."

Grégory bowed. "Thank you, Majesté. I do what I can."

"He is Friend-Brother to me now, Father," Jonathan said.

Healden looked at the little man again. "Congratulations are in order."

An easy banter began between the men gathered, and Jonathan sat back enjoying it all. He was home. He'd only thought of the palace as home once before, and now those feelings encompassed the whole of Shea-Talon, settling around him like a warm blanket.

Morning arrived. A clear sunny summer day with a breeze off the ocean. The palace windows were all open while the gentle wind touched the blooms outside and brought their sweet scent within.

"I have something to tell you." Jonathan sat in one of many chairs in his office and watched the expressions on his father's face. His mother, Tamika, and Grégory were there as well.

"What is it, dear." Michelle leaned forward in her chair.

"I am in love with a brilliant and compassionate woman."

"That is good news." Healden smiled. "Though, I may know who this is."

"We saw you kiss Tamika on the battlefield through the spyglass," Michelle said.

Grégory cleared his throat, and Tamika studied the carpet.

"*Oui*, I am in love with Tamika, and she loves me too." Jonathan waited for the inevitable fireworks of disapproval.

Healden studied him with the same frown he held whenever Jonathan got into trouble as a child. “Isn’t Tamika Shigemoris wife?” Healden asked.

“His widow.” Jonathan wanted to pace but forced himself to remain seated. “He married her when she was a child, murdered her entire family, all to get the Bracelet of the Moon and Stars.” He pointed to the bracelet on his arm. The stones still glowed amber.

“Is this true?” Healden’s gaze landed on Tamika, and she raised her own.

“*Oui*.” They were all speaking in Gil-Laelian.

“What do you plan to do?” Healden looked once more at his son.

Jonathan lifted his goblet and took a drink of his wine. “I intend to marry her.”

Jonathan called for both the archbishop of Shea-Talon from his religion and the Ajari of the Shea-Talonian faith. He watched his mother take Tamika aside and talk to her for a long time.

“Son.” Healden joined him as they climbed the steps of the stone terrace overlooking the ocean.

“I know what you are going to say.” Jonathan stepped to the wooden rail and gazed at the ocean. The taste of salt on his tongue.

Healden stood beside him. “Nevertheless, it must be said. Since the incident with that woman when you were fifteen, you have gravitated toward married women. The people may not accept her as their queen because of her ties to Shigemori.”

“You don’t understand.” Jonathan stepped away from his father and turned to look at him. “The bracelet was passed down to Tamika’s family because her grandmother was Warwyk’s wife. She was also Gil-Laelian. It was to go to her brother. Shigemori was his friend and was the only one with him when he had an accident and died. Then a fire killed her parents, and within months of both tragedies, her uncle married her to Shigemori. She was fourteen. Another fire took the lives of her uncle and his family. That left Tamika the sole heir of her family's estate, which by law, was passed to Shigemori because of their marriage. He obtained the bracelet through murder and deceit.

"I believe the bracelet came to me because I'm meant to be with her."

"I see."

Silence settled between them, and Jonathan turned back to the ocean. "I love it here. I can think things through."

Healden came to his side and set a hand on his shoulder. "I'm proud of the man you've become, son. But, I must say, your mother and I were terrified when that dragon charged you."

Jonathan laughed. "Me too."

After a while, they returned to the palace for lunch, and he was happy to see Tamika and his mother laughing at something.

The meal before them was lighter than the dinner of the night before. Once more, Grégory joined them. They remained at the table for more than an hour until word came that the two religious leaders had arrived. Then, all of them went to the throne room for the meeting.

Grégory took quill and paper, sitting at the scribe's table. Three elaborate chairs were brought from the house for Healden, Michelle, and Tamika, and Jonathan sat on his throne without his heavy crown. He'd already given the Carmelidrium sword and ring back to his father, and Healden wore both along with the matching lightweight crown.

Nathanaël announced the two men. "Archbishop Raphaël and Ajari Yabūchi."

The two entered wearing their respective robes. A cone hat for the archbishop along with a gem-encrusted white robe. The ajari wore a simple red robe with fringe around the sleeves and hem. A cap covered his head.

Both bowed in unison and said, "Excellency." Then, turning toward Healden and Michelle, they said, "Majestés."

"I don't believe either of you will be surprised by this, considering our previous discussion. Lady Shigemori is now a widow. There isn't a need for a divorce. I wish to marry her."

"Excellency, there must be an appropriate amount of time for Lady Shigemori to mourn her husband." Archbishop Raphaël waved his hand toward Tamika.

"She doesn't grieve him."

"Still, to wed so soon is unseemly."

"By law, a year must pass." Ajari Yabūchi kept his head down.

"There's a law for this?" *How ridiculous.*

"Yes, Excellency. There's a law for everything."

Jonathan stood. "I'm not waiting a year."

"Jonathan." Healden rose from his chair. "They speak the truth."

He knew it must be so since Healden wore the crown of Carmelidrium, which gave discernment regarding truth and lies to the one wearing it.

Jonathan turned to his father. "A year!"

"You are the emperor. Therefore, you must obey all laws. If you disagree with a law, you may change it, but until it is so, you must obey and be an example to the people."

Jonathan groaned, sat back down, and clutched the arms of the chair. "Very well, make arrangements Archbishop Raphaël. One year from now, on the anniversary of Shigemoris death, I will marry Tamika."

Tamika stood then. "May I?"

"Of course." Jonathan waited.

"Ajari Yabūchi, I have been a good servant to Ye Tai," Tamika said.

The old man nodded.

"When his dragon flew forth on the battlefield, our god didn't come with it. So, I believe Ye Tai's time has come to an end."

"No." Ajari Yabūchi shook his head.

"It is so," Tamika continued. "It is now the time for Jonathan's God to rule us. As a future empress, I am bound by the will of God and must obey. Therefore, Archbishop Raphaël, I must become His servant. Will you admit me and school me in all I need to know?"

The Archbishop smiled. "With pleasure, Highness."

"My Lady," Ajari Yabūchi said. ōJust because Ye Tai didn't come in person doesn't make him any less magnificent."

"If I am to be married to Emperor Jonathan, then my God must be his God." She sat, and both religious leaders bowed once more.

"Dismissed." Jonathan watched the two men leave.

Later that evening, Jonathan stood before Tamika to wish her goodnight. She would return to her home just below the bluffs along with her servants and a contingent of soldiers to keep her safe. He kissed her and asked that she come to dinner in the future. When she was gone, he turned to find his mother just behind him.

She smiled and walked to him, putting her arm through his. "It seems a little morbid to marry on the anniversary of Shigemoris death."

"You heard what the law says."

They walked toward the palace doors.

"Oui. I also heard that you may change the law. Do so."

Jonathan stopped, turned toward his mother, and smiled. "I thought I couldn't change it until the year ended."

"Nothing of that sort was said. On the contrary, your father said to obey the law until it is changed."

He grinned and kissed her cheek. "Genius."

Michelle smiled.

Immediately, Jonathan set into motion, changing the marriage laws of Shea-Talon. If all went well, he would be able to wed Tamika in three months.

Former Governor Marlon and his wife arrived in chains and stood quivering before Jonathan several days later. He sentenced them to Furuya Jun Prison and set up a court for the people to pass judgment on the pair. He also gave back money from the chests the Marlons had to the poor of Shea-Talon.

Most of the Gil-Laelian army returned through the mountain pass a short time after Shigemoris death.

Now, in mid-August, Jonathan stood before the Gil-Laelian ships that arrived to take his parents home. They were set to visit his twin brother, Emperor of Shea-Eoforwic, an island nation only two weeks away by ship and once a vassal country to Shea-Talon during Warwyk's time.

Jonathan hugged his mother. "Say hello to Eamon and Twyla for me." His twin brother and his wife.

"I will." She kissed his cheek. "I'm sorry I won't be here for your wedding." She smiled at Tamika, who stood next to Jonathan. "I'm sure the two of you will be incredibly happy."

"Thank you, Mama. Safe trip. I love you."

Healden stepped to Jonathan. "You have done well in less than a year, and the people love you."

"Your guidance is ever in my thoughts, Father."

"Thank you, it is apparent. But now we must leave. I'm sure both your brothers will be happy to see us and hear news of you."

"And Aimée."

"Oui, Aimée and Cadmar. Liam and Galodien."

"I miss my siblings, especially Aimée. Cadmar is a lucky man to have her as his wife. Does she still have a nickname for everyone?"

"Of course, Your older brother, Liam, is Lee—"

"Since she could utter a sentence." Jonathan smiled, and Michelle laughed.

"And Galodien is Glad."

Jonathan laughed this time. "How does she take it?"

"Galodien is the soul of patience. Liam was fortunate to have found her."

Healden tapped his back and squeezed his shoulder before they walked toward the ship.

"My brothers and sister all have children. I must hurry up with that."

"In time, I'm sure Tamika will provide you with many." They stopped at the boarding ramp.

"May the Great Créateur bless you and your bride." Healden stepped away and took Michelle's arm. She wiped tears from her eyes with a kerchief.

"Safe voyage. I love you." Jonathan watched as his parents boarded the grand vessel. As it departed, his parents stood waving at him, and he returned their goodbye. Tamika, still beside him.

When the ship was swallowed by the horizon, Jonathan turned and helped Tamika into the carriage. On their way back to the palace, they passed the gallows where Marlon and his wife paid the price of their sins by the people's will. He hoped he wouldn't have to deal with any more treachery.

Epilogue

The breeze off the ocean rose along the bluff and brushed Jonathan's graying hair away from his forehead as he looked out over the view. He'd recently injured his leg and held a wooden cane before him with both hands over the curved handle.

"Papa, grandmama has sent a letter."

Jonathan turned to watch his oldest son climb the stairs and approach. Maniwa was twenty-five and had Tamika's dark eyes and his father's straight nose. He took the letter and opened it.

Dear Jonathan,

Your father is dying. He desires to see all of you before the end. Bring your family home at once.

Love you with all my heart.

Mama.

Jonathan sank onto the bench attached to the wall. He leaned forward, and put his head in his hands.

"What is it, Papa," Maniwa asked and sat beside him, setting an arm around his shoulder.

Jonathan sat back and turned toward his son. "Grandpapa is dying. My mother has asked that we go before he is gone."

"All of us? I should remain behind in your stead."

"No, Maniwa. Grandpapa has requested to see us all. I will ask Nathanaël to sit in my stead. He has no desire to be emperor and is wise in his own way."

In times past, he'd have asked Grégory, but the little man died several years ago, leaving behind his Romani wife, Isabella, and their two children, both of average height. She had since rejoined the Romani camp.

Within a fortnight, they set sail and arrived at one of the southern ports in Gil-Lael two months later. From there, they took two carriages and a wagon with their belongings toward the City of Terrel and Château de Talaith. A two-week journey if the weather held.

The long days of summer were upon them, and the heat was a good twenty degrees warmer than the north of Shea-Talon ever reached. Since he left, several hotels had been built along the way. They stopped for the night at one of them, five days in. Jonathan looked forward to a bath and good food after his guards had made a campsite on the previous nights.

In the morning, they continued their journey west, stopping one last time six days later. When at last they reached Terrel, his children, Maniwa, Eoin at twenty-three, and his daughter, Terada, twenty, behaved like they were still young, hanging out the windows to view the city. Soon, high on the hill, Château de Talaith came into view. From there, it was only an hour to the gates of the château.

For Jonathan, seeing the park that spread out before Talaith and the great bronze tree fountain again brought such warm memories that a tear touched his eye. Tamika sat beside him and took his arm. Her smile was a comfort to him, and he patted her hand. A great love remained between them even after all these years later.

His guards took the carriages and wagon to the back to be unloaded, and from there, he'd given them a two-week holiday. He selected men whose families lived close.

Tamika took his arm as they climbed the grand staircase to the entrance with his three children behind.

At the door, the butler bowed. “Excellency, please come in.”

The interior of the château was cool. He stood in the great entrance as his eyes wandered over-familiar portraits, tapestries, and marble busts. The curved staircase hugged the wall and had wooden carvings in likenesses of animals every few steps to replace the rails. His children were asking a flurry of questions.

“Who’s that?”

“Look at this.”

“I’ve never seen such a staircase.”

“Where was your room, Papa?” Their voices echoed, and while they spoke Shea-Talonian, they had been schooled in multiple languages.

A young man with curly hair walked toward them down the hall. “Uncle,” he said. “I am Aleron. It’s good to finally meet you.”

Jonathan hugged him. Of course, Aleron would be Liam’s oldest. He had Galodian’s curly hair and would replace his father and brother as King of Gil-Lael in time. Releasing the young man, he turned.

“Let me introduce my wife, Tamika. My sons Maniwa and Eoin and my daughter, Terada.”

“I look forward to our talks. Maniwa, you and I will one day be in charge. I’d like to spend a lot of time with you and Julian, getting to know you both.”

“I know Julian, of course,” Maniwa said. “Shea- Eoforwic is but a two-week journey by ship. We have traveled there often.”

Aleron nodded and turned to Jonathan. “Grandpapa is taking a nap. Amaury will show you to your rooms where you can freshen up. Come down when you’re ready.”

Amaury, the man who let them in, bowed and led the way up the grand staircase. It curved slightly and let them out at the long landing with a view of the entry below.

“We made ready your old room, Excellency. The young princes and princess have rooms beside yours.” Amaury stopped by a door so familiar to Jonathan that once more, memories of childhood flooded his mind

A little more than an hour later, Jonathan made his way down the stairway and along the curved hall to the family dining room. No one was there. He took the familiar sight in and walked toward the section that held the grand piano. Behind it were French doors leading outside to one of many terraces overlooking the west gardens.

He stopped. There, sitting in a wheelchair, was his father. He was slumped in the chair, and his mother sat beside him, holding his hand. The sight caught his breath. His father had always been a strong man, wise and true, who held himself straight.

They'd brought the wheelchair back from L'Amérique after Aimée was born. His mother had needed it then for a short time. Now, his father used it.

"Brother."

Jonathan jumped and turned. He hadn't heard Liam come in. His older brother looked exactly like their father except for blue eyes and now had gray hair, which reminded him of Healden when he last saw him during the uprising twenty-eight years before.

"How long?"

Liam didn't need any more information. "He's been in the wheelchair for two years now. He lives mostly in the past. But he is aware enough to know all of us and still takes an interest in how we are doing. Especially his great-grandchildren."

"You have grandchildren?"

"Don't look so surprised. Aleron and his wife have two children. They named them after papa's parents."

"Father must have liked that."

"Oui. He was pleased, as you can imagine. I know he is anxious to see you, shall we?"

Jonathan opened the patio door, and, together they stepped outside. The gardens had always been impeccable. The layout featured square beds between walkways and benches scattered throughout. The scent of grass drifted his way.

He rounded the wheelchair and turned to greet his father. “Father.” He bent and gave Healden a kiss on both cheeks.

A light came over Healden’s expression. His wrinkled hand trembled as it took Jonathan’s. “Son. All the way from Shea-Talon.”

“Oui, I brought my family. They will be down soon.” He turned then to his mother. Her hair was now gray, and her face wrinkled as was his father’s.

She stood. “Oh, my son.” Lifting her arms. Jonathan accepted her hug. “It is so good to see you.”

He smiled, then sat, and they spent time chatting about all their family news.

One of the gardeners came close to pull a few weeds along the edge of the patio stairs. Jonathan looked toward the man. He didn’t recognize him.

“Come say hello, Jasper.” His mother always treated the servants as if they were just as important as anyone else. They loved her for it.

The man stood, bowed with his hat between his hands, and climbed the stairs.

“Jonathan, you remember Merle. This is his son. Master gardener just like his father and his father before.” Michelle smiled and nodded.

“Highness.” Jasper bowed again.

Jonathan didn’t correct him. “It’s good to meet you, Jasper.” When the gardener looked up, there was a flash of darkness that ran through his eyes. Only a moment, but it startled Jonathan and made him wonder. Jasper turned and left to continue his work. But Jonathan couldn’t shake the feeling and watched him labor for a while.

"Son, I can't quite remember. You married Tamika, did you not?" Healden's hazel eyes were watery.

Jonathan gazed at his father, still unable to come to grips with how frail he was. "Oui, Father. We have three children, two sons, and a girl."

Healden smiled then and lifted his trembling hand to pat Michelle's hand resting on his knee. "You broke the curse, my love. For generations, the royal house only had one living heir. And then, we had four."

Dinner would be served earlier than usual. His mother told him his father would retire immediately afterward. Jonathan waited with Tamika and his children in the family room.

"Will we hear music?" Tamika gazed at the grand piano.

"No doubt." Jonathan had left his violin back home.

"Johnny!"

Only one person called him that in the entire world. Jonathan turned to see his sister, Aimée, hurry toward him. She gave him a great hug.

"Aimée, my wife, Tamika."

"Tamika." Aimée treated her to a hug as well. "I've heard about your exotic beauty since mama met you."

His sister's blonde hair only had a few strands of gray. Behind her came her husband, Cadmar, whose thick black hair had thinned and gone gray.

"Jonathan, Tamika," he said.

They introduced their grown children then, two boys, all married and toting their own young children between the ages of two and five.

"How is your father and mother, Cadmar?" Jonathan asked.

"They have passed on." Cadmar put his arm around Aimée's waist.

"I'm sorry."

"Liam gave us the house." Aimée smiled. "It will no longer pass to a friend-brother but go to our heirs."

"That is good news. Where will the friend-brother live?"

"They're building a new estate a little west of here for Aleron's friend-brother." Cadmar pointed west.

Before long, all Jonathan's siblings and their families joined them. The room became noisy with the giggles and laughter of the young ones, a total of eight in all. Jonathan's sons and daughter had yet to marry.

A small table was brought in where the children would eat along with their nannies. Michelle wheeled Healden to the head of the table and sat next to him. Jonathan and Tamika sat across from Liam and Galodien while the adult children sat at the other end. His twin, Eamon, squeezed in next to Jonathan and punched his arm. They both laughed.

The meal started with chicken soup. Jonathan watched as his mother dipped the spoon in the broth and brought it up to Healden's lips. They spoke of small remembrances as they ate. Within half an hour, Healden's head began to nod, and Jonathan watched as his eyes drooped to a close.

"Time for bed, I think." Michelle wiped Healden's mouth before standing. She went around the chair, wheeling him back.

Jonathan stood as well and followed his mother. "Where are you going?"

"We converted my old office into a bedchamber." She gave him a pat on his arm.

Her office was through a door on the other side of the grand piano. Jonathan opened the door, and the three of them entered.

"We must change him."

"You don't have a servant do that, Mama?"

"No, I want to be with him as much as possible."

"What is he dying from?" Jonathan lifted his father under his arms and transferred him to the bed.

"The doctor doesn't have a name for it. I guess you could say old age."

They worked together to remove Healden's clothes and put a nightshirt over his head. Lastly, Jonathan lifted his legs, and Michelle pulled the covers up over him.

Healden took Jonathan's arm. "I'm proud of you, son."

"Thank you, Father. I love you." Jonathan bent and gave him a kiss on his cheek.

His siblings joined them, each speaking a few words to their father before kissing his cheek. Aimée sat on the bed and lifted Healden's hand, kissing the back and whispering. "I love you so much, Papa." She was the only one who still called him papa.

Healden's trembling hand patted her cheek.

Michelle stayed behind when they left, only to emerge a few minutes later. After finishing their meal, the servants cleared the table. They all gathered around the grand piano where there were sofa's and chairs. This was the music room. In addition to the piano was a harp and Eamon's old drum set.

Liam took a seat at the grand piano.

"Are you going to play the flute, Mama?" Jonathan stood next to her with one of the sofas in front. Aimée, Cadmar, Eamon, and Twyla all sat together. Tamika waited for him on another sofa with Liam's wife, Galodien.

"No, Jonathan. I no longer have the breath to play. But Liam is a brilliant pianist…" Her words trailed into a whisper. "Healden, what are you doing?"

Jonathan looked up. His father had emerged from the bedroom door walking on his own. As he watched, his bedclothes became a suit with a doeskin jacket, his stooped body became tall and straight, and his wrinkled face smoothed into the man Jonathan remembered. His hair was no longer gray but light brown. Then another man stood beside him, one Jonathan knew only from the portraits, King Llewelyn, his grandfather. Next, a woman and another son, whom she held for only a moment as a baby in her arms, grew into a child and then stood beside his mother as a man, identical to Healden. The baby Llewelyn and Avril had lost, now a man.

Healden smiled and waved a hand to indicate all of them. Every person in the room had gone quiet, looking at the ghosts. Apparitions that appeared as flesh and blood. Healden gazed at Michelle and smiled, then he faded along with his family and disappeared.

Michelle caught her breath and ran to the bedroom. Jonathan followed. His mother sat on the bed and took Healden's hand before she laid down on his chest. She kissed his cheek and whispered. "Goodbye, my love, for now."

Jonathan hadn't heard Tamika enter. His heart hurt, and tears filled his eyes. Tamika wrapped her arms around his, and he turned, holding her.

Coming Soon:

The Curse of Renwyk, Book 4 in the Chronicles of Gil-Lael. Autumn 2022.

King Julien, a Gil-Lael book. Summer 2023.

Thank you for reading. I would appreciate an honest review.
N. R. Williams

About the Author

N. R. Williams lives in New Mexico with her husband and has two grown daughters and two grandchildren. "I have found such a release in writing. I do hope that my stories will entertain you. All my best." I post stories on my blog too. Check out the pages: My blog: http://nrwilliams.blogspot.com/
Another way to connect with her is through her Facebook page. https://www.facebook.com/authornrwilliams
And her website: https://authornrwilliams.com/
When you sign up for her newsletter, you'll receive a free short story. Sign up on her website.

Also By N.R. Williams

The Bewginning of a Legend, A Chronicles of Gil-Lael Novella

A giant emperor rules through the murder of innocents and the destruction of men. By the use of black magic, human sacrifice and the drinking of blood. Druas-Bradwr has lived for 500 years. Now, Arnoux, a farmer's son, will lead a trio of friends on a quest to rid the kingdom of Bradwr. Aided by elves and a wizard, can Arnoux inspire the masses to follow him, to wage war, and kill Bradwr? Or will he and all those he loves become victims of Bradwr's blood lust?

Website: https://authornrwilliams.com/

The book that started it all:

The Treasures of Carmelidrium, Book 1 of The Chronicles of Gil-Lael:

Missie, an American flutist, is thrust through a portal into a medieval world where her music is the key to empowering The Treasures of Carmelidrium to defeat the evil tyrant, Renwyk, Lord of the Symberveen. Immediately, her life is in danger. The Symberveen hunt her, an assassin attempts to kill her, Renwyk's men plot to kidnap her. While Prince Healden tries to protect her.

Will she survive to fulfill the prophecy regarding her arrival or will Renwyk take over Gil-Lael and then America too?
Website: https://authornrwilliams.com/

The Rise of Lord Sinon, Book 2 of The Chronicles of Gil-Lael

The Kingdom of Gil-Lael has defeated the evil sorcerer, Renwyk, Lord of the Symberveen, and High King Healden has put up walls to defend itself from the same tragedies happening again.

So, why is it that when Lord Sinon Aweirgan is appointed tutor to one of the king's sons, Friend-Brother Cadmar, is troubled by an elfin prophecy? And, how can Cadmar alone stand up to Sinon?

Chaos, murder, and mortal illness to king and crown prince come to pass before Cadmar's eyes.
Investigate the intrigue in Gil-Lael before treachery changes Friend-Brother Cadmar's life forever.

Website: https://authornrwilliams.com/

The Emperor of the Moon and Stars

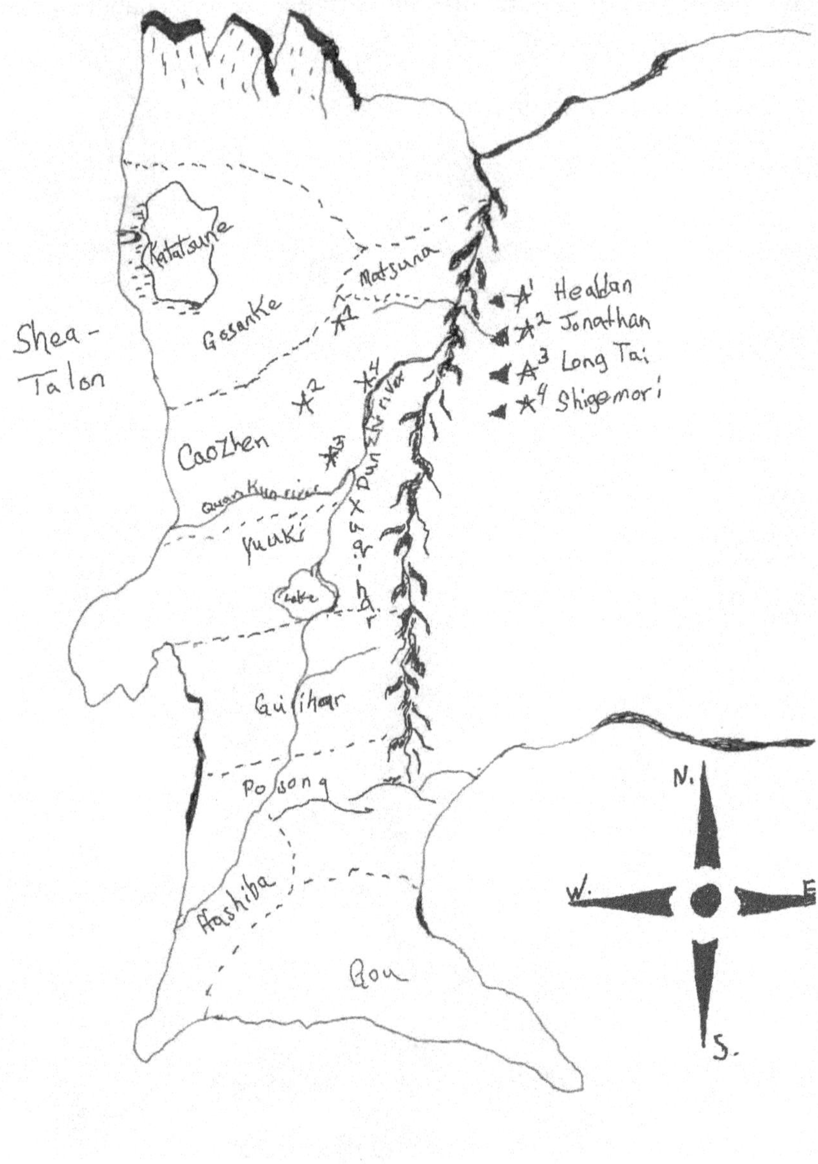